Of Mistress, Friends, and Wealth

S.J. Cunningham

Of Mistress, Friends, and Wealth
by S. J. Cunningham

© Copyright 2024 S. J. Cunningham

ISBN 978-1-964369-04-4
Paperback Edition

This is a work of fiction. All the characters in this book are fictitious, and any resemblance to actual persons, living or dead, is purely coincidental. The names, incidents, dialogue, and opinions expressed are products of the author's imagination and are not to be construed as real.

This edition published by S.J. Cunningham:
www.sjcunningham.net.

For Mom

Though fickle fortune has deceived me,
She promis'd fair and perform'd but ill;
Of mistress, friends, and wealth
bereav'd me,
Yet I bear a heart shall support me still.

From *Fickle Fortune*
—Robert Burns—

Chapter 1

Ah, the dreary, lonely week following the holiday season. The world seemed to slow its turning, and demanded its inhabitants adjust to a stark new year by diving over a cliff of laughter, tears, and champagne.

Auld Lang Syne, indeed, Liza Ramsay thought to herself as she sat in the quiet office of the Ramsay Castle. She stared out the window at the expansive, sodden grounds which stretched toward the Creagan River.

This January was even drearier than most, with tepid temperatures and rain. So much rain.

And without the cheer and laughter of family, the only distraction in the castle was the sound of workers pounding and sawing in the chapel adjacent to her first-floor office.

Liza's laptop glowed in front of her, but she barely glanced at the screen.

There were quieter places in the residence to sit— one of the conference rooms on the second floor, the cozy drawing room, or the library where a fire could have been built. But Liza craved the sound of activity.

Besides the installation of an elevator, the renovation of the chapel was the only interior construction that remained since her near-death experience in the castle dungeons six months earlier. The guest rooms had been redecorated and refreshed, the kitchen rebuilt after the fire that had nearly claimed the castle, and the centuries-old facades had had a fresh coat of paint.

Finally, after all the legal proceedings, all the travel and the trials, and the recovery—physical and emotional—the eight-hundred-year-old Ramsay Castle was finally in Liza's possession.

The holidays had been a period of victorious celebration of survival, with Liza's grandparents traveling to the Lowlands of Scotland from the United States and Lachlan's family joining them for the holiday festivities. They had forgiven, they had laughed, and they had healed.

And then, on the most glorious Christmas morning, overseen by the mural depicting the Ramsay stronghold's role in the fight for Scotland's freedom and its place in history, Lachlan had sunk to one knee and asked Liza to be his bride. Lachlan, who'd been wrongly suspected of murder for years, yet had none of the scars, trauma, or resentment that any normal human should hold due to such treatment, had turned out to be Liza's knight in shining armor. Her *fear-saoraidh.*

Liza studied the diamond winking on her left hand. She was happy, but the smile she wore also held just a hint of sadness. She couldn't say she was the same person she was before she'd first visited the Ramsay Castle. Not that she should have been. But there was a suspicion in her that hadn't existed before. A wariness and vigilance that made her just a little bit afraid of herself.

This new aspect of her personality was mirrored in her appearance. Gone were the long, soft brown waves, replaced by a straight sleek bob, razor cut at the ends and highlighted with streaks of auburn. Her body had changed as well. While she'd always been thin, now there was not a centimeter of excess weight on her. That leanness was visible in her sharp jaw and cheekbones.

Liza shook herself out of her reverie. She was wallowing in her post-holiday blues. She needed to snap out of it.

With a sigh of determination, she looked back at the laptop screen and studied the architectural design for the new chapel, meticulously scheduled to be completed later that summer for the wedding of Liza Ramsay and Lachlan McClaren. She only had to endure the six long months until then.

Lachlan strode into the office, his sandy-brown hair falling in a damp swoop over his right eye. He looked like a rogue whose spurned lover had put him out in the rain. He smiled at Liza, and all that had been wrong in her world righted. She felt the familiar combination of delight and anticipation deep in her belly.

This was one rogue she'd always bring in out of the cold.

"There ye are." His lilting brogue was deep and rich. "Bruce would like tae know if ye're acceptin' of the Fleming Company comin' to start the restoration of the stained glass in two weeks."

"Is that your recommendation?"

"Aye. The whole timeline is tight, but the sooner the better, fer sure."

She nodded. The castle may have been in her name, and the late Laird Callum Ramsay's inheritance hers, but Lachlan was about to become her husband. She wanted him to know that he didn't have to check with her on every decision. This was his home, too. She told him as much, then added, "And can you tell Bruce again that he can just talk to me directly if he has a question?"

Local construction contractor Bruce Baxter was not Liza's biggest fan. A Scotsman to the core and native to the town of Bonnyrigg, the village just outside the castle grounds, the man could not seem to get over the fact that an American, no matter what her lineage happened to be, had inherited one of the oldest and most historically important inhabited castles in the

Scottish Lowlands. Bruce had not been moved by the crimes at the Ramsay Castle last summer, nor had he been rooting for Liza to emerge as the heroine in the story.

Callum had been a well-respected and revered leader in the tight-knit community. His murder hit its people hard. The fact that Callum was Liza's relative or that Liza had nearly been murdered herself had done nothing to soften Bruce's feelings toward her. Knowing Bruce, he would have preferred the castle to have been claimed by the Royal Kingdom Trust and returned to country and kin where it belonged.

Bruce was fond of Lachlan, however, and as Bruce was the best contractor around, and someone who wanted to restore the Ramsay Castle to its former glory, Liza tolerated his disdain. She tried to steer clear of the cantankerous old man who was currently living in the workers' cottage near the river.

"And you're sure the windows will be complete before the wedding?" she asked Lachlan.

"Aye," Lachlan said. "Bruce has gotten that in writing."

Liza nodded, pensive.

"What's botherin' ye, *m'eudail*?" He used the Gaelic phrase for 'my darling' when Liza was brooding.

She forced a smile. "Just feeling a bit down after the holidays. Nothing to worry about."

"Want tae venture into Edinburgh fer dinner this

evening? Have a proper date night?"

They had been so busy with home improvements, interior decorating, and legal matters, followed by the busy holiday season, that they'd barely gone out since Liza had relocated to Scotland from Boston.

But there was more to it than that. When you lived in a location as lovely as the Ramsay Castle with a commercial-grade, fully stocked kitchen, sometimes Liza felt going out to dinner was a downgrade.

This time, though, she answered a quick and enthusiastic, "Yes."

"Ye pick the place."

Liza turned to her laptop to search for somewhere they could relax for an evening, but when she moved the mouse to wake up her monitor, she noticed the new mail icon on the bottom right of her screen. She clicked on it.

The message was from a sender named Robert Rose, with the subject: 'Requesting a Visit to the Ramsay Castle, Former Home of My Dear Friend Callum'.

It was the 'Dear Friend Callum' that prompted Liza to open the message.

Dear Ms. Ramsay,

I hope this message finds you in good health and good spirits.

I am writing with a special and unusual re-

quest. I belong to a group of unique individuals who have interests across the globe and spanning many industries, countries, missions, and visions. We gather on a bi-annual basis, and the location for our upcoming New Year meeting has become, shall we say, compromised. Sir Callum, a friend and acquaintance of old, had always told me that the Ramsay Castle was an option for our assemblies. I am, of course, aware of Callum's awful fate and your resulting inheritance. My deepest sympathies for your loss and congratulations for your gain.

While I realize this request is last-minute and details are scant, I figured I had nothing to lose by sending this inquiry to find out if you, in memory of my dear friend Callum, might find it in your heart to open your home for a few days from 23–26 January, to an old man and a few of his closest cronies. ;)

I've included my private and secure phone number below in the event you'd like to inquire further. I'd appreciate a response no matter your decision.

Robert (Rabbie) Rose
President and CEO
Spirits Rose

Liza must have been frowning deeply because

Lachlan said, "Everythin' all right?"

"Do you know a Rabbie Rose?"

He laughed. "The only Rabbie Rose I know of is the billionaire who owns Spirits Rose up in the Highlands. Glencoe, I believe."

"I think this is the same person." Liza turned the laptop toward Lachlan, who peered at the screen. When he straightened, Liza said, "Do you remember Callum mentioning him?"

While Callum and Lachlan were not related, Lachlan's family had worked at the Ramsay Castle and for Callum and his ancestors for several generations. Lachlan had grown up both in the castle and on the grounds. Callum had been like a grandfather to him.

"No, but Callum knew a lot of people."

"Including the late Queen," Liza mumbled.

Lachlan pointed to the phone number below the signature. "Call 'im up."

Liza picked up her phone from the desk. Then she hesitated. "What if the request is legitimate?"

Lachlan shrugged. "What if it is?"

"We're not ready to host visitors in the castle."

"We just held Christmas here," he reminded her. "The only room not fully renovated yet is the chapel. I dinnae think they'll be requirin' church services."

"We don't know who *they* are," Liza argued. "And it's one thing to entertain our families here, but it's quite another to host a group of strangers. We have no idea how many guests there might be—and we have no permanent staff." She thought of Sadie Gilbraith, the young housekeeper they'd hired less than two months earlier. While Sadie was agreeable and eager to please, she did not have the experience to deal with a crowd.

"Why don't ye just ring up this Mr. Rose before ye get all fussed up?"

Liza made a face at Lachlan, but he was right. She picked up the phone.

"I'll be in the chapel with Bruce if ye need me."

Lachlan exited through the back door of the office which led through a hallway to the chapel's entrance on the first floor. She heard her fiancé call out to Bruce.

Liza input the numbers listed in the email message. The tone trilled three times before a smooth accented voice sounded over the connection.

"Aye, Rabbie here."

"Mr. Rose?"

"That's what they call me." The voice held a note of good-natured humor and just a flicker of playfulness.

"My name is Liza Ramsay, I—"

"Ach! Ms. Ramsay," he interrupted. "I just sent ye a message not ten minutes ago. Ye're fast."

"Well, I was curious about the veracity of the message. Obviously, I was also intrigued by the mention of Laird Ramsay. I don't recall seeing you at the memorial service."

"Such a shame," Rabbie said solemnly. "He was a

lovely man. Ye've my deepest sympathies."

"He was. And the memorial service was lovely too," she said, a reminder that he hadn't yet responded to her implied question about his absence from the service. Up until six months ago, it had been in her nature to trust everyone until proven otherwise. Now she wasn't quite as naïve as she had been. She had no reason to trust that Rabbie Rose was who he claimed to be.

"I'm certain it was," he said. "I'd been out of the country and only learned of Callum's passin' when I returned home to Scotia."

In her more artful of moods, Liza would have appreciated his use of the poetic nickname of Scotland, which she also now considered home. But she was becoming impatient.

"Mr. Rose, your message referenced a request to stay here in a few weeks with some sort of group?"

"Please, Ms. Ramsay. Call me Rabbie. I dinnae suppose ye're on a secure line."

They had invested in a number of security measures at the castle, including a new alarm system and had strategically placed cameras around the estate's entrance and grounds. And after inheriting not only the castle, but over twenty million dollars from Callum, she had changed her phone number, but she had not felt any need to further secure her mobile phone connection.

"No," she answered slowly.

"Then ye'll forgive me if the details that I'm able to provide are hazy."

"And you'll forgive me if my acceptance of your proposal is equally as hazy."

There was a pause. When Rabbie spoke again, his voice had lost some of its cheerfulness. "Ms. Ramsay, bein' from the commonwealth of Pennsylvania in the States, would you happen to be familiar with the South Fork Fishing and Hunting Club?"

The question was so unexpected that Liza found herself speechless. He had done his research. Rabbie clearly knew much more of Liza than Liza knew of Rabbie.

"Have I lost ye, lass?"

"I'm here," she said. "I assume you're referring to the secret retreat that was owned by the group of industrialists in the late nineteenth century?"

"Ye ken yer history." Rabbie sounded pleased.

"It was the site of a dam that gave way as a result of a lack of maintenance. The resulting flood killed over two thousand people. Is that correct?"

Rabbie didn't respond to that. He said, "My great-grandfather, then president of Spirits Rose, was a good friend and peer of fellow Scotsman Andrew Carnegie and a part of that group. While the club and surrounding property were sold in the early twentieth century, the group of the leading minds in industry, finance, and more recently, technology, continue to meet on a regular basis."

Rabbie paused. Liza sensed that he was waiting for some reaction from her. "So, you're saying that such a group still exists today?"

"Aye."

"And this is the group that is referenced in your message?"

"Aye." He sounded relieved.

Liza might have continued to think this was a scam, but the mention of the South Fork Fishing and Hunt Club had been so obscure and specific that she found it hard to believe a grifter would go to the trouble of researching it.

The club had been built on an old dam high above the railroad town of Johnstown, Pennsylvania, where the titans of industry had, arguably, allowed the use of shoddy engineering to raise the level of the man-made lake. They subsequently built massive cottages and a clubhouse for its members and their families.

After winter snow had rapidly melted and heavy rains drenched the area, the dam burst in late spring of 1889, flooding and killing nearly half the town. And while it was widely agreed that the South Fork Fishing and Hunt Club was to blame, its members took no public responsibility and largely escaped legal prosecution.

It may have pleased Rabbie Rose that she'd heard of

the club, but given its reputation, he was going to need to do a better job of convincing her she wanted any group associated with its original members to be welcome in her home, even a century and a half later.

"Mr. Rose, I'm afraid that in addition to having little information on which to make a decision, given the last-minute nature of your request, I'm finding it difficult to even entertain your entreaty."

"Ms. Ramsay, I don't think ye understand me. What I'm telling ye is that a number of the world's richest and most influential people are members of this group, which is making decisions and implementing changes affecting the future and, in some cases, the very survival of the human race." His voice had become irritated and clipped, showing something of the aggressive businessman he must have been to count himself among the wealthiest men in Scotland.

While part of her resented his arrogance, another, deeper part of her paused. She knew at least some of the names that may have been included on a list of the world's wealthiest people. If this man's claims were legitimate, did she really want to bypass the opportunity to host a meeting about, and potentially contribute to, the most cutting edge of topics?

Her former business and consulting background came rushing back to her. She was intrigued.

But still, other than Sadie, the Ramsay Castle had no onsite staff or security personnel. She said as much to Rabbie.

Some of his cheerful nature returned. "That is quite all right. This group tends to be self-sufficient. My team can take care of the secure catering staff, who won't need onsite accommodation. I'll have my assistant communicate securely with yours about attendees and requirements for a lean skeleton crew. Actually, the less people at the castle the better."

"Your assistant can communicate directly with me," said Liza. Of course she had no assistant. "But I haven't yet agreed, Mr. Rose."

"Ye will, Ms. Ramsay. Ye will."

Chapter 2

Over an elegant dinner at Pantry, the swanky restaurant in New Town, Liza and Lachlan discussed the potential gathering of billionaires and weighed the pros and cons of hosting the meeting. After two glasses of wine, Liza had become enthusiastic about the possibility, as long as the event did not in any way delay completion of the chapel. Lachlan wasn't quite as enthusiastic, but he couldn't articulate his specific concerns.

Still, Liza's agreement was prefaced by the legitimacy of the inquiry. She couldn't be absolutely certain the man she'd spoken to was indeed the Rabbie Rose of the Rose family, who laid claim to the oldest and finest whisky distillery in Scotland.

It wasn't until early the following morning, after Liza had spoken over the phone with Mr. Rose's supremely competent assistant, Jane, that she felt confident not only that the inquiry was legitimate, but that with the help of the contract kitchen staff used by the Rose family, the feat of hosting the guests could be accomplished.

But to Jane's, and likely to Rabbie's, chagrin, Liza had refused to give anything more than a tentative consideration until she saw the names of the people who would be staying in her home.

And while Lachlan had been briefly distracted by the Rose name and the family's centuries-long heritage of providing the most well-known single malt Scotch whisky in the world, his skepticism seemed to grow. He became sullen, before going back to his task of overseeing the chapel remodel and leaving the planning of the event in Liza's hands.

When Liza finally received the list of names of Rabbie Rose's billionaires' club through Jane's encrypted email late in the day, it was in the fading light of the chapel where she found Lachlan.

A crew of woodworkers sawed and sanded at one end of the massive room, as Lachlan spoke with a burly African man. When Liza approached, the man tipped his head toward her and moved hurriedly away.

Was it her imagination, or did the sound of sawing and pounding increase with her entrance?

She glanced over and found Bruce Baxter glowering at her from beneath bushy gray eyebrows.

"He despises me," she said to Lachlan.

"He's like that with everyone."

"Not with you."

"I grew up in the village."

"Yeah, well if he's not careful, he should know that

we can give the general contracting job to someone else. Maybe even someone American."

Ignoring the threat, Lachlan nodded to the papers in her hand. "What have ye got there?"

Liza glanced around again and motioned Lachlan out of the chapel and into the quiet hallway that ran between the room and the castle's kitchen.

"Mr. Rose's assistant just sent me the list of potential attendees for this secret society meeting."

The document had been sent through a secure file transfer service requiring three-factor authentication including facial recognition. Liza had thought those measures overly cautious until she'd read the names. She and Lachlan had speculated about the potential guests, but seeing the names in print had left her at first stunned, then awed, and finally apprehensive.

She handed the printout to Lachlan who scanned the brief biographies.

"Is this real?" he murmured.

Liza had no idea. "I'm going to call Marion Dean this afternoon."

Detective Chief Inspector Marion Dean had been the lead investigator of the murders that had taken place at the castle not long after Liza had arrived earlier that year. She, along with Lachlan, was the reason Liza was still alive, and they had developed a sort of prickly friendship in the months that had passed, with Liza helping Dean out from time to time on the periphery of her investigations.

Lachlan nodded in agreement. While Dean had initially suspected Lachlan of not one, but three murders, Lachlan had been easier to let bygones be bygones than Liza would have been.

"Dean'll ken what tae do."

Inside the chapel, Bruce shouted something to his crew.

A sudden panic washed over Liza. Their wedding date, that two days earlier had seemed long into the endless gray months ahead, now loomed very close indeed. There was so much work to do.

Lachlan was still studying the list. "Petrus Bothas is the richest man in the world."

Bothas, still relatively young at forty-nine and notoriously reclusive, ran five companies that Liza knew of, ranging from space travel to next-generation energy sources to information platforms. He was also a polarizing and controversial figure who angered many people, from government officials and world leaders to the most common of laborers, with his abrupt and insensitive pronouncements and sometimes off-center views of the world and its future.

But as many people as he angered, he seemed to bolster and enliven even more world citizens who held opposing political and social viewpoints.

There were also those who claimed the man didn't exist at all. He was rarely spotted in public, and the only photos Liza had ever viewed of him were grainy and from a distance.

Assuming that he *did* exist, Liza was not sure his alleged vast accomplishments outweighed his reputation.

Lachlan continued reading the list, making comments on each of the names.

Aaron Scott owned three of the world's most used social media juggernauts and was in the process of acquiring Tempo, a popular video-based platform that had originated in Asia and was now growing rapidly in other parts of the world. He was also heavily invested in next-generation artificial intelligence technology, and his liberal views on the subject had received attention at the highest level of world governments.

Matthew Carter was the second richest man in the world, and the creator of the Sybl software system that was the basis of all cloud technology. There had been rumors that if Sybl became disabled or hacked, the entire world would shut down in a matter of minutes, plunging the population into a pre-industrialized state. Energy and financial systems would be immediately disrupted; not even the world's military systems were insulated to the point that those systems would be functional without Sybl.

Ironically, Matthew was also the most celebrity-minded of the group. He owned a popular American football team, and many people knew of him as a result of that venture, along with his beautiful young influencer wife, and not for his more ominous involvement in Sybl and the software's role in global defense systems. But having once worked for a major consulting firm, Liza was well aware of the man's other more lucrative and invasive contributions to the world.

Sergei Popova, the Russian oligarch, was rumored to be behind some of the most complex geopolitical negotiations. No one knew exactly how much wealth Sergei held, though there was a very good chance his affluence may have exceeded that of Bothas and Carter combined. He was not a trusted person, and one had to wonder if his admittance into this group was a matter of keeping friends close and enemies closer. In the little verifiable information that Liza had been able to discover about him, she'd discovered a few obscure references to the Russian Space Race, which may have explained his relationship with Bothas, at least.

Anne Kane, the forty-five-year-old beauty and heiress, was perhaps the most surprising member of the group. Her grandfather, Samuel Kane, had founded their namesake department store, the largest retail chain in the world, beginning with one store in Jackson, Mississippi in the late 1940s following World War Two. Anne's father, Asher Kane, had died early, leaving the retail giant to his children—Anne, the oldest of the children, and her two brothers.

Liza recognized Anne's name in particular, however, because Liza had taken a few art history classes in college and had learned a decade earlier of Anne's vast collection of art and the facilitation of its movement around the world. The woman had been instrumental in ensuring that works of art and collections from cultures past had been returned to families and museums in their rightful countries. Liza did not believe that Anne was involved in the day-to-day operation of the retail establishment, and as far as Liza knew, the woman was fairly 'off the radar'. Clearly her wealth was not.

Finally, Rabbie Rose. Neither his fortune nor reputation was on a par with the others. Given Rabbie's reference to the South Fork Club and his great-grandfather's association with steel and philanthropic titan Andrew Carnegie, Liza suspected that Rabbie was grandfathered into this group because of his ancestors rather than Rabbie's own position in the world.

As Lachlan continued to read the list, Liza watched for his reaction. Even he, who had grown up surrounded at times by nobility and royalty, seemed stunned.

"I'm not sure what tae say."

"I don't know that we could turn them down, even if we wanted to. These are the types of people who don't seem to take 'no' for an answer."

"It's not these characters who are askin' though, is it? It's Rabbie Rose. It would be easy enough fer any one of these other men or women to make a phone call and stay anywhere on earth. Hell, most of them likely own properties that dwarf the Ramsay Castle."

"So, why is Rabbie so insistent on hosting this group here?" Liza mused.

"Could be as simple as wantin' tae show off his native land. Might also be the appeal of stayin' in a dark castle at the darkest time of the year."

They looked at each other. They had both become suspicious of the motives of other people over the past year.

"I'd be interested to hear what Dean has to say," Lachlan said.

Liza fired off a text to the chief inspector and waited.

It was after dinner, as Liza had been conducting an inventory of the bedrooms on the third floor, when a chime on her phone indicated activity near the front gate. She opened the app to see, in the eerie night vision of the camera, Dean's sleek black sedan drive slowly into the castle's front parking.

Liza resisted running to the front door, instead allowing Sadie to do her job.

But a minute later, when the deep chime of the front bell sounded, Liza descended the back staircase in time to watch Sadie lead Chief Inspector Dean to the drawing room to the right of the grand staircase.

Liza didn't care how many times she'd walked down the main hallway toward the sweeping entrance, she never grew tired of passing the portraits of centuries of Ramsay lairds, warriors, and commanders that stood sentinel over the passage. And she would be forever awed by the mural of the battle for Scotland that adorned the high wall above what had once been the interior of the castle's drawbridge.

When Liza entered the drawing room, Dean was sitting in one of the brocade-upholstered chairs, frowning at something on her phone and mumbling under her breath.

"Chief Inspector," Liza said. Dean looked up.

"Liza Ramsay." The older woman smiled. "Ye're a sight for sore eyes."

"Am I?"

"I spent the day with the medical examiner and his…guests."

Liza arched an eyebrow. "I would hope my company is just a bit more lively," she quipped, but stopped herself from asking if the case to which Dean was referring was the recent homicide of a prominent professor at the university along with his wife and three young children. "Thank you for making time for me."

"Ye said it was urgent."

Liza pulled the printout of Rabbie's email from her back pocket and handed it to Dean, who set her phone on the small antique table beside her. She took a pair of thick black reading glasses from her tangle of dark curls and perched the frames on the bridge of her nose, knitting her brow as she read.

"Petrus Bothas," she murmured, just as Sadie entered the room with a glass of water. The young girl's eyes widened at the sound of the name.

Liza watched Sadie peer over Dean's shoulder at the printout.

Dean quickly noticed and laid the papers face down in her lap as she took the glass with a nod of thanks.

"Somethin' fer you, Ms. Ramsay?" Sadie asked. She'd made a lovely chicken and leek pie for dinner, and Liza was still sated from the meal.

"No, I'm fine, thank you. Please shut the door on your way out." She smiled, attempting to soften the sting of the dismissal.

Sadie nodded her head and snuck another look at the papers in Dean's lap. "Yes, ma'am."

Dean took a sip of her water and watched over her glasses at Sadie's retreat. She waited until the girl had left the room and the door latched before she spoke again. "Where did ye find her?"

"She came through a recommendation from Lachlan's family." James McClaren, Lachlan's father, was Scotland's Permanent Secretary, and oversaw thousands of people working for the government in the country.

"Pretty girl," Dean said, then studied the papers more closely. "Tell me about this."

Liza began with the message she'd received from Rabbie Rose then summarized the communications with both Rabbie and his assistant.

Liza nodded at the list. "That is the list of people who have confirmed attendance for this *meeting of the minds.*" She emphasized the last phrase, and had meant it ironically, but the words emerged almost reverently.

"So. What are ye askin' of me?"

Liza leaned forward. Her straight hair fell against her cheek, a sleek auburn curtain brushing her arm. "For one thing, I just felt as if I needed someone with the police to know that an extremely high-profile group of entrepreneurs, inventors, and financiers may be in the jurisdiction. But beyond that, and more importantly, I'm asking for your expert opinion. Do you think it's safe to host a gathering like this?"

Dean leaned her head back, considering. "I'm assumin' they have their own security."

Liza nodded. "Rabbie's assistant told me they like to stay in secure locations where their security can guard the venue but not be present in the residence itself. The leaner the staff, the better." Liza gestured around. "As you can see, we're pretty lean."

"Will background checks be performed on everyone at the castle?"

"Yes. And I need at least one experienced house manager and probably one footman."

"I can recommend some candidates, if ye'd like. I'll

need tae make a few calls."

"That would be great."

"When is this gathering set to take place?"

"In two weeks."

Dean nodded. "I'll notify Police Scotland without providin' any details. Don't want the names on this list gettin' out, otherwise ye'll have a much bigger problem on yer hands. The local constables can be assigned to make regular patrols to supplement any private security. By tomorrow, ye'll have the names of some contract staff members to vet."

Liza sat back and exhaled. But a frown still creased her brow. "When Lachlan and I decided we'd open the Ramsay Castle for gatherings—weddings and the like—I didn't envision a secret society of billionaires."

Dean laughed. "Ye weren't expectin' an evil cabal at yer dining table?"

"Do you think they're evil?" Liza asked, taking her seriously. Some of the stories she'd read in the media certainly might lead her to that conclusion.

"Nothing illegal, if that's what ye're askin'. At least, nothing that'll affect ye for a few days. Come on, Liza. This is the world ye live in now, like it or not." Dean gestured around the drawing room with its crystal chandeliers, hand-crafted woodwork, and high molded and ornamental ceilings. "And who knows—maybe ye'll make a few connections. It won't hurt to hold a couple of billionaires in yer debt."

"I suppose not." But she still wasn't happy. Because she was being selfish. She'd envisioned the first group in residence at the Ramsay Castle as the guests of her own wedding.

Dean leaned forward, peering into Liza's face. The older woman's expression softened, and she transformed from Detective Chief Inspector Dean to Marion, Liza's friend.

"What else is botherin' ye?"

Liza's eyes filled with tears. She dashed them away quickly and swallowed. "The last time there was a large gathering of visitors in the castle, three people died."

Both Dean and Liza fell silent, thinking of Charlie Campbell, Brodie Graham, and Callum Ramsay. Liza had very nearly been the fourth person on that list.

Dean patted her hand. "Don't ye worry. We'll secure the place so there's no risk of any danger makin' its way in. There'll be no more murders at the Ramsay Castle, Liza. Not on my watch."

Chapter 3

Over the next week, Liza and Lachlan held interviews for the open staff positions in the cozy and understated sophistication of the library, surrounded by the comfort of books and the warm glow of a roaring fire.

Not only was the space conducive to a more relaxed conversation, but the walk to the chamber, tucked behind a sitting room close to the back staircase, also allowed Liza to observe the behavior of the candidates as they ascended the elegant grand staircase and made their way past the portraits and antiques displayed along the main hallway.

The journey also allowed visitors a glimpse of most of the rooms on the second floor—two conference rooms, a music room, the grand ballroom, and the main formal dining room.

Dean had recommended three candidates for the position of house manager, one of whom had also been suggested by Rabbie Rose, and two candidates for the position of footman. Lachlan's father had recommended one apiece, and Niall Murphy, Liza's attorney, had proposed a few more.

Liza and Lachlan had then narrowed their list to three candidates for each position, with Liza leaning heavily on Dean's list.

Lachlan disagreed with that strategy. "It's not that I don't trust Dean," he'd said, though the look of displeasure on his face indicated that may well have been the case. "We should be able to make up our own minds without the influence of the police."

In the end, they'd split the difference, though the candidates had spoken for themselves. Carolyn Turner, who had been a Dean recommendation, had been in the Royal Household as a senior staff member, serving at the pleasure of Her late Majesty. A tall and ramrod-straight woman in her fifties with a short sensible haircut and shrewd eyes, she'd been unmoved by yet complimentary of both the castle and its priceless contents. She had asked questions about the duties, and had outlined her past experience in a no-nonsense manner.

Ms. Turner had worked for the Royal Family for over two decades, most recently at Witton Castle, but had served at nearly all of the properties frequented by the late Queen. When the woman had ended her employment with the family upon the monarch's death, she'd been in the most senior housekeeping position, and had departed on her own terms, not because she'd been replaced by His Royal Highness or his family.

"I'd always known that my tenure with the Royal Family would end upon the death of the dear Queen," Ms. Turner explained in her prim, received pronunciation. Even Liza, who had yet to distinguish between the accents in Scotland, let alone in England, understood that, despite her position as domestic help, this woman was the epitome of *upper class*.

"Both Chief Inspector Dean and Mr. Rose, whom I've known for quite some time, have explained about the position without providing myriad details." She took a sip of a cup of Brodie's Afternoon Tea that Sadie had prepared. Liza noticed the woman's long tapered fingers and short unpainted fingernails.

"And what details did they provide?" Liza asked.

"Only that you are looking for contract house help—management and oversight—from the 23rd through the 26th of January."

"Do ye have any questions about that?" Lachlan asked.

"Since we are already into the second week of January, I expect that you'd like me on staff as soon as possible so that I may understand the inner workings of the house and what adjustments may need to be made before the guests arrive."

She took another dainty sip of her tea and looked at them levelly.

Lachlan and Liza exchanged a glance.

"And you have no curiosity, Ms. Turner, about the identities of these guests?"

The woman deliberately set down her fine bone china teacup and saucer. She smoothed her plain black skirt and straightened in her chair. "It was Marion Dean who gave you my name and curriculum vitae, was it not?"

Since they'd established this fact earlier in the conversation, her pointed question came across as more of a censure than a legitimate inquiry. Still, Liza found herself answering, "It was."

"As such, I can only assume that the guests are high profile in some way. But, Ms. Ramsay, I must remind you, in my former employment I often encountered heads of state, leaders of industry and academia, and celebrities of the day. It is of no matter to me whom I serve. Likewise, it makes no matter if I serve in that same capacity for you. I'm here because I was asked to be here, not because I need to be here."

There was a long pause, eloquent in its silence.

It was Lachlan who spoke next. "Thank ye, Ms. Turner. Do ye have any additional questions for us?"

Carolyn Turner shook her head, looking very proper and stern. "No, Mr. McClaren," she said and stood. "I expect that you'll call me if you need my services."

Liza silently noted that the two other women they'd interviewed for the house manager position had referred to Lachlan as 'Mr. Ramsay'.

Lachlan seemed more irritated at having been addressed by his proper name.

When the door was shut behind Ms. Turner, Liza said, "She's perfect", at the same time Lachlan said, "She's not the one fer us."

They looked at each other, both stunned and perplexed.

"There's somethin' familiar about the woman," Lachlan said. "I've seen her before. I just can't make out where."

"Could she have been at the castle before? Perhaps one of the Queen's visits, when you were very young?"

"If she had been, why would she not have said? She wasnae shy about sayin' everythin' else."

Liza didn't want to discount Lachlan's concerns. On the other hand, Carolyn Turner had been their last candidate, and the others hadn't even come close to her level of experience or professionalism.

"Shall we start over?" Liza gave him a worried look. As Ms. Turner had pointed out, they were running out of time.

Lachlan shook his head. "It's up to ye."

Ultimately, Liza decided that hiring Ms. Turner was the best choice, and they compromised by leaving the fulfillment of the butler position to Lachlan. He chose Shaun Fraser, an experienced footman in his mid-thirties trained in martial arts and having last worked for a footballer from Sheffield. "I like the idea of havin' just a bit of muscle on our side," Lachlan said. Liza couldn't argue with that.

The next morning, a little over a week before the guests were set to arrive, Liza opened her morning email as she nibbled a soft-boiled egg. The subject line that caught her attention came from the Rose secure server and was titled 'Entertainment'.

Dear, Ms. Ramsay,

Mr. Bothas has informed us of his plans to engage the services of the Luna Chorus, which will perform at the Ramsay Castle on the evening of the 23rd of January. The festivities will kick off the event in a lighthearted and revelrous manner, reminding the participants of their friendship and cooperation, before the group begins their more pressing discussions on the 24th.

Mr. Bothas will organize the participation of the Luna Chorus. However, a performance location is required. Mr. Rose informs me that the Ramsay Castle has ample space for such a show, and this should be but a minor adjustment for you. Do let us know if there is any way that we can assist.

The email was signed by Jane and CC'd to Robert Rose. Also included was one line of postscript, which appeared to have been added by Rabbie.

Setup for the performance will take place early in the day on the 23th of January. Mr. Bothas tends to resist taking no for an answer.

Liza swore under her breath, leaving her egg mostly untouched. She quickly searched for Luna Chorus on her phone and found no official website, only a few obscure references to 'a dark, mysterious, erotic, and acrobatic performance that audiences, who may unwittingly become participants, won't soon forget'.

Liza shut her eyes and massaged her temples, her elbows resting on the white linen tablecloth.

"Are ye all right, ma'am?"

Liza looked up at the earnest face of Sadie, her big brown eyes innocent, hopeful, and concerned. Sadie was just a decade younger than Liza, but the girl seemed like a child in comparison. From the small village of Queenswick nearly an hour west of Edinburgh, Sadie's residence at the Ramsay Castle was a world away from her quaint upbringing.

Sadie was competent in the kitchen and methodical about her housekeeping duties. She didn't venture out much and kept to herself, but she always had a kind smile for guests and immediately inquired after, and sometimes anticipated, their needs. If Liza had one complaint it was that Sadie was just a bit too guileless, reflecting poorly on the air of sophistication that Liza wanted guests of the castle to sense.

A week ago, that hadn't mattered so much. It did now.

"Do you happen to know where Mr. McClaren is?" Liza's voice was clipped.

Lachlan had risen about an hour before Liza. He always kept himself busy with the maintenance and oversight of the renovations, but also with minor tasks—clearing downed tree branches, changing lightbulbs, troubleshooting faulty wiring or plumbing issues.

"He left in the truck." Sadie wrung her hands together. She was wearing a pair of black pants that were lightly dusted with a soft coating of white flour. Her rose-colored top was long and well-made but clung to her full figure in an unflattering manner. Liza would need to talk to Sadie about her wardrobe so that staff appeared professional to their guests.

"Would ye like me tae call him fer ye?"

Liza shook her head. "I'll catch up with him later." She put the subject of the Luna Circus out of her mind for the time being. "But Sadie, there is something I'd like to talk with you about." She gestured to the seat next to her. Sadie hesitated then sat.

Liza thought Sadie viewed her as some sort of celebrity. Even in Sadie's remote village of Queenswick, news of the murders at the Ramsay Castle had been reported. And the subsequent romance of Liza, the American heiress, and Lachlan, who'd once been a suspect in her murder, had seemed like the happy ending of a modern fairy tale. Liza and Lachlan had been the subject of more than one news magazine feature.

Over the past six months, the country had moved on, and yet here Sadie was, living this relatively normal life in a castle with these two characters from the tabloids.

Liza tried to keep that in mind in her interactions with the timid Sadie.

"I know you overheard some of the conversation I had with Chief Inspector Dean last week regarding the group of people who'll be visiting soon. And obviously you've noticed that we're doing some interviews for additional help around the castle."

Color flooded Sadie's cheeks. "I didn't pay any mind to that, ma'am."

Liza nodded once. "It's time you know about it. In a few days, Carolyn Turner, who you met briefly, will be joining us on staff. She'll be acting as head house manager, and you'll be reporting to her for the remainder of the month. We'll also have temporary catering staff for a few days, so you won't be expected to cook. Ms. Turner will give you your assignments. It'll most likely include housekeeping and cleaning duties and serving."

Sadie nodded. If she was unhappy with the development, she gave no indication.

Liza hesitated. "The guests who will arrive at the end of the next week are…special."

"Is it Petrus Bothas?" Sadie asked, then clamped her mouth shut as if she couldn't believe she'd just spoken. "I'm sorry. I heard Inspector Dean—"

Liza held up a hand. "I can't confirm anything until you've signed a non-disclosure agreement, which Mr. Murphy will be delivering for everyone in the house to sign. Are you willing to do that?"

At Sadie's confused expression, Liza explained that an NDA was a legal document preventing the external release of sensitive information.

"I would never say a word," Sadie promised, her voice deep and solemn.

"Once you sign the document, if you do say a word, you can be charged with breach of contract." Again, when Sadie looked confused, Liza added, "You could go to jail." That got the girl's attention. "If you're unwilling to sign for any reason, then I'm afraid you can't work here. At least not for the next few weeks."

"I need this job. I'll sign."

Liza looked at the girl carefully. While there was a time that Liza would have been quick to take at her word this virtuous young woman, Liza's swift and erroneous trust in Mrs. Boyle, the former housekeeper at the castle, had destroyed any sense of immediate faith.

"We'll meet in the conference room at the top of the stairs when Mr. Murphy arrives this afternoon, and you'll meet Ms. Turner and Mr. Fraser then."

"Mr. Fraser, ma'am?"

"I'm sorry. Shaun Fraser will be our new butler."

Sadie nodded slowly, a worried line creasing her brow.

"Is something wrong?"

"It's just that I knew a boy called Shaun Fraser from the neighboring village…"

Liza recalled the lean, clean-shaven man with the observant eyes the color of honey. She hadn't remarked on his age, but he'd seemed much older than the round-cheeked Sadie. "I don't think he's the same person," Liza offered. "It's a common name and a big country."

Sadie bit her lip and nodded. When Liza took a sip of tea, Sadie said, "Will there be anythin' else, ma'am?"

"Not for now. I'll take care of clearing my breakfast dishes and washing up. You can enjoy the morning." Liza had a feeling that after Carolyn Turner was on staff and preparations were underway, Sadie wouldn't have the opportunity for much downtime.

Not that there was much to enjoy. It was another

dreary, dark day. The weather, while cold, offered a mix of rain and sleet, and made the world seem hostile. And to Liza's chagrin, her mood was following suit.

Chapter 4

Two weeks later, Liza stared at the man with shaggy brown hair and a tiny patch of beard just beneath his lower lip.

"No," she said curtly. "That's impossible."

If he noticed her frustration, he gave no indication. He reached up and scratched his head. A shower of dandruff landed on the shoulder of his black T-shirt. He looked around the grand ballroom on the castle's second floor with a dubious expression on his face.

Liza continued. "The show must be set up in here. It's our only option. Otherwise, we can't do the performance."

At that, the man laughed, as if she'd just told a joke.

In the hallway outside the ballroom, his similarly dressed crew stacked large scuffed black boxes on the cream-colored antique carpet runner. A ponytailed man with a distended belly slid one of the cases onto the hardwood floor with his shoe.

Liza cringed. "Please, be careful."

He looked at her blankly, then turned and walked toward the staircase, passing three other crew members, their arms filled with cables, lights, and huge metal beams.

The shaggy-haired man was talking again. "It's not that the room isn't large enough..." He stroked the patch of hair on his chin. "...it's just not configured the right way. And if we set it up in here, some of the equipment we'll have to disassemble and assemble again. Not to mention the spectators will be cramped. And if Petrus sees that we've made this more complicated than it needs to be, I'm going to get an earful." He blew out a breath. "The room I saw on the lower floor would be perfect."

"That is the chapel, and it's currently being renovated."

"I heard that excuse the first three times you mentioned it, and I understand. But, as I also pointed out three times, the renovations don't have to be complete for the show to go on."

Clearly this man was *not* hearing her. She tried again. "We have workers on their way from London as we speak to start their restoration work on the stained glass in the room. That work cannot be interrupted. We're on a very strict schedule."

"It's only a day's delay."

He did not seem to understand that Liza had no control over the schedule of the Fleming Stained Glass Company, nor would they care about the reasons for a delay. As anyone who had dealt with any construction project knew, a forced delay of a day could postpone the schedule by weeks, if not longer. She would *not* delay her wedding because of this gathering.

Sadie, who was wearing a brand-new tailored white blouse and crisp black trousers, appeared from the front staircase in the drum tower. Walking right into the commotion on the grand staircase, her eyes were huge round orbs, as if she couldn't quite work out how she'd found herself in this situation.

"Ma'am, there's a gentleman here who is with Mr. Bothas's security team. He'd like a word."

When Liza turned around, she nearly ran into an androgynous-looking woman—a cross between human and sprite. She sported a short cap of shiny dark hair styled in a pixie cut, and Liza swore her ears were pointy, like an elf's. She was ageless and nubile, and even though it had begun to snow at some point in the middle of the night, this creature wore a sheer flesh-colored tube top over her small breasts which were clearly outlined beneath the gauzy material.

"Ki," the guy with the dandruff cooed. "I didn't expect you here this soon. Did you come on your own?"

"The earlier the better," she said. "An will be here soon." Liza couldn't quite identify her accent. She sounded faintly Australian. "I wanted to see the venue." She peered into the ballroom and scrunched up her face, clearly displeased.

Liza was immediately defensive. "This room has hosted centuries of royalty," she announced.

No one looked at or acknowledged her.

"Don't worry," the man said to the sprite-woman. "We're working it out."

Ki lifted her hands to the skies; Liza noted her unshaven armpits. It gave her a slight shock, though she wasn't sure why. Ki floated into the room, spinning around slowly as she walked with her arms in the air. Was she dancing or performing a ritual?

Lachlan came barreling toward her, his face stormy. "We're moving to the chapel?"

Liza held up her hands. "No."

The man in the black T-shirt faced Lachlan. "Look, man..." He gestured behind him. "...this room just isn't going to work. I don't want to assemble everything and then have to disassemble it all again. It's going to take twice as long, and I really don't want to answer to Mr. Bothas." He arched an eyebrow. "And neither do you."

Ki drifted from out of the ballroom. Liza thought Lachlan's eyes might pop from his head when he noticed her see-through top. His gaze traveled down to her skintight leather pants. She was close enough that her scent wafted toward Liza. She smelled musky and faintly of body odor. It was animalistic and alluring, rather than off-putting.

Lachlan appeared to have forgotten what he'd been

about to say.

Ki looked up at Liza's fiancé. Her lips curved into an enigmatic smile. "Well," she said in her pretty accent, drawing out the syllable.

He smiled back.

"Lachlan." Liza's voice was sharp, and the spell was broken. He looked at her, as if he was trying to remember why he'd rushed up the stairs in the first place.

She reminded him. "Can you please explain to these people that we cannot delay the work in the chapel, even by one day? I have to go meet…someone else." She exhaled, unsure which way was up.

She turned her back on Lachlan, Ki, and the man with the dandruff, then turned to Sadie, who was taking it all in.

"Where is Ms. Turner?" Liza asked.

"She's with the catering manager, ma'am."

Liza nodded, and they both headed toward the drum tower stairs at the front of the castle to avoid the scrum on the grand staircase.

As they walked, Liza wondered if she should have hired more help. She had not expected such immediate chaos.

"Do ye ken who that is?" Sadie's voice broke into her thoughts.

"Who?"

"That woman…with the—" The girl gestured toward her chest.

When Liza didn't respond, Sadie continued. "That's Ki. She's dating Petrus Bothas."

They entered the dimly lit drum tower with its rarely used staircase. "What's she doing here already?" Liza asked more to herself than to Sadie.

"She's a performance artist and a dancer. She must be performin' in the show tonight. She's released multiple…*erotic videos*," Sadie finished with a whisper.

Of course she had. Liza felt the pulsing pressure of an impending headache behind her eyes.

When the two women emerged at the bottom of the staircase, they found Shaun Fraser standing with a hulking man wearing mirrored sunglasses despite the dreariness of the day. He was dressed in a suit and was immediately recognizable as private security.

"Ms. Ramsay," Shaun said. "This is Petrus Bothas's head of security. His team is here to do a sweep of the premises."

Liza had received communication from Jane about this process, and had then been sent separate emails directly from the security team. However, she'd thought the security checks would have happened in an orderly and controlled manner, not when two dozen roadies were setting up for some sort of show right out of the seedy underbelly of the Las Vegas strip.

"That's fine," she said to Shaun with a sigh. She nodded to the large man. He would have been intimidating, but she was too harried to feel apprehension. She pulled her phone from her back pocket and swiped to her message app to let Marion Dean know that security was on the grounds. "Shaun, please help Mr. Bothas's team with anything they need."

"Ma'am, we're going to need to confiscate all phones."

She looked down at the text thread with the chief inspector, and then up at the man. "No, it's fine," she explained. "I own the castle."

"It's one of the requirements. You should have received this information. No one on the premises, including the hosts, will be permitted a mobile phone or outside communication device during the gathering. It's for the security of everyone."

He opened a silver briefcase that already held a few mobile phones inside. "This will be locked and stored in a secure location until the gathering is complete on the twenty-sixth of January."

Liza opened her mouth and then shut it again. She was too stunned to even argue, but she managed to ask, "What if there's an emergency?"

"There is no landline?"

There was, of course, though it was rarely used.

She hated that she couldn't see this man's eyes behind his sunglasses. She drew herself up to her full height. All five feet four inches of herself. The man was at least a foot taller.

"I understand that you have requirements and your orders," she said, letting him know that *she* knew he didn't have nearly as much power as he liked to pretend. "I'll be keeping my phone with me."

A muscle ticked in his jaw, but otherwise his expression did not change. Neither did his tone. "It's a requirement, ma'am." He pushed the briefcase toward her.

It wasn't as if Liza was tied to her phone. In fact, there were days she left the device charging next to the bed, forgotten until she needed to send a text or make a call. Still, the idea of being forced to give up her primary means of communication with the outside world in a house full of strangers left her feeling exposed and powerless. And maybe more than that, she felt indignant. Who did these people think they were, anyway?

"You signed a non-disclosure agreement, I believe," the man said.

It wasn't a question. He knew that she had done so. She hesitated. She hadn't asked Niall Murphy to review the agreement, and she hadn't read it carefully enough apparently. Everyone in the residence had been required to sign the NDA.

She glanced again at the briefcase before biting out a grudging, "Fine", through barely clenched teeth. "At what point do you collect the phones from everyone?"

He shook the metal box at her. "As soon as everyone enters."

"Do I have to give him mine too?" Sadie whispered from behind her.

"You too, miss," he said.

As Sadie placed her mobile in the box, Liza managed to quickly send one text before placing her device atop the others. "Guests have arrived. Security tight. No phones."

Before the man snapped the lid shut, she heard her distinct three-pulse vibration with what she could only assume was a response from Dean. She felt untethered and a bit naked.

"We're going to need any laptops and other devices that you have, too."

Liza thought about lying and telling him that there were no laptops or computers on the premises. Then she decided that, from a legal standpoint, it wasn't worth going toe-to-toe with the lawyers of a bunch of billionaires.

She stomped to the office, grabbed her laptop, marched back, and handed it over without another argument. Then she ran her hands down the back pockets of her blue jeans. How many times was she going to have to go through this for the peace of mind of her guests? "Will the security teams of the others also be arriving soon?"

"Mr. Bothas is providing the service for the gathering," he said tersely. "Once we've swept the location and ensured we have all devices, we'll exit the premises, though we'll have people placed at the entrance to the property. Mr. Bothas, especially, doesn't like outsiders onsite."

He set the silver case back on the antique console table behind him and walked outside to summon the other members of his team.

Shaun leaned in close. "I have a bad feelin' about this, Ms. Ramsay. We're basically cut off."

"The landline extension is in the castle office," Liza said, indicating the room behind them and to their left. "There is also an extension in the back conference room on the second floor, and a third in our apartment."

She didn't mention the hidden extension in the third-floor lounge.

Shaun didn't respond further before the five-person security team—a group of huge men dressed in matching conspicuous suits—ascended the main staircase and tangled with a few of the unsecured roadies.

Amidst the chaos, Liza eyed the silver case of cell phones, but just when she was about to walk over to flip the lid up, one of the security team members reappeared and snatched the case away with a sideways glance in Liza's direction.

He handed it to another man who held it in his huge hands, Liza assumed to collect the phones of anyone walking through the front door. She didn't ask how they were going to collect the phones of the roadies, though maybe they weren't as concerned about visitors as they were about the people who lived in the castle.

As the security team scattered, Liza found Sadie watching her with a look of fascination and confusion. The girl clearly didn't know what to do next. "Go find Ms. Turner and see if she needs help," Liza said. She tucked a stray strand of hair behind her ear. Liza wished that she also had a Carolyn Turner to tell her what to do next.

When she turned back around, the T-shirt-clad roadies who'd just carried all of the electronics, equipment, and large black cases up the grand staircase, were now carrying them back down. They rushed past Liza like a river of bodies so that she was boxed into a corner of the entrance hallway.

"What are you doing?" she asked a short scrawny man with wispy black hair and a thin matching beard. He shrugged and jerked his head upwards. "They told us to bring the stuff down." Without another word, he followed the rest of his crew past the castle office and toward the chapel.

A moment later, the unmistakable voice of Bruce Baxter barked out, "What in bloody hell do ye think ye're doin'?"

Liza was about to join the flow of black T-shirts on

their journey toward the chapel when Lachlan rushed past her.

"Hey," she said. He half turned.

"Gotta talk tae Bruce."

"You need to talk to *me*." But he was already heading to the chapel.

By the time she'd navigated her way through the throng of bodies, Lachlan was gesticulating to Bruce whose beefy arms were crossed in front of his barrel chest. His chin jutted out as he listened impatiently.

Liza marched up to them, just as Ki also slinked forward.

Where Liza's face was thunder, Ki's was smooth and fluid, like water. She placed a childlike hand on Lachlan's arm, and Liza couldn't help thinking about the information Sadie had shared with her about this woman's vocation and reputation.

"This space is so much better," Ki purred. Her voice was calm and positive, and even Bruce's face softened in response.

Lachlan smiled down at Ki and seemed to notice Liza in the same instant. His smile faded. "It's all goin' tae be fine," he said to everybody at once, while he made smoothing motions with his hands on the air in front of him.

"The Fleming people are on their way here now," Bruce argued. "It's snowin' out there and the temperature's supposed tae drop through the day. Can't tell 'em to take the windows if we're going to hae people in here tonight."

"Just call them and tell them to come tomorrow," Lachlan said.

"They're comin' from London." Bruce threw his hands in the air. "Who knows when they'll be able or willin' to drive back up."

"We'll pay them," Lachlan said. Liza's mouth dropped open. It's not as if they didn't have the money, but it wasn't Lachlan's money to promise. At least, not without a conversation.

She turned toward Bruce, who right now, was her closest ally. "There's a very easy solution to all of this," she said. "The show should take place, as planned, in the ballroom, not the chapel."

"I agree wholeheartedly." They both stared at Lachlan, Bruce triumphantly and Liza defiantly.

Ki watched them all, amused.

The shaggy-haired crew chief walked in behind them and nodded. "This is much more suitable," he said, surveying the chapel. "Yes, this will do nicely."

Liza turned to Bruce. "Is delaying the stained glass going to delay the wedding?"

"Most likely, lass."

Lachlan leapt in before Liza had a chance to verbally pounce. "Before we jump tae any conclusions, let's call up the Fleming Company." He looked hopefully at Bruce.

Bruce grumbled something under his breath but pulled out his ancient mobile phone—a flip phone, no less. One of the black suits was on him in a second, silver briefcase open on his massive palms. "The phone needs to go in here." He thrust forward the case revealing over a dozen phones already inside.

Lachlan held up a hand. "This is castle business."

"So is this," the man said, nodding at the case. There was just the hint of a threat in his deep voice.

Bruce looked from Lachlan to the muscular man who was now scowling at them all.

"An takes this *very* seriously," Ki said, emphasizing the word 'very'. "Better put the phone in."

It was the second time the woman had referenced 'An'. What, or who, the hell was An? Liza wondered.

Bruce shook his head and dropped his phone on the pile. "Ach," he said disgusted and clomped away.

Liza glared at Lachlan. "What now?"

"Both of you too," the suit said to Lachlan and Ki.

Lachlan reached into his pocket and tossed his phone in. He did not look at Liza.

The man looked at Ki, who said, "Does it look like I have anywhere to keep a phone?"

Their gazes all drifted to Ki's see-through tube top and skintight pants. It may have been Liza's imagination, but she thought Lachlan's gaze lingered a bit longer than everyone else's.

"Well, this is just great," Liza said. "Now we're

going to have to postpone the wedding." It shouldn't have been that big a deal, she supposed. Save-the-date notifications had not yet been sent. But Liza had wanted the wedding to take place before the anniversary of Callum's murder. Somehow, she thought her wedding to Lachlan in the place where Callum had been killed might cleanse the castle of any remaining negativity.

"No one's wedding is going to be postponed. I'll talk to these stained-glass people." Ki flung her fingers forth. "I'll pay for their inconvenience and any schedule changes."

Liza did not want this woman's money or help. This wasn't about a wave of a hand or a swipe of a card.

But before she could decline the offer, Lachlan gushed, "Thank ye, Ki. Ye are too kind." He smiled over at Liza as if the problem had been solved.

Liza snorted and walked from the room, trying to hold back a sudden flood of tears. She'd thought maybe Lachlan would sense her angst and follow her, but when she turned back around, he was still in the same spot, gesturing around the room to his new 'friend'.

In the grand scheme of life, a small delay to their wedding wasn't important. And the events of last summer had taught her, to some extent, how to keep minor inconveniences in perspective. But another, more emotional part of her couldn't help but note that the way Lachlan was acting right now was exactly how

Owen, her ex-fiancé, had acted in the past. And that relationship had ended when Liza had found suggestive text messages from another woman and subsequently fled to Scotland.

Perhaps she was being silly, but watching Lachlan with Ki brought back all of those same insecurities.

At least the main hallway was now clear and quiet, she thought, as she ascended to the second floor. She could hear voices above them, likely the security team with Shaun. And voices drifted up from the kitchen, a hive of activity with Ms. Turner and Sadie directing the catering staff.

Liza entered the drawing room to catch her breath, expecting to find it empty. Instead, she spotted an old man studying the intricate and colorful tapestries on the wall with his hands clasped tightly behind his back. He was dressed in a pair of woolen tweed trousers and a green jumper. A red and white silk tartan scarf with blue and green accents coiled around his neck like an ascot.

So much for the security of Petrus Bothas.

"Can I help you?" she said.

Startled, he turned to her, then smiled. Liza guessed that he may have been in his seventies. For just a moment, she had the oddest sense of déjà vu. Something in this man's bemused gaze reminded her of Callum.

"Ah, pardon me. I was just studyin' this beautiful

piece." He nodded toward the tapestry on the wall. "Ms. Ramsay, I presume?"

Before she answered his question, she asked one of her own. "You are?"

"Robert Rose. But most people call me Rabbie." He tapped his tongue to the roof of his mouth as he pronounced the 'r's in his name, producing a poetic alliteration. "I'm a bit early. I hope ye don't mind."

Liza gave him a tight smile. "Mr. Rose." Remembering her manners, she approached him and held out a hand. "I'm sorry someone wasn't here to give you a proper welcome. It's been a bit chaotic this morning."

He made a noise meant to blow away her concern. "As I said, I'm early. And I heard the…voices from below after that brute stole my phone."

"He's with Mr. Bothas's—"

"Security detail," Rabbie finished. "Aye, I've met him before. Or one of them. They're all the same, aren't they?"

"And he just allowed you to walk in?"

"Aye, to the castle. But there is a team checkin' everyone's identification at the entrance by the road. Got a good barrier set up there."

That made Liza feel marginally better. She wondered if Dean had sent anyone out yet to patrol the area. If these people were going to have their security, she wanted her own too.

"Can I get you something to drink, Mr. Rose?"

"Please, call me Rabbie. And no, I don't think so."

She nodded, then hesitated. Carolyn Turner had planned the room assignments, and Liza couldn't remember which room was Rabbie's. She looked around for a suitcase or overnight bag. "Can I send someone to fetch your bags?" she asked, distracted.

She supposed she'd have to wait until the security team was finished with their sweep of the building before installing everyone in their accommodations. And where was Shaun? She glanced about, hoping he'd magically appear. Hoping at least one thing would go right.

Sensing her frustration, Rabbie placed a hand on her arm. "Don' worry about me, Ms. Ramsay. Ye should ken, it's always like this."

"Like what?"

"Pure chaos. That's how they like it."

She wasn't sure if it was the laughter in his voice or the underlying kindness that caused her to pause. "But why?"

"These people may not be artists, but they do create. And often what they create is born of confusion and drama. They're disruptors at their core. Nothing that any of them do is straightforward." He chuckled. "I've got to confess—I used to be a bit like them. But I've grown out of it. I'm an old man now, who likes my rest. Along with a wee bit o' entertainment." He winked.

Suddenly, Liza felt weary. She eyed the sideboard of the drawing room which had been stocked with alcohol, much of it the Spirits Rose brand, three cases of which had been sent over earlier in the week. She could use a drink herself.

Rabbie laughed at the direction of her gaze. "Go ahead, lass. I have a feeling ye're going to need it."

She shook her head. "Can't have the hostess of this gathering incapacitated."

"It wouldn't be the first time," he said with a laugh. "Won't be the last, either."

"Well, it's not going to be me. Not at the Ramsay Castle at least."

"That's quite all right. I'm certain there'll be plenty of other occurrences this weekend that will capture our attention and sense of mystery."

"Mystery?"

"Perhaps *mystery* is not quite the right word. What I'm tryin' to say is this is a group that will keep ye on yer toes."

Liza wasn't sure what Rabbie meant by that. But before she could inquire further, Carolyn Turner rushed into the room. "Ms. Ramsay," she said in her prim and proper accent. "I'm sorry to bother you, but we've just gotten word that one of the guests—Matthew Carter—has demanded *hot dogs* for the evening meal." She appeared to be scandalized by this command.

Rabbie Rose let out a bark of laughter. "See what I mean?"

This wasn't so much a mystery as it was an absurdity. Liza thought for a moment. "Since tonight's entertainment seems to be acrobat-themed, let's have the menu reflect the playful nature of the performance. Do the caterers have the ability to serve American carnival food—hot dogs, hamburgers, popcorn, funnel cakes? We'll wash it all down with craft beer and Mr. Rose's best Scotch whisky."

Ms. Turner grimaced, but nodded briskly. "I'll see what we can do."

After the woman had taken her leave, Rabbie tipped his head toward Liza. "Aye," he said then tapped the side of his nose with his index finger. "Ye're goin' tae do just fine with this group, Liza dear. Just fine, indeed."

Chapter 5

Sergei Popova was the next guest to arrive. The rotund Russian barreled through the front door as if he were taking possession of the castle, and his strong cologne that smelled of tobacco and pine made Liza's eyes water.

He barely glanced at Liza and instead thrust his bag toward Shaun.

Liza noticed that the man's driver wasted no time in speeding back down the castle's long drive. The driver's haste could have resulted from the rapidly falling snow. But perhaps his retreat had more to do with his passenger.

Sergei gave a quick once-over of the interior.

"You Scots and your castles," he said in his thick, guttural Russian accent. "Rossiya has buildings twice this grand." He snorted. "My own place would have been a far more suitable location for this gathering." His short fat fingers were adorned with rings that shone as he gesticulated. "And we would have been attended by proper servants. Bah!"

Liza glanced at Shaun before responding. "My

understanding is that Mr. Bothas was insistent on a lean staff."

"Bothas. What a fool." Sergei pushed forward, apparently intending to climb the staircase despite having no idea where he was headed.

Shaun intercepted the man. "We have ye on the third floor in a well-appointed room close to the back staircase. Each of the rooms has its own working fireplace, which has already been set for ye."

"Where is the lift?" Sergei interrupted.

It took Liza a moment to realize he meant 'elevator', but Shaun understood immediately. "No lift, but as I said, we have ye right next to the stairwell."

A red flush of anger began to creep up the man's neck. He opened his mouth ready to erupt anew, but Shaun spoke first. "Yer room is the only one with a wet bar, and ye're right across the hall from the third-floor bar and sittin' room. Closest one. Fully stocked."

This information seemed to quell the imminent outburst, though Sergei still looked perturbed. "Stocked with what?"

"Only the best whisky." Shaun tilted his head a bit closer. "And I was able to find ye a bottle of Russo-Baltique vodka. But please dinnae ask any questions about exactly *how* I was able to procure it."

There was a short pause and then a bark of laughter. "You have done research, my good man. Perhaps we will become friends after all." He clapped Shaun on the back.

Liza mouthed 'Thank you' to Shaun, and the younger man responded with an almost imperceptible tip of his head. He picked up the Russian's huge suitcase easily and headed up the grand staircase. Sergei spared no backward glance at Liza.

Lachlan joined her just as the other two men disappeared out of sight.

"I'm sorry," he said, somewhat out of breath. "The Fleming people have just left. They're tryin' to get out before the snow gets too heavy. We may get a blizzard. It's really comin' down out there."

Liza was still angry about the chapel, but she didn't want her hurt feelings and frustration to impinge on their guests. She did her best to breathe and let it go, vowing to address her disappointment with Lachlan after the weekend had passed. She and Lachlan didn't often argue, but she knew she wouldn't be able to ignore her feelings. "What did they say?" she asked, her voice neutral.

"There's good news and bad news."

"Give me the bad news."

"They aren't able to return until the first week in February, and that is obviously goin' tae push back the schedule."

Liza shut her eyes, scrambling to swallow back anger and look on the bright side. She still had time to adjust the dates, and she might even appreciate an extra few weeks as they approached the date later in the summer months. Perhaps the spirit of Callum would smile down upon them and send them pleasant summer weather in the notoriously unpredictable Scottish climate.

"The good news?" Lachlan asked tentatively.

Liza shrugged.

"The owner of Fleming knew all about yer story and is going to push the team to do everything in their power to finish in time fer our original date. He wants ye to be happy."

Liza couldn't help but quip, "I'm glad someone does."

Before Lachlan could respond, Liza held up a hand. "I'm sorry. That was unnecessary."

He was quiet for a second, and Liza knew that her comment had hurt. He continued softly, "Ki wants to pay for the restoration. All of it. As a wedding present."

Liza immediately bristled. "That gesture is also unnecessary."

"She really is a sweet girl," Lachlan said. "Her real name is Stephanie."

That bubble of jealousy in the pit of Liza's stomach threatened to burst, and Liza pushed it down. This was Lachlan who had proved his loyalty to Callum time and time again, she reminded herself. This was Lachlan who had *saved her life.* He was not her ex-fiancé Owen, nor had he ever acted like Owen. It was Liza who was acting like a child.

She did her best to show some interest and keep the conversation light. "So where did the name 'Ki' come from?"

"That's a little murky. It's her performance name, and she's in the process of legally adoptin' it. It comes from an ancient Sumerian myth." Lachlan looked as though he might try to explain something to Liza and then thought better of it. "Anyway, she's a nice person."

Liza just nodded and started to walk toward the kitchen to find Ms. Turner. She was doing her best to avoid acting petty, but she also didn't want to hear about how *nice* Ki was. What she really needed to do was make sure things were going smoothly with the catering and that Sadie felt comfortable with her assignments.

"You didn't hear the best news of all," Lachlan called after her.

Liza slowed and looked over her shoulder. "What's that?"

"Bruce Baxter is on yer side. Told me I'm an idiot fer allowin' this evil show tae take place in the chapel, and that I should be listenin' to my soon-tae-be wife, before ye're my one-who-got-away."

Liza forced a smile and made a benign comment about Bruce coming to his senses. But she wasn't feeling either charmed or confident. Something of

Lachlan's words had an ominous feel to them, as if they were a portent of peril to come.

The American Matthew Carter was next to arrive, but was completely overshadowed by the tall, gorgeous younger woman on his arm. Liza immediately recognized her as model and influencer Daphne St. James, daughter of British multi-billionaire Hugh St. James, a chemist, engineer, and businessman who had founded the James Pharmaceutical Company. Daphne was also considered a successful businesswoman in her own right—the *Daphne* brand included a line of cosmetics, beauty supplies, and high-end fragrances. Liza had also read that the woman was preparing to launch a designer clothing label.

Despite the otherworldly beauty of the young woman, her face was fixed with a vacant stare that bordered on vapid. Liza had to assume that she had plenty of help on the business end of her empire.

Matthew Carter reminded the group of his presence when he thrust out his hand. "Liza Ramsay," he said. "I've been very interested to meet you."

"Me? Why?"

"I followed your story closely last year. As a fellow American, I always love to see a success narrative. Especially if it means besting the rest of the world. I'm afraid we've started to lose that race a bit."

The man had a hard look about him, and though he was friendly enough, there was an underlying impatience that made Liza imagine he didn't suffer fools lightly.

She supposed if you'd managed to create the biggest software platform in the world before buying one of America's most successful sports teams and investing heavily in the defense industry while befriending numerous world leaders and politicians, you might tend to become intolerant of any nonsense.

Liza glanced at the man's wife, who seemed as inconsequential as a bit of dandelion fluff. At first glance, it appeared that Matthew was with the woman for her youth and her looks. But Liza knew that looks could be deceiving, so she tried to avoid prejudging their relationship.

He smoothed back his unnaturally dark hair, not a strand of which was out of place. "This is my wife, Daphne," he said.

Daphne stepped forward and offered first Liza then Lachlan her cool, limp hand. Her movements were forced and robotic. "Pleased to meet you." Her accent wasn't unlike Ms. Turner's, though there was something less refined in her words and the over-enunciation of her vowels.

"Of course, Ms. St. James," Liza said. "We didn't have you on the guest list, but we can prepare a room.

Unless you'll be staying with your husband."

Matthew answered for his wife. "Better give her some space. God knows she's got enough clothes with her to fill three of your guest rooms."

Daphne didn't react to that, just moved her mane of sleek blonde hair from one shoulder to the other.

Two men appeared from behind the couple, each carrying two large suitcases and a number of smaller valises, along with bags of varied shapes and girth. Both Shaun Fraser and Carolyn Turner stepped forward. "We'll take care of the luggage," Ms. Turner said, not about to let the unsecured drivers into the castle. "Just place everything right there," she directed, pointing to a spot by the door. "Ms. St. James, I have a lovely room for you on the fourth floor, if that suits."

Daphne nodded and asked, "Has anyone else arrived?"

"Robert Rose and Sergei Popova," said Liza.

"And Ki," added Lachlan.

Matthew's head snapped up. "Sergei is here?"

"Were you not expecting him?" Liza assumed that the participants of this gathering would have been made known to each other.

Matthew shook his head. A shadow crossed over his face. Suddenly, instead of the arrogance, there was a hint of self-doubt; an apprehension. But as quickly as the expression appeared, it was gone again, replaced by the intense confidence.

Daphne stepped forward and looked around the entrance and toward the antique chandelier. A placid smile spread across her face. "This place looks exactly as I remember."

"You've been here?"

"When I was a child. Teen, I guess. With my uncle."

Before Liza could inquire as to the identity of her uncle, Rabbie Rose appeared at the top of the staircase.

"Ah, the lovely lassie Daphne has arrived."

Daphne's serene face lit up at the sound of the thick Scottish accent. "*Uncail*," she called back, and her voice slipped into a Scottish brogue, before shifting back to her earlier English accent. "Uncle Rabbie, it's so good to see you." Abandoning her bags and her husband, she ran up the stairs and threw her arms around the old man. "It's been ages," she said in her euphonic English dialect. It was the first sign of life that Liza had detected in the woman.

Rabbie broke the hug. "How's yer mither?"

Daphne's expression changed. "She's fine. The same."

"Okay, Daph," Matthew called up. "Let's get our bags to our rooms and freshen up. There'll be time to reminisce later."

She looked from Matthew back to Rabbie, who gave her a nod of his head. *Go on.*

Daphne walked back down the stairs slowly to

rejoin her husband.

Shaun picked up Matthew's bags first before shooting a look at Daphne's luggage piled up inside the front door. "I'll come back fer those."

Liza smiled and indicated that Matthew and Daphne should follow her up the grand staircase where Rabbie still stood.

"Can we have a climb up through the drum tower?" Daphne asked.

"Ye ken the stairs in the drum tower?" Lachlan looked taken aback. "Those stairs had been closed off fer years."

Daphne gave him a sheepish look. "The last time I was here, I met a rather well-known…boy. We explored. There were plenty of secrets in the castle worth exploring." Her smile was childlike, deep, and dimpled. Much different than the woman who had greeted them just a few minutes earlier.

"Secrets?" Liza asked.

Daphne winked at her. "I'll wager I may know a few more secrets about this place than even you do," she said. Then she turned, offering no additional explanation.

Liza looked at Lachlan, who shrugged. There was clearly an interesting story that the young woman wasn't telling.

They obliged her anyway and led both Matthew and Daphne up the dimly lit staircase. Daphne ran an elegant hand with carefully manicured nails along the bricks as they climbed.

They kept moving along the staircase until they reached the reading room on the third floor where the staircase ended. There was no fireplace in this room, but the vintage radiators kept the room warm as snow blanketed the ground outside. Liza glanced out the ancient window and noticed that at least two inches had freshly fallen within the last hour, and the squall continued to reduce visibility across the Ramsay estate grounds.

"You don't have an elevator?" Matthew asked, unimpressed with the reading room. It was the same question Sergei had asked, using different terminology.

"Not yet," Liza answered. "We hadn't planned to host guests this early."

"Then what are we doing here?"

She wasn't sure if his question required a response. She bristled. "Mr. Rose is the one who came to us. Despite our hesitation, he was quite insistent and persuasive."

Daphne gave a little laugh and clapped her hands together, clearly thrilled by anything to do with her uncle. Matthew shot his wife a contemptuous look. She put her hands down quickly as the laugh faded from her lips.

Ms. Turner had assigned Matthew a room on the right side of the hallway. Shaun deposited the man's suitcases inside and headed toward the back staircase to gather Daphne's bags. Matthew peered into the room which was decorated in deep hunter greens and burgundies. It was a masculine room, and Liza silently gave Ms. Turner thanks for anticipating the personalities of their guests so well.

Matthew seemed to be searching for something to complain about. His gaze stopped on the fireplace, which had been laid with fresh logs, yet to be lit.

"Does this thing work?" he asked.

"It does," Lachlan responded. "Would ye like me to get it started fer ye?"

Matthew eyed the comfortable leather armchair next to the fireplace. "Yes."

As Lachlan stepped in front of the hearth, Liza said, "I'll show Daphne to her room."

Matthew didn't answer nor did he acknowledge their exit.

The two women climbed the back stairs to the fourth floor, emerging in the rear of the hallway. Again, Liza noticed Daphne's eyes taking it all in.

"Does it look much different?" Liza asked, curious.

Daphne lifted a shoulder, still concealed by her long double-breasted coat with its layered sleeves and unique plaid lining. "It was dark, and we weren't supposed to have been up here," she said.

Liza's curiosity got the better of her. She leaned in close. "Who was it?" she whispered.

Daphne's gaze snapped to Liza's.

"The boy…" Liza prompted.

Daphne was quiet, and for a moment, Liza thought she'd overstepped.

Then a slow smile spread across the younger woman's face. "If I told you, I'd have to kill you."

Liza laughed, and Daphne continued. "Let's just say he's now extremely well-known for having run off to the States with his American wife." Her smile faltered. "Rather as I have with my American husband, I suppose." She waved her hand as if shooing the thought away, and recovered the memory. "We were kids, though *he* at least, was old enough to know better. But it was fun. Truth be told, I think Uncle Rabbie knew and was all for it. He would have liked to have a royal niece. He's all about tradition."

Liza had certainly figured that out about Rabbie Rose, but she couldn't quite reconcile this girl who had emerged in the absence of her husband, with her surprising impish grin, to a position in the stolid, staid Royal Family. Though maybe she would have been something they sorely needed.

Shaun Fraser came bumping up the back servants' stairs with two huge bags in his hands and two smaller bags under his arms.

Liza moved forward to help him, and he allowed her to take the two smaller bags, which were both heavier than Liza had expected.

"Be careful," Daphne exclaimed. "Those are my cosmetics."

Just as Liza was wondering why one might possibly need that much makeup, Daphne said, "You won't mind if I do some photo shoots inside the castle, right? I can't have my phone," she said and made a face. "But I did bring my Nikon and tripod." She nodded to one of the oddly shaped bags.

Liza hadn't considered how much publicity that might bring the location.

"I thought this was a private, secretive meeting."

"The photos won't be posted until after we leave. And of course, no one will know *how* I came to be here. The brands I represent will be thrilled to be featured in a medieval castle."

Liza gave her permission to have the photos taken with the caveat that she'd need to check with Mr. Murphy regarding the use of the actual location. Daphne seemed unconcerned with that detail.

Shaun walked toward a room on the right side of the hallway, nearly directly above Matthew Carter's room. "Ms. Turner said this is the best room in the place," Shaun said with a quick smile at Daphne. Indeed, the space was lovely. It had been decorated in soft lilac and creams, and the toilet had been renovated with a jacuzzi bathtub. While the fireplace was not yet laid, the grate was clean below the white brick mantel. The space was fit for royalty, and in fact Her Majesty had stayed in this room once upon a time. She hadn't even been the first royal woman to reside in the space.

But Daphne frowned, her pretty brow revealing a crease between her eyes. She pointed out the door and across the hallway to another room. "Would you mind if I moved over there?"

Liza hesitated. It was the room Liza herself had first occupied upon her visit to the castle last summer. Lady Catherine's chambers. She remembered the strange occurrences that had taken place: the ghostly visitors, the voices, the feeling of her body being electrified.

"I'm sure you'd be more comfortable in this room," Liza said lightly, motioning toward the space that had been assigned to Daphne. "It's bigger and brighter."

Daphne looked between the two spaces, then walked purposefully toward Lady Catherine's quarters. "I think I'd like to stay here."

Shaun looked at Liza, who shrugged then exhaled. "Let's go."

When Daphne's bags had been deposited on the decorative bench at the foot of the bed, Liza said, "Would you like me to send Sadie up to unpack for you?"

Daphne walked over to the wall next to the fireplace, and Liza caught the mournful eyes of Lady Catherine studying them curiously. Liza looked quickly away from the painting. Still, she could vividly picture the sorrowful brown eyes, the dark hair, the feminine curve of the cheek, so lifelike it would seem as if that face might turn and mouth an otherworldly secret. Or a warning.

Liza shivered. She noticed that Daphne was also distracted. It was a struggle stepping out of Lady Catherine's spell, but Liza forced her attention back to the present and repeated her offer of help with Daphne's luggage and clothing.

"No," Daphne answered absently. Gone was the personable, bright woman that Liza had spoken to just moments earlier. "That'll be all."

As Liza and Shaun left the room and descended the back staircase, Shaun said, "She's more beautiful in person than in her photos."

Liza glanced over her shoulder at the man. There was nothing sinister in the way he'd said the words, but something of the comment reminded Liza of Sadie's reaction when the name Shaun Fraser had first been uttered. Nothing more had come of Sadie's concerns, and as far as Liza knew, Sadie had been interacting with Shaun for the past week without incident. She didn't want to invite trouble, but maybe she should ask Sadie if all was well.

When they reached the first floor, they discovered that Aaron Scott had arrived and had carried his own bags to his room on the third floor with the help of Carolyn Turner.

Liza swore under her breath. She'd spent too much

time with Daphne St. James. Both she and Shaun hurried back up to the third floor, and by the time she reached the top of the staircase, Liza was out of breath and her quadriceps burning from all the climbing.

Aaron Scott still had a few snowflakes in his hair, and his long beaked nose was red on an otherwise pale face.

He looked at Liza with wide blue eyes when she said, "Mr. Scott, my apologies for leaving you to your own devices." He had a sanguine expression, though he didn't smile. "I'm Liza Ramsay." She walked forward with her hand outstretched, displaying a confidence she did not feel. This man single-handedly had control over the world's largest communications platforms, and likely other technologies and decisions that Liza couldn't begin to fathom.

Unlike the prickly and arrogant Matthew Carter, Aaron Scott appeared thoughtful and observant rather than reactionary.

He took her hand and studied her. "You're younger than I'd expected."

She wasn't sure how to respond to that comment, even though she'd thought the same about him. Though he was in his late thirties, he possessed a boyish quality. In fact, he seemed almost shy.

"I had wanted to be here to welcome you," she said. "How was the travel to the castle?"

"The plows are out, but the crews seem to be having trouble keeping up with the snowfall." He glanced out his window that overlooked the northeast end of the castle grounds. From his vantage, he had a view of the long drive leading to the main road that wended into the village.

"It's beautiful, though," Aaron murmured.

Liza tried to reconcile this man with the cutthroat executive who had initiated multiple hostile takeovers of rival media conglomerates and was a leading proponent of monopolized artificial intelligence, much to the chagrin of his peers. Aaron's company Ajna had made incredible strides in AI over the past few years, but all rather quietly. Liza had had no idea the company existed until she'd done research on Aaron over the past two weeks.

Ajna had made a number of stealthy strategic investments and partnerships with a limited number of tech companies, all but ensuring digital dominance in the field. This meant that Ajna was in a position to use its monopoly to manipulate users while thwarting efforts at regulation, putting the company in a position of near-complete power over all artificial intelligence assets across the globe. And because neither the field nor the technology was well understood, not many people were asking questions. Scary stuff indeed.

One person who had been extremely vocal against the implementation of closed AI practices was Petrus Bothas, who saw artificial intelligence and its rapid development as one of the future's greatest threats.

"You have a beautiful home," he said, so sincerely that Liza felt disoriented.

"Yes," she said. "Thank you."

"Has An arrived?"

"Anne Kane? No, not yet," Liza said.

"Sorry. I meant Petrus." Aaron looked as if he might say something else, but he left the words unspoken.

Liza repeated the names of the guests in residence. They were now only waiting for Anne Kane and Petrus Bothas. "We plan to gather in the dining room on the second floor for dinner and then head to the chapel for Circus Noir."

Aaron gave a short laugh. "I see Ki got her way."

"Her way?"

He answered her question with another. "Have you seen the show?"

Liza shook her head. "I believe the performers are rehearsing now, but I've been busy with the guests."

"You said the performance will be taking place in the chapel."

Liza pursed her lips but said nothing. It was still a sore subject.

"The gods will not like that."

"Gods, Mr. Scott?"

"Whatever you worship—gods, ghosts, spirits." He said this with a flick of his fingers and a hint of derision. "And call me Aaron."

"What makes you think I worship any of those things?"

He studied her again, and the careful way he looked at her made her even more uncomfortable than the hard gaze of Matthew Carter had. It was as if Aaron Scott could see into her soul. "Because of the way that you lovingly observe your environment and the energy that you've put into your surroundings. I can feel love for the past and the unseen coming off of you in waves."

Liza was taken aback by his assessment. She didn't know if she should feel complimented or violated.

After a moment, she said, "And what about you, Mr. Scott...*Aaron*? What do *you* worship?"

"Science. And progress. At any cost."

Liza caught a hint of the man beneath the easy-going facade. Detached. Remote.

"Six pm, you said?" he asked.

She nodded.

"I'm going to catch a quick nap before dinner. I'm a bit jet-lagged. Honestly, these days, I can't remember what country I'm in."

"Would you like Shaun to build the fire for you?"

"No, thank you, Liza," Aaron answered. His easy charm had returned. "I'll see you in a few hours."

Liza nodded and stared back at the door as it shut behind her.

What a strange group of people. But something about the collection of personalities made her want to please them. *Be* one of them. Their big personalities, prodigious vision, and quirky out-of-touch existences intrigued her. She wasn't like them, but maybe one day she could be.

Is that what she wanted? she thought as she made her way back to the second floor. All these months, she'd thought she'd wanted to be an innkeeper. Maybe what she really wanted was to play a part in changing the world.

Chapter 6

As the dinner was laid out in the formal dining room under the watchful eye of Carolyn Turner, Liza wrung her hands. At least half a foot more of snow had fallen, and though the grounds of the Ramsay Castle looked like a crystal-encrusted wonderland, Petrus Bothas had yet to arrive.

Anne Kane's plane had been delayed, and later she'd entered the castle in a rush of snow and cold, uninterested in pleasantries. Liza had read the mood of the woman, who was as icy as the weather she'd brought in with her. In her late forties, Anne was taller than many of the men, with a taut lean body under her long black coat. Her silver-blonde hair shone brighter than the snow that had covered it.

Despite her delay in arrival, she was the first one in the dining room for dinner, dressed immaculately in a sapphire blue A-line sheath dress, her accessories platinum and elegant, and her makeup impeccable. A cloud of rich, spicy floral followed her, and Liza inhaled deeply as the woman swept forward.

Sadie shrank back and retreated in Anne's powerful

wake.

"I must apologize, Ms. Ramsay, for my mood when I arrived."

Anne Kane was American, but the precise way she formed her words made her sound vaguely British, though her speech bore no resemblance to the stiff patterns of Ms. Turner or the round soothing dialect of Daphne St. James.

"Please, call me Liza, Ms. Kane."

"Then you must call me Anne." She tilted her head back and sniffed the air. "Is the rumor of frankfurters true?"

"I'm afraid so. But there are also hamburgers and salad. And if you'd prefer something else, I'm sure we can arrange it."

When Anne laughed, she revealed a mouthful of impossibly white teeth. "I'm not that hard to please," she said. "I may have had a privileged upbringing, but my grandfather was a humble man. Despite the excesses of my father, Opa gave us some normal experiences. Baseball games, carnivals, amusement parks. Some of my favorite memories."

Anne looked around, noting the lack of bodies in the room. "These men are not known for their punctuality," she remarked. "Would you mind showing me around? You may be aware that I have a keen interest in art and architecture, and in my brief travel to my room, I wasn't able to properly appreciate the fine collection amassed here."

Liza agreed, glad for the distraction from the worry due to Petrus's continued delay.

She walked Anne around first the drawing room, describing the origin of the tapestries, antique furniture, and elaborate chandeliers. Then they moved to the main hallway where Liza introduced her to the portraits of the Ladies and Lairds Ramsay from the past seven centuries.

Anne inspected each piece with a keen and critical eye. Normally Liza was extremely proud of the antique collection at the castle. Anne's inspection made her watchful and defensive. "I'm sure our collection is not as valuable as many you've seen," she offered meekly.

Anne arched an eyebrow. "Do you know much of the value of art, Ms. Ramsay...*Liza*?" she asked, remembering herself.

"I wouldn't say that."

"Often what makes a piece valuable is its history. Its heritage. The way that it ties the past to the present in a shared story, and the potential it has to remind future generations of the lessons of the past, even when we fail to listen to those lessons ourselves." Anne pointed up at the mural above the doorway. "Who painted this?" she asked.

"A man named John Macpherson," Liza said. "It was completed in 1879, so it's relatively modern compared to the rest of the castle and its pieces." Liza gazed up at the battle scene that may have depicted a number of periods in the history of the Ramsay Castle. The location of the stronghold at the gateway to the Highlands on the banks of the Creagan River had made it valuable to the Caledonians for the defense of *Alba*. Its location had made it equally as valuable to the English when it had changed hands and become a fortress from which to march English troops north-ward. From King Edward I to William Wallace to Oliver Cromwell to Mary Queen of Scots—great leaders and warriors had all appreciated this place and the status of the Ramsay Clan in history.

"Ah, but you see..." Anne pointed up at the mural. "...that's precisely what makes this piece valuable—the story that it tells about this building, this family, this land. That is what I'm interested in, Liza. And that's what makes me a good art historian. I understand that art is...life."

Liza smiled at that. Perhaps Anne Kane was not as cold as she'd first seemed.

"And what of the art collection from your own history?"

Anne looked at Liza and cocked her head. "What do you mean?"

"Your grandfather immigrated to the United States from Germany, didn't he?"

A shadow darkened Anne's face. "No, you're mis-taken."

"I'm sure I remember correctly. I took a number of art history classes, and I vividly recall a professor mentioning that Samuel Kane had immigrated to the United States as a young man following the outbreak of World War II. He was able to salvage a few of the family pieces. Is that where your love of art was born?"

"I'm afraid your professor is wrong." The ice had returned to Anne's voice. "Perhaps you should seek a refund from whatever unaccredited school you attended." Anne didn't wait for Liza to respond before she swept away in her cloud of perfume.

Confused by the sudden change in the woman's mood, Liza whispered a meek, "It was Harvard," in her wake.

Lachlan climbed the stairs in time to note Liza's baffled expression. "What's wrong, *m'eudail*?"

Liza let out a short, mirthless laugh. "I'm not sure what just happened, but I don't think Anne Kane likes me very much." She noticed that Lachlan's cheeks were flushed. "Have you been outside?"

"No, down in the chapel. It's freezin' in there."

"I thought they were finished setting up?"

"I was takin' a peek at the rehearsal."

He did not meet her eyes. Liza nearly asked about his reticence, but decided not to plumb those depths at that moment. They had bigger things to worry about.

"Petrus still isn't here," she said instead.

"Aye, he's on his way."

"How do you know that?"

"Ki mentioned it." Again, the lack of eye contact and the flushed cheeks. She was beginning to suspect the flush wasn't due to the cold.

Liza studied him. "How would Ki know?" she asked. "She doesn't have a phone. Or at least, she *shouldn't* have a phone."

"She says they have a soul connection—she can communicate with him telepathically."

Liza stared at Lachlan, who didn't appear to be speaking ironically. "And you believe that?"

"I've heard stranger things."

He didn't elaborate, but Liza knew he was referring to the role that the ghost of Sir Alexander Ramsay may have played in Liza's own survival in the castle dungeons. She did not appreciate the implication.

"Anyway," Lachlan continued, "Petrus's security team are huddled in their vehicles by the main road. I'm sure if Petrus isn't able to make it, they'd have come up and knocked on the door."

That was true, Liza supposed.

"I was just about to dress for dinner. Care to join me?" he asked, a suggestive tone coloring the words.

Maybe it was Liza's sensitivity to Lachlan's fascination with Ki, or maybe it was her apprehension about the guests. It could have been her anxiety about the continued delay of the main player on this stage. Whatever the cause, Liza was irritated by his innuendo.

"We don't have time for that."

Lachlan grabbed her hand and started moving toward the heavy mahogany door of their apartment near the end of the second-floor hallway. "Sure, we do."

"Anne is already in the dining room."

"She's the only one, and ye said she disnae like ye. Let's give her a reason fer it."

"Lachlan, no!" Liza snapped.

Noting the hurt look in his eyes, she opened her mouth to explain her reaction, but he held up a hand. "Nah, ye're right. I shouldn't hae pushed ye."

"It's not as if I don't want to…" But that's exactly what it was, and they both knew it.

"No need to explain. I'll just go and freshen up before dinner. The *help* has tae look good too." He didn't look at her again before opening the door to their apartment and shutting it behind him.

Liza sighed.

She followed him into the chamber, but gave him a wide berth as she also dressed for dinner. They spoke in short questions and one-word answers while Lachlan dressed in a white shirt and crisp gray trousers. His hair curled roguishly over his ears.

He caught her watching him. "Is this not appropriate fer yer important guests?" he asked, a challenge in his tone. He was looking to pick a fight.

She was not.

"You look amazing," she said, then added, "I'll be happy to marry you in just a few short months."

"Oh, we're goin' tae dredge up that fight again, are we?"

"What fight?" Liza asked. Now she was irritated too.

"I told ye, we'll do everythin' we can tae make sure the chapel is done in time. But it's just not good enough fer ye, is it?"

Liza's face burned. She did not want to do this now, but how dare he turn the delay back around on her. "Well, if you hadn't been so eager to please the naked woman in our home, perhaps there would be no delay."

"Ye're the one in charge of this gatherin'," he yelled. "Perhaps ye shouldn't hae invited these people here in the first place."

"It's too late now," she said.

"It sure is," he agreed, and stomped out of the room.

When he shut the mahogany door behind him, more forcefully than was necessary, Liza jumped. Her heart beat heavy in her chest, and she took a few deep breaths, trying to calm herself.

She washed her face in cold water and dressed in a form-fitting red dress that was much brighter than she felt.

When she left the apartment and walked down the

passage to the dining room, most of the guests were present. Lachlan held a whisky glass of amber-colored liquid and didn't look her way when she entered.

Ms. Turner clapped her hands together. When the guests settled, she announced the menu as a team of catering staff entered the room with silver platters filled with American fast food. If anyone was disappointed by the informality of the dinner, they gave no indication.

As they munched on hamburgers, hot dogs, chili, popcorn, and French fries covered in cheese sauce and gravy, the guests reacquainted themselves.

Daphne, in a simple rose-colored dress, huddled together with her uncle in one corner of the room, while Matthew Carter frowned and watched them. Lachlan had made some progress with Anne, who appeared more charmed with him than she had with Liza. And Liza watched it all, fretting about Petrus's absence while noting that Aaron Scott was also missing. She attempted to put her quarrel with Lachlan out of her mind. They would work out their differences later.

Sergei Popova, face florid, lurched toward Sadie, who was refilling glasses with soda, beer, and Spirits Rose single malt.

"You are a little *Zaychik*." His heavy vowels sounded menacing rather than complimentary.

Sadie ducked away from his meaty hands. Liza had

no idea what the word meant, and she assumed Sadie didn't either.

Sergei was on the girl again in a minute, causing her to spill the bottle of soda she'd been pouring.

Liza moved quickly toward them. Before she could reach Sadie, Anne, a red solo cup in her hand, swept in. "Sergei, you brute. Leave the girl alone."

With a glance at Liza, Sadie abandoned her duties and left the room. A minute later, Shaun Fraser seamlessly picked up where the girl had left off.

"Anastasia," Sergei slurred, transferring his attention to the older woman. "It's always my pleasure to see you." His accent seemed to have become more pronounced with his inebriation. "Bah," he said when he looked around and found that Sadie had escaped. "I'm looking for a woman anyway, not a little girl. Care to accompany me to my room?"

"I'm surprised your equipment still works under that belly." She gave a pointed look at his ample midsection. "With as much drink as you've already consumed, I doubt you're good for much besides perspiring on a woman."

"I perform just fine in the bedroom," he said. "Just ask Ms. St. James." He laughed heartily at his own secret joke.

Before Liza could react to that comment, the deep chime of the doorbell sounded from the front of the house. Liza jumped. Shaun made a movement to walk toward the door, but Liza stopped him. "Stay and keep an eye on Mr. Popova. I'll greet Mr. Bothas." At least she *hoped* it was Petrus Bothas.

She rushed down the stairs and opened the door, expecting to find a driver delivering Mr. Bothas's bags. Instead, she encountered a tall snow-encrusted man wearing a long woolen coat, toboggan cap, and black gloves designed more for driving than for hiking in frigid temperatures. His face was red from the cold and wind, and he smelled of skin and winter. In one hand he held a small black bag. The other hand was shoved deep in his pocket. His teeth chattered. Liza ushered him inside.

She looked around him for a car, but the driveway was empty of all but the steadily falling snow.

"I'm sorry, this is a private residence," she said, wondering how this man had made it past security. But she couldn't in good conscience leave him out in this weather. "Come in and warm up, and I will call someone to collect you."

Sadie had appeared from the kitchen.

"Can you prepare some tea? As hot as you can make it."

"C-c-coffee," the man said through chattering teeth.

"Right. Coffee," Liza amended, and she huddled the man into the castle office, placing a chair next to the radiator heat. With frozen fingers, he attempted to peel off his gloves, and Liza reached forward to help him. She took his icy hands between her palms and rubbed vigorously. As he started to flex his fingers, she released her grip. He placed his hands dangerously close to the radiator. "Be careful," Liza warned, and gently guided them away from the scalding metal.

This time, she kept hold of his large hands between her fingers.

As she stood over him, he looked up into her face. "Road impassable," he managed. "Had to walk. Car stuck."

She supposed that explained his presence. The castle was powered by its own small electric grid and large backup generators. With the snowstorm, she suspected that at least some of the town may not have had electricity from the main grid. The light from the castle would have been a beacon to him as it had been to so many in the past. It still didn't explain how he'd managed to make it past the security team. Unless they'd not been able to see through the snowsqualls. Which was another concern altogether.

"You're lucky you didn't freeze to death out there," she said, wondering if she should call Dean on the landline for her own peace of mind.

A minute later Sadie came in with the coffee, and the man reached for it quickly. "It's hot," Liza said, intercepting it and forcing him to move more slowly.

He took a small sip and gave a sound of pleasure.

"Better," he said. He took another swallow and began to return to a normal color. She glanced down at his boots, which were more weather appropriate. Still, depending on how far he'd walked, the risk of frostbite remained.

Ki burst into the room before Liza had a chance to question the stranger more aggressively, and if Liza had thought the woman's earlier outfit was inappropriate, she'd been mistaken. Ki was now dressed in a sheer white mesh dress with nothing underneath. Liza could detect no undergarments of any kind. The woman might as well have been completely nude.

"An!" she cried. "Finally. I was getting worried about you."

Ignoring the mug of hot coffee, Ki nestled herself on the man's lap and snuggled into his wet wool coat.

Liza watched this coupling for a long moment before the knowledge of the man's identity clicked into place. "Mr. Bothas," Liza exclaimed. "Oh, my goodness. I'm so sorry. I didn't know it was you. Are you okay? What were you doing?"

He took another long drink of the coffee then set the cup on the desk.

"Ms. Ramsay, I presume," he said after a minute. He flexed his thawing lips over his mouth, testing his ability to speak. Finally, he continued, "You were quite kind when you thought I was a wayward soul. There will be a special place in the afterlife for you."

Ki had begun planting small kisses on Petrus's jaw and neck. Petrus stared straight at Liza, and his pronouncement seemed to hold some weight, as if he were certain about her acceptance into an afterlife.

Liza blinked. "Can I show you to your room so you can get out of those wet clothes?"

The question held an innuendo that Liza had not intended, and Petrus chuckled and smiled. He reminded Liza of those portraits of Maine longshore-men—heavy clothes, woolen cap, ruddy cheeks. He certainly did not look like the richest man in the world. Other than for the naked woman currently sitting on his lap, Liza supposed.

She sputtered, "I-I just meant—"

"I know what you meant," he interrupted, letting her off the hook. "And I'm fine." He stood, and Ki slid down the length of his body and positioned herself in front of him. She clung to him even as he shrugged out of his coat.

He handed the garment to Liza. "If you can have someone take my things to my room, I'll join the party now. I assume there's a party?"

Ki nodded, and Liza looked around for Sadie who was still lurking in the doorway. She handed Sadie the coat and directed her to take it, along with Petrus's lone bag, to his room on the third floor.

When Liza turned back, Petrus was kissing Ki deeply and intimately. She cleared her throat softly and

Petrus looked up at her without breaking the physical connection with Ki.

Liza couldn't look away.

His eyes flashed.

She pointed to her head, trying to indicate that she could take his hat.

With one hand still on Ki's exposed backside, he reached up and plucked the cap from his head, tossing it in Liza's direction. His hair was still damp and stood up in short brown strands.

Liza caught the cap and walked from the room. She handed the article of clothing to Sadie who hurried toward the drum tower staircase.

When Liza walked up the grand staircase, she did not turn to see if the couple followed. She entered the dining room, still shaken from the entire encounter, and caught Lachlan looking at her curiously from across the room. He was now standing with Matthew Carter, but he offered her a slight smile.

Liza smiled back, relieved.

Rabbie approached her, a cup in his hand. "Have ye eaten anythin', hen?"

She realized that she hadn't and shook her head. A moment later, a hamburger on a plate was delivered to her. Rabbie winked. "Knowin' this crew, it's goin' tae be a long night."

There was a collective flutter among the guests as Petrus walked into the room. Rabbie pumped Petrus's hand aggressively, and Sergei boomed something in his slurred words about it being nice that Petrus had decided to join them. Matthew crunched on a handful of popcorn and scowled, and Anne Kane circled warily, eyeing the naked Ki.

"Nice to see you again, Petrus," she said.

"Is it?" Petrus smiled at Anne. Something passed between them. Anne had to be nearly twenty years older than Ki, but she was much closer to Petrus's age. And in Liza's opinion, the heiress and former model was twice as beautiful and more interesting than the attention-seeking Ki.

Liza glanced toward Lachlan, who couldn't seem to tear his eyes from Ki's body. Liza wondered if she could tell Ki to cover up. As the host, what was the etiquette when one of your guests refused to wear proper clothing?

After Petrus had served himself from the sideboard, he asked, through a mouthful of food, "Where is Aaron?"

Everyone quieted and surveyed the room. Sure enough, Aaron was not in attendance. In fact, Liza could not remember seeing Aaron since she'd left him in his room hours earlier. Perhaps, in his jet-lagged state, he'd fallen deeply asleep.

Sadie was on the other side of the room, keeping her distance from Sergei who had lost interest in everything but the tumbler of Spirits Rose single malt in his hand.

Liza approached her. "Can you go and gather Mr. Scott? He may need some help waking up."

Sadie nodded and hurried away.

Petrus snorted. "He's avoiding me."

"He can hardly avoid ye here," Rabbie said.

The other man poured himself a cup of soda. "Oh, yes he can. This is our annual airing of grievances, and this year, my grievance is with him."

"Everyone has a grievance with everyone else here," Matthew said.

Sergei burped loudly, and Anne said, "My grievance is that we keep inviting *him*." She jerked her head toward Sergei. "Whose idea is that anyway?"

"Ask Matthew." Petrus raised his glass in Matthew Carter's direction, and Matthew scowled and looked away.

Liza frowned. When he'd arrived earlier, Matthew seemed surprised that Sergei would be in attendance. Liza turned to Petrus instead. "What is your conflict with Mr. Scott?" She was emboldened by her initial encounter with the billionaire.

"For one thing, he started that company of his—Ajna—even though I explicitly told him not to."

"I didn't realize we were required to take direction from you," Matthew shot back.

Petrus stared at him intently, and Matthew's gaze slid away from the more powerful man.

"You do," Petrus answered slowly, "when there is a signed legal agreement that you will not start a privatized company dealing in the rogue development of artificial intelligence. That is the entire point of open-source AI. The market is supposed to regulate itself. Aaron is trying to create a monopoly on the technology. And he's watching everyone else, but no one is watching him."

Anne lifted an elegant shoulder. "I thought it was you who said not three months ago that AI was going to develop beyond human capabilities whether we like it or not. Aaron is simply proving your own point."

Petrus shook his head. "You're taking my comments out of context just like everyone else does. While I did, indeed, verbalize those words, you're missing the part where I went on to explain that it's going to be important to regulate the development. And I don't mean government regulation. I mean we must regulate each other. Aaron believes that AI is the next evolution of our planet, human consciousness be damned."

"What on earth does that mean?" Rabbie asked.

"It means that he doesn't care if AI destroys and replaces humans," Petrus said. "Once it takes over, the progress will be insidious. And there will be nothing we can do to stop it."

"That might be bothering you," Matthew said, "but I think you're angrier that Aaron poached some of your people."

Petrus scowled but didn't say anything.

Ki jumped in. "An cares about the divine spark." Her voice was hot, passionate.

"Oh, for god's sake, quit calling him that," Anne said. "People are going to confuse him with me, and that's the last thing I want."

"Who is An?" Liza asked.

Anne went to pour herself another drink.

Carolyn Turner picked up the cup that Anne had just abandoned and discarded it almost imperceptibly. Liza had barely noticed that the woman was in the room.

"An is the Anunnaki god of the sun," Ki announced. "Petrus Bothas is An reincarnated. And I am Ki, his queen consort."

Anne laughed out loud. "Your name is Stephanie, and you're from Canterbury, New Zealand," Anne shot back.

Sergei laughed loudly, too, but Liza had no idea if his amusement was directed at the conversation or at something else entirely.

As this argument was taking place, Daphne walked into the room, smoothing her long champagne-colored hair behind her ear. She appeared flushed and out of breath.

Her dress was an icy blue and flowed past her knees. Liza could have sworn the other woman had been wearing different clothing earlier in the evening.

A few minutes later, Aaron Scott joined them, and Ki announced that the performance would begin in twenty minutes. When Ki took her leave, Liza breathed a sigh of relief.

"Aaron," Petrus said. "We have some things to discuss."

The other man piled a plate high with food and poured himself a generous tumbler of whisky. "Tonight is not the time, Petrus," he said evenly. "Tonight is for friends and fun. We can discuss all of your issues and complaints tomorrow during the meetings. That's what this gathering is for, isn't it?"

"Yeah, except that on my way here, I got word that Gerald Ellis was leaving my company to join Ajna. That's the third intelligence engineer you've poached from me in the past year."

"That's not my problem. I'm a better leader than you are. Not to mention, my salaries are higher." Aaron smirked.

"To what end, Scott?" When Aaron took a bite of a hamburger and declined to answer, Petrus continued. "I'll tell you to what end. To the end of the human species."

Aaron sighed heavily and finished chewing before he said, "You know how I feel about this. Evolution is a bitch, but she's nothing if not predictable. And evolution does not favor humans. That much has become glaringly clear over the past few years."

"It doesn't have to be that way, and you know it."

"I know nothing of the sort."

"Now, lads," Rabbie said. "There's no need tae fight tonight."

Sadie appeared at Liza's side. "Ma'am, can I talk to ye for a minute?" She indicated that Liza should follow her into the hallway.

Liza trailed Sadie out of the room. "What is it?"

"I wasn't goin' tae say anythin', but I feel funny about keepin' this secret." She hesitated so long that Liza finally said, "Sadie, spit it out."

The younger woman took a deep breath. "When I went up tae collect Mr. Scott, I knocked softly but got no response. I could hear somethin' in the room. Shufflin' and breathin'. I got nervous, so I tried the door, and it was unlocked." Her gaze slid to the floor, and she swallowed.

Liza glanced into the dining room to ensure that Petrus and Aaron had not come to blows. Petrus's arms were gesticulating wildly, but Aaron continued to eat his hot dog.

Sadie took another breath then continued. "When I opened the door, I saw…Ms. St. James."

"Where was Mr. Scott?" Liza asked.

"He was there too."

"Okay," she said slowly, and waited for Sadie to continue.

The younger woman licked her lips and shifted her

weight from one foot to the other.

Liza was becoming impatient with Sadie, and she tried to remain calm. The woman's intimidation was understandable, but unhelpful.

"Bullshit!" Petrus's word punched through the air and shot across the distance of the room.

Liza looked over her shoulder and saw a smug smile on Aaron's face—condescending and superior. Petrus's fists were now balled at his side.

"Sadie," Liza said. "Can you hold that thought for a second?" Before Liza had a chance to go back into the room to diffuse the tension, Ki appeared, now completely nude, at the top of the stairs. "It is time," she announced loud enough for everyone in the drawing room to turn toward her voice. "It is time for the show to begin."

Liza shut her eyes. It seemed to her that the show was already in progress.

Chapter 7

The space was black as pitch as the guests entered the chapel. Liza bumped into a body that she assumed was Lachlan's, but they'd entered as one amorphous group, and the bodies jumbled and reconfigured in the darkness.

There were a few murmurs of discomfort, and someone—she thought Rabbie—laughed nervously. Anne Kane asked in her unmistakable plummy American accent, "Is the electricity out? Should we be worried?"

Just as Liza was preparing to retreat to check on the power, a single beam of red light washed toward them from an unknown source, illuminating a group of ten chairs.

They shuffled in, haphazardly and disoriented, toward the ominous-looking oasis of seating. Liza found that she was on the opposite side of the mob from Lachlan. She became sandwiched between Sergei Popova and Petrus Bothas, both of whom appeared demonic in the dim red light.

Petrus grinned at her, and she half-heartedly returned a wan smile. She did not share his sense of, what seemed to be, anticipation.

They sat in the red glow for long minutes that stretched into a distortion of time and space. A metal-on-metal noise echoed from the front of the chapel and then faded again, until the only sound was the shuffling of the people in the chairs. A light cough, and a whisper—Daphne perhaps. Then a giggle, and an answering chuckle.

Beside her, Sergei breathed forcefully, and his body gave off a surprising amount of heat. He smelled of booze and sweat. No matter the high cost of the premier alcohol he'd been drinking, at the end of the day, a drunk was still a drunk.

Liza found herself leaning close to Petrus on her right side to escape Sergei's rancid aura. Compared to Sergei's suffocating warmth and smell, Petrus gave off a different kind of energy—vibrant and clear. She accidentally brushed against his arm, then whispered an apology to which he did not reply.

When she'd leaned far enough from Sergei, she felt the chill of the rest of the room and smelled the piney scent of recent construction—varnish and fresh-cut lumber. But underneath was the rich, dusty essence of the past. A reminder of the ritual and sacredness of the chapel itself. In the darkness, the ghosts danced and co-mingled with the living. As a light breeze kissed the back of Liza's neck, her skin electrified. She was tuned to the frequency of another realm.

A loud crack cut through the silence. Liza, along with a few other faceless guests, let out a startled gasp.

There was another charged silence, and then a click after which a sudden flow of buttery-yellow light illuminated the makeshift stage.

Ki stepped forward, her naked body bathed in luminescence. Behind her stood two ladders that reached the ceiling, along with what looked like a large bird's cage hanging in the center of the spotlight.

She lifted her arms heavenward, and a deep, low tone pulsed from a hidden amplifier. The tone reverberated through Liza's body and into her core. She shifted in her chair.

Two large swarthy men, their stomachs and nether regions covered in slinky gold cloth, stepped toward Ki. They were heavily muscled and oiled in the bright light. But as impressive as they were physically, it was Ki who held the attention. Her small body glowed nearly white, as if she was illuminated from within or possessed by an otherworldly source of light.

A low thumping beat, not unlike a heartbeat, began pulsing in time with the primal tone. The men knelt down while Ki stepped into their hands and then onto their shoulders, finally resting the soles of her feet on the tops of their heads. She balanced effortlessly, the music building with her climb.

Liza had been so focused on Ki and her companions that she had not noticed two figures climbing the tall ladders on each side of the stage, until they swooped down on their trapezes, one of them ensnaring the elevated Ki by her outstretched wrist.

Liza let out a small cry, and she was vaguely aware of Petrus chuckling beside her. Then he leaned closer. "Just wait," he whispered, and his warm breath tickled her ear and caused shivers down the right side of her body.

Back and forth, Ki flew through the air between the two acrobats. She twirled and tumbled with the pulsing beat of the music. There seemed to be no control, and yet every twist of her body was effortlessly beautiful in its wild abandon.

It was difficult for Liza to take her eyes off of the electrifying Ki, and when she tried to focus on the acrobats who were now flinging the young woman around, Liza found they were moving too quickly. They could have been men or women, humans or creatures, angels or devils.

Finally, with a sudden burst of orange light, Ki was tossed nearly to the ceiling. The music reached a crescendo, culminating in silence. For a terrifying second, Ki was suspended in space and time. Then, her arms crossed over her chest, and her legs tight together, she spiraled down toward the floor, like a high-diver gracefully soaring toward the water's surface.

Except there was no water—only the cold stone ground, on the exact spot where baptisms, marriages, and funerals had taken place for centuries. Liza leapt up and screamed, "No!"

The light extinguished. In the darkness, there was another crack.

Then silence.

Her heart pounding, Liza attempted to scramble over the legs of Petrus, who grabbed her around the waist as her feet clumsily entangled with his.

"Liza," he said, his voice a mixture of amusement and bafflement. "It's okay."

It was not okay. Someone had just dived headfirst into the floor from a height that precluded survival. She pried at the fingers which held her captive.

The lights snapped back on, and Liza blinked. Ki lay prostrate on the hands of the two oiled, muscled men. Liza's companions erupted into applause.

"Bravo!" called Rabbie Rose, while Sergei laughed heartily. "*Очень хорошо!*" he called in his heavy voice. "Very good!"

Liza's heart was still beating furiously, but now a rage bubbled up from inside her. Part of her was embarrassed by her overreaction, and the other part was angry over the unnecessary risk that had just been taken. In her house. In a church.

What was wrong with these people?

Still held by Petrus, she struggled against him, but

he pulled her down so that she was sitting on his lap. "It's all an illusion, remember?" he asked, his words so close and hot that they nearly manifested into something tangible to worm their way into her mind.

She didn't know why, but she stopped struggling when she was engulfed with the sense that her body was melting into his. In the darkness and the silence that followed, she couldn't tell where she ended and he began.

The lights illuminated the stage again, this time with a sapphire blue glow. Ki was now inside the cage with two other genderless figures. They didn't seem to be wearing any clothes at all, and their bodies were completely smooth. Their eyes and faces were hidden behind golden masquerade masques. Ki, still naked, kissed one of the figures deeply as the cage began to undulate. The hands of the other figure began a slow ascent upward, exploring Ki's body. The music, now louder and more insistent, was punctuated with human voices, low masculine and feminine keening and whispers.

When Liza realized what was happening, she slid away from Petrus, and he let her go. She felt for the chair beneath her and perched at the edge of her seat.

As the cage swayed higher and higher, Ki alternated between kissing each of the figures as hands roved her body, fingers exploring. Ki arched forward. The tongue of the other licked a path down her neck and stopped at her chest.

Liza heard heavy breathing to her left and looked over. Though the seating area was dark, she could just make out the shadowy movements of Sergei next to her.

On Sergei's other side, Daphne appeared to be sitting very close to her husband. She may well have been sitting atop him.

Liza could not see Lachlan. Where was he? What was he doing? What was he thinking?

It was all too much. Whatever was happening on that stage, it was not an illusion. Those movements were real; these reactions were real.

Liza had to get out. She stood to scramble past Petrus, and this time, when his large hands reached out to stop her, she was ready for him. She pushed him away, nearly falling over him in the process. An unoccupied end chair skittered across the floor then toppled. The interruption was enough to cause confusion, and Liza, her eyes blinded by the bright lights of the stage, scrambled free. She reached out instinctively and kicked something hard with her shin.

She sucked in a breath as her hands reached a wall. Limping, she pushed out into the dim light of the chapel hallway. She gulped in air as if she'd been underwater.

Inside, the music pulsed on.

As she stood alone, Liza anticipated that Lachlan

would sense her unease and follow her out of that spectacle to make sure she was okay. But when the door finally opened behind her, it was not Lachlan who appeared. Instead, it was Anne Kane who emerged, her blue dress and silver hair gleaming.

"Needed a moment, too?" Anne asked. She looked around the hallway as if she were in search of something.

"If I'd known what I was in for, I would never have agreed to host in the first place." Liza wrapped her arms around her stomach. Her shin was pulsing where it had slammed into the hard object.

"Are you talking about the performance or the gathering?" Anne asked with a wry smile. She didn't wait for Liza's answer. "Ki is something else. They all are, really. But when you have that much money, there's no limit to what you can get away with."

"Don't you have as much money as the rest of them?" The question was delivered bluntly, but Liza wasn't feeling diplomatic at the moment.

Anne didn't seem to be offended. "Of course." She pressed her lips together. "I'm sorry, but I really need a cigarette. Herbal joint, actually—the non-psychoactive kind. Is there a covered porch where I might duck out for a moment?"

Liza blinked at the change in subject. She hadn't had a cigarette since her freshman year of college, nor had she wanted one. But something about Anne's description piqued her interest. "What kind of herbs?"

"Just rolled tea—jasmine, rose, and honey. They help me relax, and after that spectacle…" She lifted her chin toward the doors. "…I could use a breather."

Liza was already moving toward the back stairs. "Follow me."

They emerged in the back corner of the second floor, and Liza led them into the library where Shaun had built a crackling fire. Liza switched on a low lamp that bathed the room in warm light.

"What an absolutely charming room."

"This might be my favorite room in the castle." Liza looked at the books that covered the walls from floor to ceiling.

Anne wandered over to a chess set encased in glass on a table near the back of the room.

"This can't be what I think it is…" She peered closer, her keen eyes assessing the set.

Liza didn't answer. She should have known that an art dealer like Anne Kane would identify those gleaming white pieces at first glance.

After a few minutes, Anne murmured, "This is the entire Uig chessmen set." She straightened and clutched the back of a chair. "Do you have any idea what you have here?" Her voice was filled with awe.

Liza nodded. "It's worth millions."

"Not millions," Anne corrected. "The chessmen are priceless. They should be in a museum."

Liza gazed at the distinctive figurines carved from ivory culled from the teeth of walrus and whales. Over the centuries, the pieces, sculpted in the twelfth century, had been found largely around the Uig Bay in the Outer Hebrides island chain. Somehow, however, those pieces had all eventually made their way to the Ramsay Castle. Even the chessmen that had been stolen from the castle over the years—including the piece that had started the chain of events that nearly culminated in Liza's death—had all made their way safely back home.

Although Liza agreed with Anne that the set of human-inspired figures, with their bug eyes and dour expressions, should be properly displayed where they could be enjoyed by the general public, neither she nor Lachlan had been able to part with them. She felt as though the chessmen wanted to stay put.

"We've locked them up," Liza said, indicating the padlock on the case.

"You know that's not what I meant." Anne shot her a disapproving look, but moved away from the set and took a slim case from a pocket hidden within her dress. She opened it, and a sweet potpourri escaped.

Liza inhaled. The rich floral scent calmed her senses.

Anne held the case toward her, and she plucked out one of the fragrant cylinders.

"You don't mind smoking in here?" Anne asked.

She proffered a silver lighter from the case.

Liza leaned forward and lit the end. She inhaled deeply as the scent of incense filled the room. A profound peace flowed through her body, and she rolled her neck from side to side. "Normally, I would object, but this isn't a dirty nicotine-laden cigarette." She scrunched up her nose. "Besides, I couldn't begin to count the number of cigars consumed in this library." Even so, Liza didn't plan on making a habit of smoking herbs.

Anne took a drag of her cigarette and looked around. "It's a decidedly male room, isn't it?"

Liza followed the other woman's gaze, imagining, as she often did, Sir Walter Scott sipping a glass of good spirits in front of the fireplace.

"Drink?" she asked Anne.

"Oh, hell yes."

Liza laughed and moved to the small bar in the corner where she poured them both a Glencairn of Spirits Rose.

As they inhaled their herbs and sipped their bouquets, Liza could just barely make out the pulsing beat of the music below. She scowled at what was happening in the chapel. Scowled because clearly Lachlan hadn't noticed or cared that she'd left. Scowled because he was ogling Ki and her naked body, along with her strange counterparts, in the very spot where Liza and Lachlan were supposed to be joined together in a sacred ceremony that would now be delayed because of the current sacrilege.

"We'll be gone soon enough."

"What?"

"You look incredibly unhappy that we're here."

Liza began to wave away the other woman's charges, then stopped, emboldened by the alcohol. "I am, actually," Liza said. "Unhappy that you're here," she added. "We weren't ready for guests. But it was such a shock to get Rabbie's inquiry, and when I saw the guest list, I was dazzled." She shrugged. "By the time I'd come to my senses, it was too late."

"You could have canceled at any time."

"Somehow, I didn't assume Petrus, or the rest of them, would take my rejection lightly. I didn't see a way out."

Anne took a long swallow of her Scotch and said nothing.

"And what about you? Why are you with this group?"

She stared into the fire. "A Kane representative doesn't always come. Sometimes one of my brothers is here, sometimes not. But over the years, I've found that if one of us doesn't attend, a few months later, some legislation is passed, or some regulation is introduced that hurts the retail industry in some way." She lifted a shoulder. "Maybe it's all a coincidence."

Anne didn't look like she believed that, and neither

did Liza.

She continued, "Most of the time, I'm not part of the real discussions they have. The conversations about geopolitics and world security, intellectual property, and advanced engineering, and the economic viability of the globe. But I think my presence reminds them that we exist." She laughed, a high, tinkling sound. "Maybe it doesn't. Maybe I'm crazy. But I suspect I'm here for the same reason they all are. We remind each other of our relevance. Even if that relevance is only to ourselves."

Liza looked into the crackling, dancing flames. At the end of the day, was that not the same reason she'd agreed to host this gathering? To prove to this group that she, too, was relevant?

"Anyway," Anne continued. "It's mostly just a bunch of hot air. A group of men, and sometimes women, bickering. Most of the conversations come to nothing but empty words."

"Most," Liza repeated, pulling out that one word.

Anne grinned, slow and feline.

"What about the conversations that *do* come to something?"

Anne finished her herbal cigarette and stubbed it out in the remainder of her whisky. "My dear. Those are the conversations that change the world."

Chapter 8

Liza remained in the library after Anne had retired to her room. The fire had burned down to embers, and while the sweeping hallways and high ceilings of the building sometimes caused drafts to hang in the air and travel like ghosts through the interior, because of its placement within the walls, the library nearly always felt warm and cozy. She found herself nodding off in front of the dying light.

When she could fight it no longer, she returned alone to her apartment. She glanced at a clock that hung on the wall of their room. It was well past midnight. Their meetings were scheduled to begin at 9:00 a.m. the next morning, but from what she'd seen so far, Liza suspected that this group followed a very loose adherence to schedule.

She listened for the continued relentless pulsing of the primal music coming from the chapel, but given that their living quarters were situated at the back of the castle, she couldn't catch any sounds, even when she strained to do so. Perhaps the performance had ended, and Lachlan would return to her at any moment.

Instead of immediately dressing for bed, she walked to the tall windows of the apartment's sitting area and peered into the darkness. The snowfall had eased, but cloud cover blocked any moonlight. Still, by the meager light shining at this hour from the castle onto the grounds, she could see that over two feet of snow had fallen since morning. The drive leading to the castle had long since been covered, and the roads into the small town and toward the city would be impassable well into the next day. And that was *if* the area didn't get any more snow, as had been forecasted. Who knew how long they might all be stuck in the castle together? The thought of it made her weary.

As it was, on this night, they didn't have enough rooms for the catering staff, who had been scheduled to vacate to be replaced by a fresh morning crew. And there were at least four performers that Liza had seen for whom accommodations had not been accounted.

A brisk rap on the apartment door startled her, and she turned and crossed the room quickly.

She noticed her heartbeat quicken in anticipation or fear—she couldn't tell which. She pulled the door open fast and wide to compensate for her reaction, and was relieved to find Carolyn Turner standing outside.

Ms. Turner looked exactly as she had earlier that day—her white shirt was crisp and her black pants clean and pressed. Not a strand of her hair was out of place. She looked cool, capable, and competent and reminded Liza of Chief Inspector Dean. Liza gave silent thanks to Dean for the recommendation of Ms. Turner as an addition to their staff.

"I apologize for the interruption, but I need to alert you of a situation," Ms. Turner said, and quickly summarized the same issue that Liza had just been pondering. Neither the catering staff nor the performers were going anywhere anytime soon.

"We have the extra accommodations upstairs," Liza said uncertainly. "They haven't gone through the same rigorous background investigation, but these are extraordinary circumstances." Still, she was hesitant to house contract staff in the same area as the prominent guests. She was nearly finished with caring what these people thought of her and Ramsay Castle, but there was a small part of her that was still putting her best foot forward.

"Mr. Baxter has proposed another solution."

Liza's eyebrows rose.

"He has offered to sleep in the chapel office and give up the cottage for the extra guests. I haven't been in the residence, but he assures me there is ample space for the additional bodies."

Liza had only been in the cottage a few times after Lachlan had moved out, but it did hold several bedrooms and bathrooms. And while Liza wanted to be a gracious host, she felt more comfortable with the unsecured guests away from the more prominent visitors.

"Mr. Baxter doesn't mind?"

"He says not, though it's often hard to tell what he's actually thinking through his gruff demeanor." Ms. Turner's tone tightened. "He also claims that he'd like to get an early start putting the chapel back into order after the travesty that has just occurred there. His words, not mine," she clarified.

"The performance is finished then?" Liza asked, noting the continued absence of the guests, including her soon-to-be husband.

"Mr. Fraser and I have seen the guests to their rooms, though I suspect many of them will retire to the third-floor lounges. Mr. McClaren stayed behind to help Mr. Baxter and the performers with the dismantle."

Liza nodded, attempting to keep her face passive. Carolyn Turner did not need to know that she was worried about her fiancé. "Well then," she said briskly, "that sounds like the best solution we've got."

Ms. Turner nodded and turned to take her leave. But before she did, she turned back as if she were ready to say something else. Liza waited, but the moment passed, and the older woman just nodded briskly instead. "Goodnight, Ms. Ramsay."

Liza shut the door softly behind her. She changed into a modest set of silk pajamas that would have been perfectly acceptable to wear as a casual ensemble with guests, should she be summoned for any reason throughout the night.

She felt ridiculously naked without her phone, so she stayed up reading a novel—a psychological thriller by a popular new author—until her eyes began to droop. Switching off the lamp on her nightstand, Liza tucked herself under the covers, feeling very alone indeed in her houseful of guests.

Liza awoke with a start, listening.

There had been a sound, she was sure of it. What was it?

She felt for the bedside lamp and squinted at the clock, which indicated it was 2:30 a.m. Still no Lachlan. Could the sound have been him, climbing the back stairs and making his way to the apartment?

But the space was empty, and the room quiet.

Liza blinked and reached over to switch off the lamp. There it came again—a thumping sound followed by what she thought was a low ghostly moan. She waited.

And again.

The castle walls were thick, but since moving into the building, they had not hosted this many people at one time. She was not sure how sound traveled through the thick walls, and she could not tell from where the sound originated.

She folded the covers back and climbed out of bed, shoving her feet into a pair of slippers. Then she grabbed a flashlight from the drawer of the bedside table and ventured out into the dark hallway.

She thought she heard the sound again, but she also heard other shuffling movements—creaking and ticking—that seemed to be coming from the third floor. She turned to her left and climbed the winding back stairs before slowly pushing open the door that emerged between the third-floor lounge and a storage closet.

The lounge was empty. She tried to remember the guest room assignments—the male guests were residing on this floor. She had seen most of them to their chambers upon arrival, or had welcomed them there. All except for Petrus and Rabbie. Liza peered down the shadowy, empty hallway, and felt the weight of the castle's historical darkness.

There it was again, louder this time. She thought the sound might be coming from Aaron Scott's corner room. A thump, a light clanging, and then a low sound, human in nature. A sigh? A moan?

She listened in the hush of the passageway. But this time, there was silence. Still, she stood in the shadows at the end of the hallway, waiting for something to happen.

The click of a latch was amplified in the stillness, and then the unmistakable sound of door hinges rasping open. But it wasn't Aaron's door that opened. This was on the other side of the hallway. Liza's heart leapt into her throat as she watched a large shadow emerge.

Sergei, she realized, her pulse thrumming. And he was heading Liza's way, most likely for the lounge where Shaun had stocked the best whisky.

He swayed as he moved, and Liza marveled at the man's ability to function with all the alcohol he seemed to have consumed already throughout his short stay.

If he'd been looking, he would have been able to see her, or at least her outline, in the shadows. She didn't wait; she moved quickly along the wall and reentered the stairwell, shutting the door behind her quietly. Her slippers made a light flapping noise on the stone stairs as she quickly descended to the second floor.

When she reentered her apartment, her heart still furiously pounding, she found that Lachlan's clothes had been discarded on the floor at the foot of the bed, and he was breathing heavily on his side of the mattress.

Her lamp still glowed by her bedside, and she stared at Lachlan for a moment, debating. In the end, she just sighed. There would be time for discussions in the morning. Nothing productive would come from a late-night argument. Especially one fueled by billionaires, eroticism, and alcohol.

As she slid under the covers, Lachlan inhaled and rolled over, flinging his arm over her. Liza was about to push him away. But her nerves were still frayed from her sojourn to the third floor; she leaned into his body instead.

He breathed into her hair. "*Tha gaol agam ort,*" he whispered in his sleepy brogue.

She wasn't sure exactly what that particular Gaelic phrase meant, but she couldn't help but smile. "Back at ya," she whispered, and he chuckled before his breathing regulated and he was asleep again.

Despite the fact that her heart was somewhat eased, Liza couldn't shake the feeling that something was very wrong, though she couldn't put her finger on it. She fell into a fitful sleep, lucid dreaming of bodies and flashing low lights in the snow. In one particularly vivid scene, Callum's kind face leaned over her to whisper a warning, but as he came closer, she found that it wasn't Callum at all. It was Petrus Bothas. And he had fangs.

Liza's internal clock woke her at 6:30 a.m.

It was still dark outside, and she felt as if she hadn't slept at all. Her dreams had kept her as active as if she'd been running in place all night.

She climbed from the bed and showered as quietly as possible, careful not to wake Lachlan. She wasn't being considerate. She simply was not ready to talk to him yet.

She threw on a pair of blue jeans and a long black flowing blouse that contrasted nicely with the red highlights in her auburn hair. Though she didn't often bother with makeup, she brightened her sallow complexion with a bit of highlighting foundation and smudged concealer over the dark half-moons under her eyes. Not satisfied with the paltry effect, she applied a bit of neutral eyeshadow, black eyeliner, and dark mascara, along with a plum-colored lip stain.

When she stepped back and assessed the look, she thought she looked rather sophisticated. If one took the time to look closely enough, the shadows beneath her eyes were visible. She doubted anyone here would take that time. Still, the effort had given her the boost of confidence she needed to face this group once again.

When she emerged from the bathroom, Lachlan was snoring loudly. He muttered something in his sleep, and his dreams sounded as uneasy as hers had been. *Good*, she thought.

She knew she was being petty. Even though her irritation from the night before had softened, there was no doubt that she was still stung by his lack of aware-ness of her discomfort. And what *had* he been doing until the wee hours of the morning? She didn't doubt there had been work and cleanup to do in the chapel, but she also couldn't help feeling that if anyone but Ki had been involved, Lachlan would have been in bed well before 2:00 a.m.

The beginnings of a headache stirred behind her eyes, and she left the room in search of a strong hot cup of coffee.

She passed Shaun Fraser, who had just emerged from the dining room. "Lady Ramsay." He smiled, but she could see the shadow of exhaustion on his face.

"Try to find some time today to rest," she said as she passed.

He nodded his head. "Will do." His voice was cheerful, but weary.

She didn't think he had any intention of taking her suggestion.

Sadie was in the drawing room adjacent to the dining room, fussing over a sideboard lined with coffee, teas, and fresh scones.

Liza had entered quietly, and when Sadie turned, she jumped at the sight of Liza standing just inside the doorway. "I'm sorry, ma'am," she breathed, her hand on her chest. "Ye scared me."

Liza shook her head. "We're all a little jumpy, I think. And I should have announced myself." Liza crossed the space and poured herself a mug of coffee, lightened it with fresh cream. "I don't expect we'll see many of our guests for a while. It was a late night."

"So I heard," Sadie said.

"From whom?"

"I just meant that I heard everyone returnin' to their rooms after midnight, and then movements and noises throughout the night. Couldn't sleep well what with the people and the snow."

Given that Sadie's room was on the fourth floor, Liza assumed she'd heard Ki returning to her room later than the other guests. She nearly asked Sadie what time she estimated that Ki had returned. But before she could utter the question, something occurred to her.

As Liza had been investigating the sound she'd heard on the third floor, Lachlan had returned to their apartment. But she hadn't seen Ki on the back stairwell. Liza supposed Ki could have used the servants' stairs on the other side of the castle, but why would she have done that? Did Ki even know that stairwell existed? Liza also didn't remember Ki having been one of the guests who'd explored the drum tower stairs the day before. Had Ki returned to her room? Perhaps she'd opted to stay with her performers in the cottage…

"Everythin' all right, ma'am?" Sadie asked, interrupting Liza's thoughts. Liza cradled the mug of coffee in her hands.

"Did you happen to leave your room last night?"

"No, ma'am. But I did hear some strange thumping sounds." Sadie's eyes were wide. "I thought maybe it was the ghost of Lady Catherine." The young woman had heard the rumors of Lady Catherine's ghostly appearances and seemed both terrified and desperate to receive such a visit herself.

Had Sadie heard the same sounds Liza had heard coming from Aaron Scott's room? Liza didn't ask the question. Instead, she said, "Has the catering staff made it up from the cottage yet?"

Sadie shook her head. "But the refrigerator is fully stocked and there's plenty of food for breakfast. I can cook some eggs, beans, and tattie scones when ye're ready fer it."

Liza smiled. "Let's wait and see where we are in an hour or so." She thought heavy food might be the last thing on the guests' minds after the amount of Spirits Rose imbibed. "Tea and toast may do for an early meal."

Sadie nodded and took her leave. Liza stood in the room for a long while, watching the sky gradually lighten from black to slate gray, bursting with unshed snowfall, as the night turned to day.

"An early riser," intoned the voice of Petrus Bothas in its light halting accent.

There were rumors that Petrus slept very little. Liza supposed if she were to establish, manage, and grow, five successful companies into billion-dollar corporations, she also wouldn't have much time for rest. Still, she was surprised, and a little nervous, to see him this early and all alone. The man put her on edge, and she didn't want to explore the reasons for that. She remembered the fangs from her dream and turned away from him so he couldn't see her flush or sense her disquiet.

"I'm afraid I'm the only one here," she said. An apology of sorts.

He also opted for coffee over tea, and gave a murmur of approval at the steam rising from the cup. Then he turned his intense gaze on her. "I'm pleased that it's just the two of us."

She did not respond.

"You left the performance early last evening."

"It wasn't really my scene."

"Because you're uncomfortable with sexuality? I've found that most Americans are actually quite puritanical."

Liza bristled at that, even though she didn't think it was necessarily a bad thing to view the connection between a man and a woman as private and sacred. "I just don't think intimacy belongs on display in a chapel." Especially not *her* chapel.

"It's not a working chapel though, is it?"

"It had been for several hundred years. And it will be in just a few months more."

Petrus opened his mouth to respond, but Liza held up her hand. "I'm not much interested in a debate on the semantics of the issue. It's early, and I'm tired."

He bowed his head. "My apologies, Ms. Ramsay. Sometimes I get caught up in the game. This is your home, and I am your guest."

He sounded sincere, and Liza nodded an acknowledgment. They sipped their coffees in silence, and after a moment, Liza thought that perhaps she'd been hasty. "Please. Call me Liza."

"Liza." He drew the syllables out, as if he were savoring the flavor of them on his tongue. She had a sudden flashback of this man's hand around her waist—of sitting on his lap in the surreal nightmarishness of the chapel performance.

She wasn't sure if he'd experienced a similar memory, but something passed between them. An electricity. A spark. A recognition.

When Lachlan walked into the room, the spell was broken, and Liza lowered her gaze.

"There ye are," her fiancé said, his voice booming across the space.

She wasn't sure if he had witnessed the strange moment, but she was glad he'd come in when he did. "Let me get you some tea," she said with a quick smile.

"Mr. Bothas," Lachlan said and held out his hand. "We didn't have the pleasure last night. Lachlan McClaren."

Petrus took the proffered hand. "Ah…the one who has captured the interest of Ki."

Liza glanced over and saw the color rush into Lachlan's cheeks. "She's an interestin' lass."

"She said the same of you. 'Pure and transparent', were her words. 'A heart of gold'."

"That's very kind o' her," Lachlan mumbled as Liza cleared her throat lightly.

"What about you, Liza?" Petrus asked.

Liza finished steeping her fiancé's tea and served it to him on one of Callum's fine bone china sets. Her irritation had returned, and she didn't look at Lachlan. "What about me?" she asked, addressing Petrus.

"I don't necessarily get 'pure and transparent' vibes from you." He studied her again, and there was an anticipatory pause.

It was Lachlan who asked, his voice tight, "What do you get from my Elizabeth?"

Petrus's eyebrows shot up. "Elizabeth?" The name seemed to be a revelation to him.

"It's just Liza," she clarified, annoyed that Lachlan would mention the name her father had bestowed upon her as a baby, given her complex feelings toward her late parent.

She took a sip of her now lukewarm coffee. She wanted to end this game, but not before she discovered what vibes Petrus received from her.

"When I look at you…" His words trailed off, and he stared at her as if Lachlan was not in the room. "…I get…incendiary. And passionate. A ferocity that is not seen by many."

Liza felt the heat rise in her own cheeks, and there was a long silence.

Finally, Lachlan spoke up. "Interestin', Mr. Bothas, that ye would assign those particular qualities to my wife."

Liza's head snapped up at that. She wasn't Lachlan's wife yet, but no one corrected him.

Petrus smiled, clearly enjoying the fact he'd gotten under Lachlan's skin. "Relax, my friend. No one is going to force anyone to do anything they don't want to do."

It was an odd thing to say, and Liza could think of no appropriate response. But Lachlan's mouth was open as if he were about to offer a retort.

He didn't get the chance. Before he could speak, a blood-curdling scream filled the castle.

It took the three of them less than five seconds to gather their wits and sprint up the back staircase toward the continued screams from the third floor.

When they reached the passageway, they saw the door of Aaron Scott's bedroom flung wide open. Sergei, Matthew, and Rabbie huddled in the entrance, frozen in place. Anne Kane and Carolyn Turner arrived running just a few seconds later from opposite stairwells.

Liza pushed through the men gathered at the room's edge and saw Shaun Fraser holding a pale Sadie Galbraith near the end of the bed. Her already milky white skin was ashen, as though all of the blood had leached from her body. Her wide brown eyes were focused on the other side of the room.

Liza followed her terrified gaze to the object of her horror.

The naked body of Aaron Scott hung unmoving inside the closet, attached by a thin piece of fabric around his neck to the metal clothing rod. The man's eyes were open but unfocused and unseeing, and his swollen tongue lolled to one side of his gaping mouth. Liza had a horrific flashback to the body of Brodie Graham hanging from the sycamore tree on the castle grounds. She shuddered and shut her eyes.

"Jesus," Lachlan whispered. "The man choked himself tae death."

"Good riddance, if you ask me," Matthew Carter quipped from the doorway.

"Mr. Carter," Carolyn Turner scolded.

Matthew shrugged. "If the guy wants to off himself playing stupid sex games, bully for him. He was worthless anyway. Petrus knows."

Petrus shot the other man a look of unbridled hatred.

Liza studied the myriad expressions on the faces around the room. Then her eyes locked with Ms. Turner's. She wondered if the older woman's thoughts were synchronous with hers. Because Liza had been in this situation before, and she'd learned quickly that not everything was as it seemed in times of tragedy.

Anne Kane spoke in a hushed tone. "Why on earth would he risk killing himself like this?" She sounded truly distraught.

But not one of them had any evidence that what had happened to Aaron Scott was accidental, or even self-harm, Liza thought. There was an equally strong chance that Aaron Scott, one of the wealthiest and most well-known men in the world, had just been murdered in her home. Making him the fourth victim on her property in less than a year.

Liza blinked around her.

And if he *had* been murdered, then one of the people in the room with her right now was a killer.

Chapter 9

"No one can know about this."

These were the first words Petrus uttered. Both his expression and his voice were strangely calm. Almost emotionless.

An uncomfortable silence settled over the group, and while the guests shuffled awkwardly, their gazes averted from the grisly scene in the closet, no one else said a word.

Liza stared at them, her mouth agape. Finally, she said, "Mr. Bothas, I agree we must be discreet. But surely you aren't indicating that the police are not to be informed."

"That's exactly what I'm saying, Ms. Ramsay." Gone was the flirtation of just a few minutes earlier. He was all business. "The police can do nothing for Aaron now."

Ms. Turner caught Liza's eye again, and Liza had the feeling the woman was trying to communicate something to her.

Lachlan spoke up next. "We have tae at least call Chief Inspector Dean. We can't leave the poor bastard here. Like that." Lachlan gestured toward Aaron's exposed body.

Petrus moved forward, as if to cover the body or close the closet door, but Carolyn Turner jumped forward, putting herself between the living and the dead. "Don't touch anything," she ordered.

Petrus looked so taken aback that he halted and obeyed without argument. Then he said, "I'm not suggesting we leave him here. One of the security team can take him out."

"Take him out where?" Liza asked, mystified.

"They'll know what to do." His words were ominous, and Liza shivered again.

Sadie let out a low wail, and Liza looked over. She'd forgotten about the poor girl. "Shaun, can you see Sadie to her room and get her a strong cup of tea?" Liza would have preferred that Ms. Turner take care of Sadie, but one look at the intensity on the older woman's face, and Liza knew she wasn't going anywhere.

"I agree with Petrus," Matthew said once Sadie and Shaun were through the door. "We can't have this getting out. We need to get rid of the body."

"A man is *dead*." Liza was appalled by the suggestion, and more so by the agreement between what seemed to be every one of their guests. "He was your friend."

Sergei made a noise—a cross between a laugh and a

shout.

Everyone ignored him.

"My men will handle this delicately and securely," Petrus said. His voice was more amiable, almost compassionate. "Aaron will be found in his bed at home, after a short illness. His wife will be by his side." The billionaire waived his hand. "Or something like that. The story will be plausible and tragic, and Aaron will retain his reputation and his…" He glanced at the naked man again. "…his dignity."

"I must agree with Petrus," Anne Kane said, her resonant voice stronger now. "It's always so strange to hear those words come out of my mouth," she murmured, then chuckled, before seeming to remember both herself and the tragedy. She cleared her throat. "I didn't see eye-to-eye with Aaron on a lot of issues, but the thought of him being remembered for this…" Her words trailed off as she shook her head. "The awful stories…I don't want that for anyone."

"But an autopsy must be done," Liza sputtered. "We can't simply remove the body and pretend nothing has happened."

"Of course we can," Sergei bellowed. When Liza stared at him, horrified, he continued. "The man has suffered a terrible accident, as we all can see. There is no need to cause his family more pain than is necessary." He shrugged as if the solution was extraordinarily simple.

Rabbie was the only person who seemed unsure. "I hear what ye're saying," he said, his tone consular. "But maybe we should consider notifying the authorities, to protect ourselves. I've found the Scottish police to be a trustworthy bunch."

Petrus laughed, and the sound was so out of place that Liza cringed. "The police aren't trustworthy anywhere," he said.

Murmurs of assent followed. Liza looked around. Ki was not in the room. Someone else was missing, too. When her gaze passed over Matthew, she realized his wife was nowhere to be found.

Sadie's scream had been chilling, and Daphne's room was directly above Aaron's. She inadvertently glanced toward the ceiling.

There was no way the other woman hadn't heard the shrieking.

Carolyn Turner had appeared at Liza's side. "May I have a word?" she asked softly.

Liza nodded and began to move toward the door. She was happy to get out of the room.

"No one touch Mr. Scott or anything else in the room," she directed before leaving. "Is that clear?"

"I don't see what the big deal is," Petrus said.

"The big deal is that we don't know for sure this was an accident," said Ms. Turner.

"You think this is suicide?" Anne's voice was incredulous. "I just can't believe that Aaron would ever consider ending his life. He had *everything* to live for," she said. After a second, she seemed to dismiss the suggestion outright. "Preposterous," she muttered.

Liza thought that she noticed a peculiar look on Matthew's face, but she couldn't be sure.

"I'm not saying I agree with the housekeeper," Sergei said in his thick accent, "but I have seen people check themselves out over the most minuscule of issues."

"Really, Sergei?" Rabbie's tone was dubious. "Ye've seen them commit suicide?"

Sergei shrugged. "It happens more often than you might think."

"You sure you don't help them along with the task?" Matthew asked.

"We have people for that when necessary."

Ms. Turner shot the two men a disgusted look. "Mr. McClaren, can you keep an eye on the scene please?"

"Scene?" Anne raised an eyebrow. "You make it sound as though you think a crime has been committed."

Another silence had fallen over the room as Liza followed Ms. Turner down the hallway and away from the guests and the body.

The image of Aaron Scott's sightless, naked corpse would be burned into her mind forever.

When they were out of earshot of the others, Ms.

Turner turned to her. "I do not think that man died accidentally."

Liza hated that her fears were being voiced by someone else. In an effort to avoid her own suspicions, she said, "So you think it was suicide?"

"No, Ms. Ramsay. I think he was murdered."

Liza shivered again. She looked around the hallway, desperately searching for something to anchor her racing thoughts. Her gaze settled on the smiling portrait of Elizabeth Cunningham Ramsay, the ancestor for whom she was allegedly named.

"Did you see something, Ms. Turner?"

Carolyn Turner shook her head. "I didn't need to. Nearly every person in that room has motive for desiring to see the man in his grave."

"Just because they have a motive doesn't mean they did it. We have no proof."

"Which is why we must call Marion Dean. She will be able to guide us on what we need to do next."

Liza knew Ms. Turner was right. Beyond the need for investigation was the additional concern of having a dead body in the house. And if one of Petrus's men took it away, who knows where it would end up. As much as she didn't want the Ramsay Castle besmirched by another murder, she couldn't have a potential cover-up of a crime on her conscience. Aaron Scott deserved better.

Petrus had said that the man had a wife. Perhaps he

even had children. In any case, he had a family who loved him.

Liza exhaled. "I will tell Mr. Bothas." It was a task she did not relish for a number of reasons.

As she turned, Carolyn Turn said, "Ms. Ramsay, there's something else you need to know."

Liza stopped, waited.

The older woman hesitated. Then she said, "I'm not precisely a house manager."

Liza's brows knitted together. "I'm sorry?"

"Well, I am. I was a member of Her Majesty's staff—the Household department." She licked her lips. "I also was—*am*—a member of the British Secret Intelligence Service."

Liza's frown deepened. "I'm afraid I'm not sure what that is."

"MI6, Ms. Ramsay."

A memory crawled through Liza's brain. It was of watching a cathode-ray tube television set with her grandfather. A handsome man in a tuxedo with a beautiful woman on his arm in sepia hues. She blinked at Ms. Turner. "Like James Bond?" Before the other woman could answer, Liza said, "But that's not real." Part of her wanted to laugh.

Carolyn Turner was not smiling. "It is true, I'm afraid. And while I'm technically an operative, the job is also not quite like James Bond. At least *my* position is not."

Liza ran a hand through her hair and sighed again. "I don't understand."

"I don't expect you to understand. You weren't meant to know."

The woman didn't sound contrite or regretful in any way. She simply stared at Liza as Liza stared back.

Liza had many questions, but the one that came out first was, "So why are you telling me this now?"

"Because you have a dead body in your home, my dear. And I happened to be here when the death occurred."

"Does Dean know who you are?"

Ms. Turner nodded once. "She does."

"And it was she that called you about this…position?" Liza felt like a fool, treating Ms. Turner as if she were the help when the woman was far more accomplished than Liza herself.

"Not exactly."

At that, Liza's head lifted a notch. "Then how did you know?"

"I'm not at liberty to say." She hesitated though, as if she were weighing her options.

"And the experience you said you have…managing a house and staff—all of that was a lie?"

"No, Ms. Ramsay. During my time with the Queen, I held a similar position and often posed as a member of Her Majesty's staff. It was how I'd come to be at Ramsay Castle in the past."

At that, Liza scoffed. Then she took a deep breath and threw her head back. "Well, Ms. Turner—is that even your real name?"

The woman nodded, but Liza didn't believe her. She just shook her head. "If all this is true, why do we need Dean here? Can't you investigate the potential crime yourself?"

"I'm not a detective. I gather intelligence. Occasionally, I may be tasked with a minor interaction with a target. But principally, I watch and report."

Liza looked at her closely. If Dean hadn't asked the woman to take on this assignment, that meant she'd been sent here to watch someone. But which one of their guests had attracted the interest of the equivalent of the United States Central Intelligence Agency? It could have been any one of these guests.

"Besides," Ms. Turner continued, "someone needs to process that body and the crime scene. The room has already been compromised, but that doesn't mean there isn't evidence to be gathered."

Liza nodded and reached into her pocket for her phone before she realized it wasn't there. She'd have to contact Detective Chief Inspector Dean using the landline.

From the window at the end of the hallway, she could see that the snow had started to fall again, obscuring the world outside in a curtain of gray.

"Let's go tell the guests our plan," Carolyn Turner

said, and they walked back toward Aaron Scott's room. Liza was shocked at just how much one conversation could change a relationship.

The guests still milled around the room, but when Liza entered, she found Aaron Scott no longer in his gruesome position in the closet, but rather prostrate on the bed and covered head to toe with the thick white comforter.

"We told you not to touch him," said Liza.

"More humane," Petrus said with a definitive nod.

Anne added, "It was uncivilized to leave him the way he was."

Liza stared open-mouthed at Lachlan, who spread his hands in front of him. "I couldnae stop them."

Rabbie said, "I tried, too, fer what it's worth. Not enough, apparently."

Ms. Turner clapped her hands together sharply, causing more than one of the men to jump. "All right. Everyone out." They stared at her, but again they obeyed, shuffling out of the room single file.

Once they were gathered in the hallway, Liza shut the door behind her. As committed as she was to preserving the potential crime scene, she had to admit, she was relieved that Aaron Scott's body was now hidden and resting, at peace, outside of the closet. What a sad and embarrassing place to die. Petrus was right—the man deserved a bit of dignity.

"Shall we retire downstairs?" said Ms. Turner. It

was more command than question.

As the guests headed for the back staircase in various pairings, Liza noted the continued absence of both Ki and Daphne. Lachlan was at her side, and just as he said her name, Ms. Turner placed a hand on her arm. The older woman looked at Lachlan pointedly until he sighed and followed the other guests with one half-forlorn, half-suspicious backward glance.

"No one can know who I am," she said softly. "Not even Mr. McClaren."

Liza started to protest, but Ms. Turner held up a hand. "It's not that I don't trust him. It's that I don't trust anyone. I don't even trust you."

"You think I killed Aaron Scott?"

"Of course not. I don't think Lachlan killed him either. But the more people that know my background, the likelier the killer is to attempt to cover up his—or her—crime. Lachlan means well, I'm sure, but he seems to have become rather attached to one of the guests."

Liza bristled, but as much as she wanted to deny that fact, the woman was right. Instead, she said, "That guest isn't among us right now."

"I'm attempting to minimize risk."

"What do you think they're going to do when they find out Chief Inspector Dean will be joining us?"

"I think they might try to stop it," Ms. Turner murmured.

Liza's eyes narrowed. This whole situation was becoming overly dramatic. After all, they had to keep in mind that a crime may not even have been committed. "Don't you think we're getting a bit ahead of ourselves?"

"We can always reduce speed and course correct, Ms. Ramsay." She started walking again, leaving Liza to follow. "But if we find that we are behind the killer, we will never catch up to him."

Chapter 10

While Liza gathered with the other guests in the drawing room where she would announce the plan to engage Chief Inspector Dean, Ms. Turner continued on to the castle office to make the phone call to the detective. Ms. Turner would then send Shaun Fraser to guard Aaron Scott's bedroom, before resuming her duties as house manager so she could observe the behavior of the guests.

Liza suspected there were others that Carolyn Turner would notify. She vaguely recalled a few hazy spy thriller novels she'd read involving the Secret Service as well as the long-since-forgotten 007 franchise. In most cases, unless the agent had gone rogue, there had been some sort of well-dressed handler or shady point-of-contact involved. Was it the same for Carolyn Turner?

With the other guests around her, and her suspicions piqued, she decided it didn't matter who Ms. Turner notified. The more the merrier. As long as the public didn't find out. These men and women had a lot to lose by being connected with a prominent death, even if that death turned out to be accidental. But Liza also had a lot to lose. After the deaths of Charlie Campbell, Brodie Graham, and Callum Ramsay, one more body could push the castle's reputation from morbid attraction to house of horrors.

The tea and coffee was still marginally warm on the sideboard, and the guests helped themselves, having the grace not to complain. But as soon as Ms. Turner reappeared, Liza would need to ask her to refresh their rations. She cringed at the thought of the task, given her newfound knowledge of the woman's position.

The guests also needed to eat something. Sustenance was necessary after the shock they'd had, no matter how unaffected they pretended to be.

"What is the plan here?" Petrus asked no one in particular. "We can't just sit around all day, wallowing in our grief."

Liza looked around. None of the guests looked particularly aggrieved.

She cleared her throat. "Ms. Turner is calling the authorities now."

Petrus's face flushed an angry red. "We agreed—no police."

"I made no such agreement, Mr. Bothas. This is my house, and there is a body upstairs." They all inadvertently looked to the ceiling. "In addition to the fact that we don't know for sure what happened to Mr. Scott, I won't be a willing participant in the cover-up of a suspicious death. No matter how humane the cover-up may be."

"It's not a cover-up," Matthew Carter said. "Not if we're all agreeing to the plan."

A thump sounded from somewhere above their heads, and Rabbie Rose said, "Now, what was that?"

Liza put a finger to her lips and listened intently as she looked toward the ceiling.

When no additional noise sounded, she glanced around the room. Liza noticed that Anne Kane was now missing. Had the woman been there when she'd entered after talking with Ms. Turner? Liza couldn't remember. Stress, emotion, caffeine, and lack of sleep, were catching up to her.

"Has anyone seen Ms. Kane?" she asked.

They were all glancing around when Ki burst into the room, fully clothed in a heavy coat and boots that were much too large for her and looked suspiciously familiar. She exuded cold and snow, and an earthy, wintry smell that was unexpectedly alluring.

She jumped into Petrus's arms. "Oh, An," she said, using his odd nickname. "I've just heard the news." She looked up into his face with her elven features and put her gloved hands on either side of his cheeks. "Are you all right?"

If he was annoyed with her dramatic antics, he gave no indication. "I'm quite good actually," he said. "Aside from the fact that the police have been summoned." He shot Liza an angry look.

Bruce Baxter had entered the room. "They haven't been summoned yet." Lachlan turned to the man, who continued. "Phone lines hae been cut."

"Cut?" Liza's eyes met Lachlan's. "Are you sure it doesn't have something to do with the snow?"

"Not unless the snow has a knife." Bruce put his hands out in front of his body. "And it's started to come down again. Near whiteout fer those poor bloody cooks." By cooks, she assumed he meant the catering staff.

"It was awful, An," Ki said woefully. "We had to walk through the snow, it was nearly up to my thighs. It took ages, and I couldn't see my hand in front of my face." Her accented voice was breathless. "I didn't know if we would make it."

"We should have come and got ye," said Lachlan apologetically. "Bruce, we shouldae had a plan for that."

Bruce gave an unconcerned shrug, but Ki shot Lachlan a grateful, watery smile. "You're so kind. But you had your own situation to deal with here."

Liza wondered how Ki had received the news so quickly having just arrived at the house.

"I'll get ye some tea," Lachlan said to Ki, who had nestled in Petrus's lap in one of the sitting chairs. Petrus acted unconcerned by Lachlan's attentiveness to his girlfriend.

Carolyn Turner appeared in the doorway. "Ms. Ramsay, a word?"

Liza met her in the passageway, under the watchful eye of a portrait of Sir Alexander Ramsay. "Mr. Baxter said the phone line's been cut?"

Ms. Turner nodded. "From the inside, and to the phones in the office, the conference room, and the third-floor lounge."

Liza put a hand to her neck. No one knew the third-floor landline had existed. She was sure she hadn't communicated that to the guests.

"Mr. Baxter made it sound like the line had been cut from the outside."

"That's what he originally thought."

If the cords had been individually cut, one last option existed. "There's an extension in our apartment," she said, her voice animated. She began heading in that direction, and the other woman followed.

Liza pushed open the unlocked door and went to the cordless phone charging in its dusty base. But she didn't even have a chance to pick it up before Ms. Turner pointed to the wires dangling uselessly behind the stand. It had been sliced clean through.

Liza swore under her breath. She should have locked the apartment door. She hadn't thought it necessary since anything worth stealing was out in the open in the public rooms. And aside from that, what would a bunch of billionaires want with her measly sentimental treasures? But now, she was going to have to be much more watchful. Especially if someone had a motive to cover up a murder.

"So, we're cut off," Liza said dejectedly. There was more than just disappointment in her heart. There was real fear.

"Bruce has offered to walk into town," Ms. Turner said. "I believe that might be our best option, if these brutes won't release our mobiles."

Liza thought of the security staff sitting at the end of the lane and wondered if anyone in the house had means to contact them and let them know the situation. She also wouldn't put it past any of the guests to be hiding a secret cell phone for situations just like this. Well, maybe not exactly like this one. But emergencies.

Given their current position, along with the weather, she did not trust that the security team would let Bruce exit the grounds without a fight.

Liza said, "He'll have to go down the old quarry trail." The ancient path ran through the woods, curving with the Creagan River and past the footpath to the primeval chapel ruins and Ramsay family burial grounds. The pathway eventually opened onto the back road to the small village of Bonnyrigg just a few miles away. While Dean's department was closer to the city, Bruce should at least be able to find a friendly neighbor who'd offer him use of a phone.

Ms. Turner looked at her doubtfully. "Are you

suggesting he make the journey alone in these condi-tions?"

Liza considered. Shaun Fraser needed to stay here to guard the body and attend to the guests. "Lachlan can go with him," she said finally.

"Are you certain?"

She knew it was wrong, but her mind immediately shifted to the tiny, helpless figure of Ki wrapped up in what she thought was Lachlan's coat and knit cap. She remembered the woman's tiny naked body from the night before. "We have no other choice," Liza said briskly.

Ms. Turner pursed her lips and nodded, and they left the apartment, locking it securely behind them.

Both Bruce Baxter and Lachlan agreed quickly and quietly. Lachlan didn't seem to suspect her darker motivations behind the request. She hated that she had to utter the next words.

"You're to tell no one where you're going," she warned.

"Who would we tell?" Bruce asked in his surly voice.

She glanced at Lachlan. "No one," she emphasized.

Liza's fiancé looked away. Her heart sank. He was human—they all were—and it was inevitable he might be attracted to women other than Liza. But his fascination with the colorful and eccentric Ki was so blatant that she wondered how many other women might fit the same bill.

As Lachlan and Bruce disappeared to dress for their long trek into town, Rabbie Rose approached.

Ms. Turner nodded her head at the older man. "I'll just be on my way to oversee breakfast now that the kitchen staff are back. Will there be anything else, Ms. Ramsay?" She fell seamlessly into her role as house manager, and Liza picked up the cue. "That will be all, Ms. Turner. Thank you for your assistance."

She gave a bow of her head and dip of her knees and hurried quickly away. Liza's stomach growled. She turned to Rabbie.

"What is it, Mr. Rose?"

"I'm a wee bit worried about Daphne, the dafty lass. She hasn't emerged from her room yet. I'm sure she's fast asleep." He spread his hands out in front of him. "But with everythin' else goin' on…"

Liza glanced over Rabbie's shoulder into the drawing room. Petrus and Ki were talking quietly, their heads bent close. Matthew Carter was staring out the window with a deep crease between his eyebrows, and Sergei was sitting upright on an antique ivory sofa that dated back to the fifteenth century, snoring heavily. A glass of liquid that she suspected was not tea tipped precariously from limp fingers on his knee.

Liza realized that as much as they were trying not to show it, Aaron's sudden death had affected them in more ways than one.

Liza held up a finger to Rabbie to wait and entered the room. Anne Kane had reappeared, looking regal in a pair of wide-legged black trousers and a purple jewel-toned silk blouse. A matching scarf was loosely wound around her long, elegant neck and her blonde-silver hair fell around her shoulders.

"Excuse me, everyone."

They all turned toward Liza.

"Now that the kitchen staff is back, breakfast will be served shortly. Once we've eaten, we can figure out next steps for the day ahead."

"I'm not sure what there is to talk about," Matthew said. "The feud between Aaron and Petrus was the agenda item."

"It wasn't a feud," said Petrus. "It was a debate."

Sergei, who'd been roused from his dozing, held up the tumbler. "Perhaps then we can talk about your attempts to renege on your side of our agreement, Carter."

Matthew flushed red. "Now isn't the time." His words had emerged through clenched teeth.

"Seems as good a time as any."

"Gentlemen…" Anne's voice was placating, with just a touch of condescension. "…these meetings are to air our issues, not our dirty laundry."

Liza and Rabbie left them to fight among themselves. "Should we invite Matthew to check on his wife?" she asked.

Rabbie shook his head. "As ye may have noticed, Daphne and Matthew don't exactly enjoy a happy union."

"Then why don't they divorce?"

"Financial ties create unbreakable bonds, Ms. Ramsay. Ye're new to yer money. But ye'll see."

They climbed the back stairs to the fourth floor. Despite Rabbie's spritely nature, he was breathless when they reached the doorway. Liza paused while he caught his breath. They really needed to install an elevator, she thought grimly.

They encountered Sadie in the hallway. The girl was still pale, but otherwise seemed fine, though her large eyes were wider than normal.

"How are you?" Liza asked. "Do you need some more time?"

"I'm okay." She bit her lip. "It's just hard to get the image out o' my mind." Her lilt was extremely pronounced, as if the sight of the dead body had propelled her back in time to her childhood in Queenswick.

"Ye still look a bit peely-wally," said Rabbie, leaning close.

"Can I ask you something, Sadie?" Maybe this wasn't the right time to impose her thoughts, but she needed to set something straight with the young housekeeper.

The girl pressed her lips together and nodded.

"How did you come to be in Aaron's room to discover his body?"

Sadie shut her eyes as if steeling herself, then opened them again and took a shuddering breath. "I-I'd heard a noise through the door. At first it sounded like…" Her cheeks flushed. "…I thought it was two people…together." She gave Liza a meaningful look, and Liza nodded. She wouldn't force Sadie to offer additional detail on any perceived, and likely illicit, intimacy. Liza also thought she'd heard something similar in the middle of the night.

Sadie swallowed, then continued. "But then, it sounded more like a woman cryin' and beggin', like someone was in trouble. I thought about leavin' and comin' to fetch ye or Ms. Turner, but I was afraid if I didn't go in quickly somethin' terrible might happen." She shuddered. "I knocked on the door first, Ms. Ramsay. I swear I did. No one answered, and the sobbin' stopped. Then I heard another strange noise. I dinnae usually follow my intuitions, especially after what happened last night, but I opened the door. That's when I found him."

"Obviously it wasn't Aaron who was greetin'," said Rabbie at the same time Liza said, "What happened last night?"

Sadie looked from Liza to Rabbie and pointedly answered Rabbie's question rather than Liza's. "It certainly wasn't Mr. Scott. But when I opened the door, there was no one else in the room. Just his…body." Sadie blanched again and squeezed her eyes shut against the memory of the image.

"It's okay, Sadie." Liza patted the girl's shoulder.

Sadie took a shaky breath and nodded, her eyes wide open once again. "Do ye think I could've been hearin' Lady Catherine cryin'?" she asked hopefully.

Liza hesitated. Because Liza herself had seen Lady Catherine—and heard the spirit of her ancestor—on more than one occasion, she didn't want to outright dismiss Sadie's question. But no part of her believed it was a ghost who was sobbing in Aaron Scott's room.

"I'm glad you followed your instincts and found Aaron early," Liza said, instead of addressing the question. "It will give the police more time to figure out what happened."

"I thought the police couldn't get here," Rabbie said. He seemed alarmed, and Liza hesitated. She remembered Ms. Turner's warning, but Rabbie had been the lone supporter of involving the police in the first place.

In the end, though, Liza kept her mouth shut. "Let's check on Daphne," she said instead. "She had to have heard the commotion. Her room is directly above Aaron's."

The trio made their way to the fourth floor and knocked on the door to Daphne's chamber. They listened. There was no movement and no response.

"Daphne, lass," Rabbie said through the heavy door. "It's yer uncle and Ms. Ramsay. We've come to check on you, hen. Open the door." Again, no response. "No one else is with us," he added. "And no one knows we're up here."

Liza glanced at Rabbie who didn't meet her eyes.

"Should we use the master key?" Liza asked.

Rabbie listened and shook his head. "She's coming," he mouthed, hearing his niece's soft footfalls on the floor.

A second later, the door opened, and a sliver of Daphne's face appeared through the crack.

Liza couldn't get a good look at her, but she could see that the woman was still dressed in her night-clothes.

"Are ye all right?" Rabbie asked.

"Uncle? What's happened?" Her voice was so low and thick that Liza had to strain to hear her.

"Ah, we've had a bit of a situation downstairs." Rabbie seemed to search for the right words. "Aaron Scott…he appears to have come to some harm. An accident, of course," he added quickly, wanting to reassure his niece that she was safe.

"Aaron…" It was one low, plaintive utterance from the other side of the door.

"Dinnae worry," he said quickly. "We're goin' tae get tae the bottom of the situation."

There was no response.

"Daphne, hen?" Rabbie's voice was gentle. He sounded much like Callum, and Liza was surprised to feel her throat close with emotion. It was the exhaustion, she knew. She got weepy when she was tired.

"Ye should get dressed and join us," Rabbie continued. "It'll make ye feel better to be around other living souls."

There was another long pause then an audible breath. "I'll join you in a bit." The words were slow and deliberate. Detached.

"That's all right, lassie," Rabbie said. "Do ye need some help to dress?" He looked at Sadie hopefully. Sadie's gaze slid away, but she didn't decline the offer on her behalf.

Another long pause. Rabbie opened his mouth to speak again. Daphne finally said, "No." The word was long and drawn out. She didn't sound at all like the animated woman Liza had spoken to in the drum tower staircase yesterday. She sounded as if she'd been drugged.

Liza added, "Breakfast will be served shortly. It might be good to get some food in your stomach."

The sliver of face peered blankly through the crack in the door, and the stare was fixed on Rabbie, who said, "Take yer time. We're not goin' anywhere."

Maybe he'd meant the words to be a comfort to his niece, but to Liza, they sounded ominous.

When they took their leave and the door clicked

shut behind them, Matthew approached from the other direction.

"She's all good," Rabbie said cheerfully, waving the other man away. "Just had a long, hard sleep after a late night. She's getting dressed right now."

Matthew's dark square jaw was set, and his gaze passed over the trio in front of him. In contrast to Rabbie's fake cheerfulness, Liza and Sadie's faces were tense and drawn. Liza tried to put a smile on her own face, but it felt more like a grimace than a grin.

"You needed three of you to check on her?" he asked.

"We ran into Sadie in the hallway," Liza said. "She had quite the shock this morning, remember?"

If Liza hadn't known better, she would have sworn Matthew rolled his eyes. "Yeah, well, if it's all the same to you, I think I'll check on my wife myself." He started to move past them.

Rabbie stepped into his path. "She's just gotten into the bath. Might be best to wait a few minutes."

Matthew made to move past him again, but Ms. Turner's voice sailed down the corridor. "There you all are," she said brightly. "Breakfast is served in the dining room."

Matthew hesitated, then with a shake of his head and a mutter under his breath, he turned around and joined the others as they walked back down the stairs.

Liza glanced at Rabbie, who looked relieved. She wondered why.

Chapter 11

Breakfast was a somber affair. Any morning light that may have streaked in through the sweeping panes of glass was blocked by an opaque curtain of fresh snowflakes. The mood was perhaps made even darker by the reaction of the non-Scottish guests to the traditional breakfast of haggis, black pudding, and beans. The only guest who appeared unbothered by either the food or the death of Aaron was Petrus, who ate heartily, occasionally chatting in low tones to Ki.

Ki, on the other hand, speared individual beans on the tines of her fork and looked into the distance as Petrus kept up the stream of one-sided conversation.

In the relative quiet, silverware clinked against the fine porcelain china, accompanied by Sergei's occasional snorts and heavy breathing.

Ki turned to Liza. "Where is Lachlan?"

Liza took a sip of water, buying time. "He and Bruce are working in the chapel." Liza was not a good liar, and she hadn't expected anyone to ask after Lachlan directly. Not even Ki. She should have known better.

Ki had barely been out of Liza's sight since she'd appeared earlier that morning, but Liza knew it was only a matter of time before the woman would work out that Lachlan was not in the castle. Even now, she was looking at Liza suspiciously. Liza caught Petrus's sideways glance at his girlfriend; the first indication that perhaps the billionaire was not as impervious to Ki's attention to another man as he pretended.

Carolyn Turner was simultaneously clearing plates and serving coffee. She was also closely watching these guests. Liza was careful not to make prolonged eye contact with the woman, lest she reveal her fear and disquiet.

"Are you quite all right, Daphne?" Anne Kane asked, peering closely at Matthew Carter's wife.

Despite Daphne's disoriented state, she'd joined the group shortly after the conversation with Liza and Rabbie. The younger woman was dressed in a plain navy-blue sheath and tasteful nude ballet flats, and her hair was tousled and pulled into a knot atop her head. Her beautiful face was free of makeup, and dark shadows bruised the skin underneath her eyes.

Daphne turned her head toward Anne as if she'd heard the older woman's question in slow motion. "Hmmm?" she asked after a delay of nearly a minute.

Anne stared at Daphne, then said, "God, Matthew. What has she taken?"

While Rabbie regarded his niece with a look of

concern, Matthew ignored the question. "Petrus, do you mind telling us what the agenda is for this meeting? We were set to hash out your concerns regarding artificial intelligence. Seeing how your beef on the subject was primarily with Aaron, is there a revised focus of discussion? Or can we all be put out of this misery and just head home?"

Petrus fixed a hard look on Matthew, before sitting back in his chair. Like a grade-school child, he tipped backward on the two posterior legs of the antique chair, balancing his weight. He stared up at the ceiling.

Liza barely contained her urge to chide this grown man.

Ms. Turner happened to be passing behind the billionaire, and she pushed the chair down hard on all four legs with a firm hand. "If you fall, I'm afraid none of your money will be able to summon this exact chair from the Stewart dynasty in the 1600s," she said, a note of censure and a whiff of condescension in her voice.

Anne Kane laughed.

Petrus flicked a brief glance in Ms. Turner's direction but made no comment.

Liza wondered how the woman knew the origin of the room's furniture.

Petrus turned his attention to Matthew. "We have plenty to discuss," he said. "Perhaps you and Sergei would like to discuss the deal you've been attempting to broker regarding defense weapons?"

A flush crept up Matthew's neck.

"Your intelligence is faulty, Petrus," Sergei said.

"No, I don't believe it is. My intel also indicates that the party on whose behalf Matthew is negotiating is a ranking member of the U.S. House Intelligence Committee. Would be quite the scandal if *that* got out."

"Preposterous," said Sergei. "Our great nation would never stoop to such paltry back-channel deals." He gave a grunt of derision. "As if we needed it."

"Perhaps that is why your great nation has entrusted the conversation to you. A paltry and expendable player in a very high-stakes game. If the information were to leak, your great leader would simply eliminate you and issue a pronouncement that you are a turncoat negotiating on behalf of your country's enemies. All very neat and tidy."

Sergei said nothing.

Matthew balked. "Are you accusing me of treason?"

Petrus seemed to consider this. "No, I don't think I am. But I might be accusing you of betrayal, because I don't know what kind of backdoor deals you're making with the enemy regarding the space industry. And, my friend, that is *my* domain. Not yours."

Liza was appalled by this casual conversation. As a U.S. citizen, did she have some obligation to report it? And if so, to whom? Who would even believe her?

Anne Kane had been watching Liza's face. "Gentlemen, I would caution you to engage in conversation lightly with the newest member of our group present. Ms. Ramsay has not yet had a proper orientation to our inner circle. She doesn't yet know our ways."

"I might suggest that the death of one of our friends is orientation enough," Petrus quipped at the same time Liza said, "I'm not part of your group."

Anne chuckled dryly; at which comment, Liza was not entirely sure.

"I don't hear much work happening in the chapel," Ki said and stood.

Petrus suddenly snapped. "For fuck's sake, can you at least try to hide your desire to sleep with the husband of our host?"

Ki sat back down.

He looked at Liza, his eyes intense as they bore into hers. "Apologies for that outburst, Ms. Ramsay."

This did not make Liza feel any better. The verbalized acknowledgment of Ki's motives made her feel sick to her stomach. Mostly because Lachlan likely felt the same way about Ki.

"That's rich, coming from you," Matthew muttered.

"If you're talking about the rumor that I slept with Daphne five years ago, I thought we'd cleared this up."

A heavy silence descended on the room as the remainder of the dishes were cleared. After a minute, Daphne said, "I didn't sleep with Petrus."

"Come on, hen," Rabbie said. He moved to stand behind his niece. "Let's get ye back upstairs for a rest. This is all too much for ye."

"Can I help you?" asked Liza.

Rabbie waved her off. "We'll be just fine, Ms. Ramsay. Thank ye."

Was it Liza's imagination, or did Rabbie seem colder than he had before? Perhaps he was just worried about Daphne.

"Do ye have the key to your room, dear?"

Daphne reacted to her uncle's proximity. "Where's Aaron?" she asked. Her voice had developed a fearful, tremulous quality.

"He's in his room, remember?" Rabbie began yanking on the back of Daphne's chair. "He's in his bed."

Daphne pushed her chair back, and Rabbie looked relieved. "Can I see him?"

"Not right now, lassie. He's resting."

Daphne's delicate eyebrows drew together, and she silently mouthed words, trying to manifest and vocalize a thought.

The rest of the table was watching this scene take place, but Liza noted Matthew Carter's deep scowl. He made no move to help either his wife or her uncle. In fact, he was staring off into the distance as if keeping his gaze forcefully trained away from the pair.

"I can have Sadie bring up a cuppa, Mr. Rose," Carolyn Turner said as Rabbie huddled his niece toward the door.

Rabbie glanced over his shoulder. "That would be most kind of ye."

When they were gone, Anne steepled her hands in front of her. "I hate to say it, but I agree with Matthew. It makes sense to forego the traditional meeting format we had planned, given the circumstances."

Liza said, "I'm afraid that with the amount of snow that's fallen, it might be some time before you'll all be able to leave."

She didn't plan on mentioning the dead body lying alone in the room above them; she had no intention of letting *anyone* out of the house until a police officer showed up at the castle.

"Yes, of course," Anne said. "I just don't think it makes sense to try to force a regular agenda when our primary purpose for this meeting has been…eliminated."

Petrus let out a long exhale. "I agree with Anne." No one mentioned that the original idea had been Matthew's. "I'm afraid we've wasted your time and your hospitality, Ms. Ramsay."

Liza was bemused by the apology for that and that alone.

He stood and moved to the windows. The snow continued to swirl around them as if they were in a life-sized snow globe. "I'd forgotten how dreary this country is in the wintertime," he murmured. "We should have usurped Rabbie's hosting duties."

"It's the only thing he's got," Sergei spoke up. "God knows he hasn't got the money to justify his place in the group."

"Why does he participate then?" Liza asked.

"Great question." Petrus looked at Anne. "Ms. Kane?"

"His ancestor was a founding member of the group," she said, a tad defensively. "We can't just kick him out."

Petrus clicked his tongue against the inside of his cheek. "Anne has a bit of a sentimental streak."

"He's not going to be around forever," Anne said. "Besides, he brought Daphne's father into the mix, and I believe you benefited greatly from that partnership, did you not, Petrus? Kephalē wouldn't be successful without Hugh St. James."

At Liza's quizzical look, Anne said, "Kephalē is one of Petrus's lesser-known endeavors, using implanted computer interfaces to treat complex brain injuries."

"A rather elementary definition," Petrus said with a shrug. "While it's true that I benefited from Rabbie's connection with Hugh, I perhaps did not benefit nearly as much as Matthew did."

"Or Aaron," Sergei said with a laugh.

Matthew scowled, and Sergei seemed legitimately contrite. "I'm sorry, my friend," he said in his heavy accent.

Liza had a hard time envisioning a computer being implanted in her brain. The potential for disaster—rejection, disease, *mind control*—made her shiver in terror. These people were monsters with god complexes.

"Why is Daphne's father not here?" she asked, even while she was glad that another demented and perhaps diabolical rich person wasn't sitting around her dining room table.

"He's traveling on business, and the intended subject of this meeting—artificial intelligence—wasn't of particular interest to him. At least not at this stage of its development."

"But it was to the rest of you?"

Liza's gaze went to Anne. Last night, Anne had offered Liza an explanation for her presence at the gathering. Liza still couldn't shake the feeling that it was odd Anne had chosen this particular meeting—in a remote castle in Scotland in the middle of winter—to attend. After all, the Kane retail chain was an $800-billion business and sold a variety of products to humans around the globe. Artificial intelligence seemed a distant threat to the titan of goods and services.

Anne smiled, sensing that Liza had directed the question to her. "The development of AI has a direct impact on the viability of the economic development of the Kane retail conglomeration," she said. "Depending on the outcome, our business model will need to be adjusted."

Matthew snorted. "Not to mention its effect on your precious art projects."

Anne barely glanced in his direction. "AI has nothing to do with the works of the past."

"If AI can produce a perfect replica of a masterpiece, your art would become obsolete though. Isn't that right?"

"Artificial intelligence will never be able to take the place of the talent of the masters—past, present, or future." She waved a hand toward Matthew, as if dismissing not only the concern but the man himself. "Can you imagine Michelangelo, da Vinci, Durer, Caravaggio, being replaced by a computer?" She laughed bitterly. "Absurd."

"Is it?"

Anne turned to Liza. "Ms. Ramsay, do you think AI could replicate one thing in this castle?"

Liza looked around her at the antique furniture, the priceless tapestries on the walls. "I hadn't thought about it." But now that she considered, the answer was *no*. "The history of this castle relied on humans," she said. "So, too, does its present and future." The present and future would then rise and fall like a wave, adding to its posterity and further enriching the history of the Ramsay heritage. Though she didn't say it aloud, the death of Aaron Scott had been added to the legacy of the estate, along with the death of Callum Ramsay and Liza's own near-tragic experience.

Anne nodded in agreement and gave the group a superior look.

"You think you're so much better than the rest of us," said Sergei. He sounded more amused than bitter.

"I'm certainly better than *you*," she said.

Sergei laughed.

"All right," Petrus said, looking off into the distance. "I propose we take a break and reconvene for a late lunch in the conference room that Ms. Ramsay has set up. Perhaps by that time, we'll have a better idea of the trajectory of the weather, and we'll be able to plan our departure."

Liza looked around for Ms. Turner; the woman had left the room. She wanted nothing more than for these guests to leave. But she knew she needed to keep her visitors on the premises for as long as possible. At least until they could determine the cause of death of Aaron Scott. Liza wasn't sure of much, but she did know one thing: These people were not friends, as much as they pretended to be.

What kind of friend covered up the death of another member of their tribe?

She looked around at the bored and jaded gathering of megalomaniacs. Not a tear had been shed for poor Aaron Scott. The most he'd been afforded was a confused, detached, and potentially false, memory from Daphne St. James's scattered mind.

One of the richest men in the world, and very few people seemed interested in discovering the truth behind how he'd died. Fortune for Aaron, it turned out, had been nothing but a fickle and illusory blessing.

Chapter 12

The guests began to scatter to their respective rooms, and though Liza didn't want to hover or keep tabs on the visitors, she also didn't trust any one of them.

She hoped that Lachlan and Bruce would return soon with help.

As the catering staff cleared the leftover food and plates from the dining room, Petrus, Sergei, Matthew, and Anne, walked toward the back staircase.

Liza stood in the doorway and watched as Ki headed toward the grand staircase leading to the first floor. She was, no doubt, planning to visit the chapel in search of Lachlan, who Liza knew was not there.

"Ki," she called after the woman.

Ki stopped near the top of the staircase, her back still to Liza.

Liza thought she saw the woman's shoulders rise and fall on a sigh.

When Liza approached her and Ki finally turned around, a dim smile was pasted on her full bare lips. Similar to Daphne, dark smudges of exhaustion hollowed out the crescents under her eyes.

"Hi," she said to Liza in her bright Kiwi accent that did not match her weary demeanor.

"Am I correct to assume you slept in the cottage last night?" Liza asked.

Ki nodded, the dark cap of her pixie cut sleek against her skull. She wore simple black leggings with a cozy oversized white sweater that swallowed her petite body. Her feet were clad in fashionable fur booties. She stifled a yawn. "It didn't seem fair to leave Hahana and Mariama alone. They are my sisters."

Liza remembered the two women who had embraced Ki so intimately the night before. "Your birth sisters?"

"My star sisters," Ki clarified.

Liza bit the inside of her cheek.

"Are they dating the male performers?"

"Etera and Marcus?" Ki frowned. "Not exactly. It's all very…fluid."

Liza tried to keep her voice neutral. "Meaning that everyone sleeps with everyone else."

"It's not tawdry," Ki said. "Intimacy is beautiful between everyone when there's a soul connection."

Liza didn't disagree with Ki. She just couldn't wrap her mind around sharing her bed or her body with anyone but her partner when she was in a committed relationship.

Liza had braced herself for Ki to comment on the

other woman's soul connection to Lachlan, but she surprised Liza by instead saying, "Just like you and Petrus."

"Pardon me?"

"It's okay," Ki said with a genuine smile. "He and I aren't the jealous types."

"I think there's been some misunderstanding. There is absolutely nothing going on between Petrus and me." Liza held up her hands in front of her, palms out, for emphasis.

"I can see how he looks at you. I'm sure you've seen it, too."

Liza wished she could deny the glances Petrus frequently aimed in her direction. Unbidden, her thoughts returned to his hands on her waist, sitting on his lap as the dark, sultry show had pulsed on.

Liza cleared her throat and drew herself up tall. "I'm not sure what you think you saw, noticed, or assumed, but I am quite happy with Lachlan. I'm not interested in another man, even if that man is Petrus Bothas."

A corner of Ki's mouth ticked up, and she leveled a look at Liza, a knowing gleam in her eye. "Petrus is a man who goes after what he wants. If he decides that's you, Liza, I'm afraid you'll not have much choice in the matter."

At Liza's shocked face, she gave a small tinkling laugh and started down the stairs.

She made it halfway down before Liza said, "If you're looking for Lachlan, he's not there."

"You said he was with Bruce in the chapel." Ki didn't bother pretending she was looking for anyone but Lachlan.

Liza bristled and answered, her words abrupt, "They've finished."

"How do you know? You were with us in the dining room."

Liza hesitated for less than a second. "He told me it wouldn't be long and that he was going to head to the apartment for a rest afterward. He came to bed late last night."

Liza thought she saw the ghost of a smile on Ki's lips. Was she imagining that?

Then her blood ran hot. How dare this woman act as if Liza's fiancé were up for grabs. As if he were Ki's for the taking.

Both Petrus and Ki had a problem with boundaries, Liza thought.

"I'd like to make something clear," she said and didn't wait for Ki's response. "Lachlan is mine. I will be marrying him in just a few short months. Just because you and Petrus have an open relationship—that does not mean the rest of the world operates in the same way. So, I would very much appreciate you staying the hell away from the man I plan to marry."

Ki's gaze was serene. "Considering the conversation Lachlan and I had last night, I'm not sure he feels the same way you do."

Those words caused Liza's blood to cool rapidly. She swallowed, trying to regain her composure.

Ki noticed and opened her eyes wide in an exaggerated innocent gaze. "He didn't tell you about that conversation?"

Liza didn't trust this woman, and though she assumed Ki was lying, she asked, "What did he say?" through clenched teeth.

"Only that he thought maybe you were rushing into the marriage. That he wasn't sure it was the right choice at this point in your lives, but he didn't want to tell you that and hurt your feelings. Not after what Owen had done to you. He's married now, isn't he? Owen?" Ki clarified. "After dating you for over a decade, it took him less than six months after you broke up to marry someone else?"

Liza blinked, in that very moment hating this woman with her cheerful lilting enunciation and charming upturned syllables. The only way Ki could have known about Owen and his new wife was if someone had told her. The only *someone* that could have been was Lachlan.

Liza didn't trust herself to speak.

Ki spoke instead. "I'll stay away from Lachlan if that's what you want. But just so you know, it was Lachlan who sought *me* out last night, not the other way around."

Liza wanted to ask if anything had happened between the two of them, but she was afraid of the answer.

Ki pointed to the curved wall of the drum tower on the other side of the hallway where they stood. "Do those stairs go up to the bedrooms?" She asked the question as if she hadn't just implied she'd slept with the man Liza loved.

Liza found she could do nothing but nod.

Ki turned away and walked in that direction. "I may as well explore a bit, since we're all stuck in this vile place together." She didn't look back at Liza but added, "Tell Lachlan I was looking for him."

Liza watched the figure disappear into the stairwell. She stood there for a moment alone with her arms crossed tightly over her midsection.

She thought about Lachlan, her handsome, rugged Scot who'd saved her from certain death in the castle's dungeon. She thought about the look on his face after she'd been rescued and Owen had shown up in her hospital room and proposed. She thought about the night he'd proposed, too, promising to love her forever.

After all they'd been through, had Lachlan really shared with that spooky woman that he was having second thoughts about marrying Liza?

A deep pit opened and twisted at the bottom of

Liza's belly. The only way to find out was to ask him. But she couldn't do that because she'd sent him out into the blizzard with Bruce Baxter.

Exhausted with lack of sleep and an abundance of worry, Liza wandered slowly down the hallway toward her apartment. Instead of traversing the entire passage, though, she turned right into the grand ballroom.

The ceilings were high and painted with vibrant blues, golds, creams, and reds. The cornices were adorned with representations of the virtues of Justice, Fortitude, Constancy, and Courage. And in the ornate center of the elaborate mural, the divine hero Hercules was carried by his godly chariot toward Mount Olympus.

The room smelled of lemon cleaner, and antiquity—distinguished and elegant. She breathed in deeply and shut her eyes, her head thrown back and her face lifted to the heavens. The celestial ceiling seemed to glow, casting a warm light over everything it touched.

Liza thought about the sky god An. About how Ki had referred to Petrus as the deity—a divine representation of the sky. There were similarities, she thought, to this painting.

"Now, there's a sight."

Liza spun around. Petrus leaned in the doorway, his big body relaxed in his jeans and unassuming blue sweater. He couldn't have looked less like the magnate he was. And he wasn't staring at the extraordinary ceiling, he was staring at Liza.

Liza didn't answer, and perhaps he sensed her disquiet. "Ki said you were down here."

"I was just about to head to my apartment for a rest," she said. "It's been a long morning." Her voice was brisk, no-nonsense. She did not want this man to get the wrong idea about her interests. Not after the conversation she'd just had with his girlfriend. She was no hypocrite.

He dipped his head. "Of course." Then his eyes, too, went to the painting of the heavens on the ceiling. "Who did that?" he asked.

"It's a copy of *The Apotheosis of Hercules* from the Palace of Versailles. Lemoyne painted the original, but I'm not sure who painted this one."

"Perhaps Lemoyne?"

"Perhaps." Certainly, there were stranger possibilities than the obvious but unlikely prospect that the pieces were created by the same artist.

They stared at the ceiling together in silence for a few moments until Liza moved to leave the room.

Petrus said, "I came to tell you that the snow has slowed. I'll head out to the security team soon to let them know we'll be leaving. We'll take Aaron's body with us."

And here, Liza thought, was the rub. As much as she wanted these people gone, she could not let that body leave these premises. Not without an investigation.

"I really don't think that's wise," she said, considering her next words. Could she use Petrus's obvious attraction to her to convince him otherwise? The thought made her breathless, but she was willing to try. Even if it did make her a hypocrite.

The bigger problem was that this man made her feel insecure and dry-mouthed. Like a schoolgirl. She'd had no confidence in her flirting skills when she was younger, and she had even less now, in her early thirties.

"Look," Petrus said, before she could get her wits about her and her game face on, "I know you're worried about Aaron's death. But I assure you, it will be better for all of us—and for you, Liza—if you just let me take care of this."

"What if it wasn't an accident, though?" she asked. So much for the flirtation. She went straight for the uncomfortable potentiality that had been swirling around them since Sadie Gilbraith had screamed that morning.

"You mean, what if he killed himself? On purpose?" Petrus lifted a shoulder. "I've known Aaron a long time. He had a lot to live for. I don't think he'd commit suicide, but I suppose it's possible. Sometimes we don't know people as well as we think we do."

Liza shook her head. "No. What if it was…something else?"

Petrus cocked his head, waiting for her to expound on what that something else may be.

"Murder." Her voice was just barely above a whisper. And she was acutely aware that she could be talking to a killer right now.

Petrus looked shocked. Not like a murderer. "You saw his body," he said. "What he'd been doing. That's not the way a killer would leave a man."

"If he wanted us to think it was an embarrassing accident, he might."

Petrus was quiet for a moment. Then, voice detached and without emotion, he asked, "Ms. Ramsay, are you implying that someone in this house may have murdered Aaron Scott?"

Before Liza could formulate an answer, Anne Kane was behind them in the doorway. Her eyes were immediately drawn to the ceiling. She inhaled sharply. "Liza, you've been holding out on us. Is this Lemoyne?"

"In the style of," Liza murmured, aware that Petrus's gaze was still on her. He wouldn't let her off the hook that easily. They would be continuing this conversation, she knew.

Anne's pale throat was exposed as she wheeled around slowly, head back, mouth agape. Suddenly, she snapped her fingers. "Have you been in the Palace of Holyroodhouse, Liza?"

Liza shook her head. Someday she would make it to the Edinburgh palace less than twenty minutes from her home. But that day was not today.

"This is the Dutch artist Jacob de Wet." Anne made a murmuring noise as she considered the art. "He'd been invited to Edinburgh in the late 1600s by Sir William Bruce, who was the Master of Works for the King. At the palace, he produced a series of decorative history paintings for the newly rebuilt state apartments. He must have also been invited to Ramsay Castle around the same time." She breathed. "You've got it backward. Lemoyne's painting in the Palace of Versailles—*The Apotheosis of Hercules*—is in the style of de Wet. You, Ms. Ramsay, have the original right here."

Liza wanted to share the other woman's awe—she truly did. But the air was still heavy with her conversation with Petrus, who said, "Do you think one of us is a killer, Anne?"

Petrus's question was a wet blanket on Anne's wonder. Her head jerked around. "What?"

"Liza thinks Aaron may have been murdered."

Anne's eyebrows drew together. "Oh, come now. We're not that bad, Liza."

"I didn't say you were."

"Then why would you even raise the possibility?"

Liza opened her mouth and shut it again. She felt helpless and slightly...silly. "It's just that there are so many questions."

"But no one here would want Aaron dead," Anne

said with a small laugh.

Liza's lips pressed together. She believed that every single person in this group had a motive for Aaron's murder.

Anne, also, seemed to rethink her statement. "I mean, not really," she clarified, her gaze shifting to Petrus. But he was staring at Liza.

Liza sputtered, "I-I just don't think the body should be moved. We should at least ask the police to…take a look."

"But it will be so much kinder," Anne said soothingly, practically, "if *we* take care of it. Aaron would want that. His children would want that."

Liza swallowed. She had wondered if Aaron were a father. She shut her eyes against the image of him in that closet. It was not an image she wanted passed along to his children or his family. "I would just feel better if the police knew what had happened, that's all."

"I thought the phone lines had been cut," Anne said.

Both Petrus and Liza stared at her, Petrus with a look of disbelief at the information. Liza with a look of disbelief at her knowledge.

"Was I not supposed to know that?" Anne asked. "Perhaps you should tell Mr. Baxter to lower his voice next time. I'm sure I'm not the only one who heard him."

Petrus smiled. "Well, Liza, if that's the case, I don't

think the police will get here before my team is able to remove Aaron's body, will they." It wasn't a question, and Petrus looked much more relieved than he should have been.

But Anne did not share his relief. "Where *is* Mr. Baxter, Liza? And where is your fiancé?"

Liza swallowed, aware she was alone in the room with two strangers. "They are…around."

"Around, as in they are in the castle?" Anne continued.

When Liza didn't respond, Anne and Petrus exchanged a glance.

Liza inched toward the door. Although Petrus was standing near the doorway, he didn't block her exit as she slipped past him.

"If you'll excuse me," she murmured, adding some insignificant words about needing to look after something. She hurried to her apartment and glanced behind her as she unlocked the door with trembling unsteady fingers.

She finally pulled the door open and slipped inside. It was only then, with a thrumming pulse as she closed the door, that she caught sight of Petrus Bothas's dark eyes on hers. She shut the door to those eyes and slid the deadbolt into place.

Chapter 13

The world had gone mad.

Each time Liza considered her current circumstances, it was the only explanation she could summon. If she pinched herself, would she wake up from the dream? Just in case, she shut her eyes and gave the fleshy part of her arm above the elbow a hard, painful, squeeze.

When she blinked her eyes open, she was still awake and standing in her apartment within the castle.

How was it that a young woman of modest means, who had grown up in a rural community in the Rust Belt of the United States, had ended up as the owner of a centuries-old estate in Scotland? What's more, how on earth had she come to be trapped inside said castle with the richest people in the world—one of whom was dead, and the others, potential suspects in his murder?

She stared out the window across the vast white expanse of the estate grounds. Petrus was correct. The snow had indeed slowed, and she could make out the shape of the great sycamore that stood sentinel in the snow-covered yard.

Several feet of fresh powder had fallen, and the landscape was coldly and starkly beautiful. The world was still and pristine. Any footprints left earlier by Ki and her consorts, or Lachlan and Bruce, had long since been erased.

She wasn't worried about the men's safety—not really. They'd both grown up in Bonnyrigg, and Lachlan knew the castle grounds better than Simundus de Ramesia, who had built the castle after following King David I to Scotland from the village of Ramsay in Huntingdonshire in the year 1140.

Still, the snow was deep, and the temperature was cold.

Liza turned her head. If she squinted, she could just make out what looked like one of Petrus's security vehicles nearly a mile away at the end of the lane.

What were those large men capable of, with their unconcealed weapons, unsmiling faces, and toned physiques? According to Petrus, they were perfectly capable of removing a dead body, no questions asked. What would they do to two defenseless Scots on the wrong side of the boss's orders?

A light knock sounded on the door to the apartment. Liza froze. Of course her guests knew she was in this room. Of course she'd have to answer the summons.

A wave of nausea coursed through her.

She should have taken a nap, she thought, crossing

the room. But when she'd lain down, fully clothed on the bed, all she could picture was Aaron Scott's grotesque face and naked, slumped body.

She leaned close to the door. "Yes?" she asked, hoping her voice sounded stronger than it felt.

"Ms. Ramsay?" the feminine Scottish voice asked. "It's Sadie, ma'am. May I speak with ye?"

Perhaps Sadie had brought some coffee or tea, Liza thought with a surge of hope. Tea and biscuits would be lovely. Or perhaps some of the sweet, sugary Scottish tablet. Her mouth watered in anticipation.

But when she opened the door, there was no tray of tea and biscuits. There was just pretty and timid Sadie who, since their guests had arrived, had looked as though she was perpetually on the verge of tears.

"What is it, Sadie?"

"I'm sorry tae interrupt." The girl's voice was quiet. "Ms. Turner asked me tae fetch ye."

Liza hoped that Carolyn Turner—the woman masquerading as her house manager—only had a question about the menu for the midday meal. Her gaze wandered behind Sadie to the empty hallway. "Is she in the kitchen?"

"She's with Ms. St. James."

Liza's heart sank as she remembered Daphne's altered state during the breakfast meal. But Liza said nothing more on the subject. She just nodded and glanced around, before pulling the door shut behind her and locking it with the bronze skeleton key.

They should have upgraded the locks on the interior doors.

It was past the lunch hour; she asked Sadie if she'd heard from the catering staff.

"Aye, ma'am," Sadie said as they climbed the cold, bare servant staircase in the southeast corner of the building. "They're preparin' cold meats and cheeses and fresh bread. Somethin' simple for the midday meal."

That was good. There was certainly no longer any cause for an elaborate celebration.

And while she wished the entire event had been a great success, given the occurrences that had transpired over the past few hours, she supposed that none of their high-profile visitors would dare to speak ill of the accommodation or of their hosts. It was the one saving grace in the midst of the utter failure of the affair.

When they reached Daphne's room on the fourth floor, Sadie knocked softly, then pushed open the door and slid inside without waiting for a response.

But something—a movement or a shadow—caught the corner of Liza's field of vision. She cast her gaze around, scanning the empty passageway. She listened carefully.

Nothing but a soft voice coming from inside Daphne's room and the sound of Liza's own stomach softly rumbling.

After following Sadie inside, Liza latched the door behind her. As she looked on the portrait of Lady Catherine staring back at her, the same cold finger of apprehension tickled her spine as it did every time she entered this room.

A breath of chilled air swirled around her, and she shivered.

Daphne St. James lay on the bed. Her eyes were shut and she seemed asleep, though her breathing was uneven and labored. Her eyebrows were drawn tightly together, as if in slumber something greatly troubled this beautiful woman.

Liza looked at the bed. A small streak of vomit soiled the side of the thick purple comforter and puddled on the floor beneath.

Carolyn Turner stood beside the prostrate woman while Rabbie Rose sat on the bed, the girl's limp manicured hand in his.

"What's happened?" Liza asked as her gaze settled on the small orange bottle on the nightstand. "What is that?"

"Diazepam," Ms. Turner said grimly.

"How much has she taken?"

The older woman shook her head slowly. "The label indicates there were one hundred pills in the bottle, but we have no idea what she arrived with." She gestured toward the sickness on the floor. "She's regurgitated roughly ten partially digested pills."

"Is the bottle empty?" Liza asked.

"Just about."

Liza swore under her breath. "She needs a doctor."

"This is that dobber Matthew's fault," Rabbie spat vehemently but quietly, as if he didn't want Daphne to register his words. "He's turned her into this."

While Liza thought that Matthew Carter was likely a terrible husband, she had a hard time believing he'd forced Daphne to ingest the pills. "You've said their marriage isn't a happy one. Do you have reason to believe Matthew would want his wife dead?"

"Dead?" he scoffed. "Why would he want that? She's worth much more to him alive. It's *she* that would prefer death than to spend one more second on this earth with the basturt."

"Then why wouldn't she just leave?"

"She can't leave him. He's got connections to everyone and dirt on everybody all over the world. He'd destroy her and he'd destroy her family if she tried to escape. Besides, Hugh St. James has already sacrificed his daughter for his business interests. He'd disown her in a heartbeat if she brought shame to his reputation. He's a basturt, too, that one."

"Sometimes peace of mind is more important than money," Liza said softly. "Or family."

But she knew it wasn't that simple. A woman who'd grown up accustomed to the lifestyle Daphne had lived wouldn't know how to navigate the world without the resources she'd been born into. Though Liza herself had nothing in common with Daphne, she thought she understood the other woman's predicament.

She looked at the beautiful face, far too pretty and kind for Matthew Carter. Then she wondered what Daphne's life would have been like if she'd been encouraged to pursue her own relationships. Perhaps even the relationship with the boy from the Royal Family with whom she'd explored the Ramsay Castle a decade earlier.

"Once Lachlan and Bruce arrive with Chief Inspector Dean, we can get Daphne to hospital. In the meantime, I'm afraid we just need to keep an eye on her." She wasn't sure what else to do. She looked at the putrid puddle next to the bed. "Can we clean that up?"

"I'd rather not, Ms. Ramsay. At least until we're sure of the cause of Daphne's distress." Ms. Turner gave Liza a meaningful look.

Liza understood the significance of that look all too well, having herself been poisoned not long ago. Then again, Liza hadn't ingested ten Valium.

She threaded both of her hands through her hair and pulled the skin of her face taut between her palms. Then she took three deep breaths, trying to remain calm. But what she really wanted to do was to let out a primal scream.

Ms. Turner gave her a hard look as if to silently communicate that Liza needed to hold herself together. Then she glanced at Rabbie before shifting her gaze back to Liza.

"Sadie, perhaps you should share with Ms. Ramsay what you shared with me."

Sadie, standing quietly by the foot of the bed, widened her eyes. "Do I have tae?"

"Yes." The older woman's voice was gentle, yet firm.

Sensing more bad news, Liza didn't want to hear whatever Sadie had to say as much as Sadie didn't want to say it. But she exhaled, and said, "Come on, then." She turned to Ms. Turner. "I'll let you know as soon as the men return."

The older woman nodded, and Liza left the room with the perpetually distressed Sadie. No doubt Liza would be looking for a new housekeeper after the guests finally departed.

In the hallway, Sadie turned to Liza and wrung her hands together. "I saw somethin' last night." The words came out in a rush, as if she wanted to get the conversation over with quickly.

But Liza gave a slight shake of her head. "Not here." Though the passageway still appeared abandoned, Liza was well aware that either Anne Kane or Ki may have been lurking in the shadows. She didn't rule out the hidden presence of Matthew Carter either. The man would certainly be interested in keeping an eye on whatever was happening with his wife, wouldn't he?

Liza led Sadie to the sitting room at the end of the hallway, a comfortable space next to the north stairwell, decorated in rich burgundies and soft creams. A fire crackled in the hearth, and Liza thanked the stars for Shaun Fraser's attention to detail, though she wondered when he'd had time to build a fire if he'd been keeping watch over Aaron Scott's doorway on the third floor.

She shut the door behind her. "What is it?" she asked Sadie.

"Last night..." the girl said in a halting voice. Then she paused. Whatever courage she'd summoned moments earlier appeared to have fled.

Realizing this conversation would not be quick, Liza indicated that Sadie should take a seat. The younger woman complied, perching on the edge of an overstuffed decorative chair facing the flames.

Liza sat in the chair opposite. "What happened last night?" she asked in as patient a voice as she could muster.

"When ye asked me tae check on Mr. Scott during dinner..."

Liza nodded and waited.

"Well...I knocked but didnae get a response. I heard a noise, so I opened the door just a wee bit. It wasn't locked," she said quickly. "I wouldn't hae opened it if it had been." The color rose in the girl's face and her breath quickened.

Liza really wished she had a cup of tea. Or something stronger. "And what did you see?" she finally prompted.

"I saw Ms. St. James."

Liza frowned and the information that Sadie had attempted to share with Liza last evening came back to her. She'd interrupted Sadie and had not followed up with her employee.

Sadie stared at the antique rug on the floor.

In the long seconds that followed, Liza had a good idea of what might have been going on in that room, but she pressed Sadie anyway. "What was she doing there?"

"She was…" The girl swallowed. "Well, ma'am. She was…atop Mr. Scott." Sadie put her hand to her throat.

And because Aaron Scott was now dead, Liza felt the need to be extremely clear. "Were they having sex?"

Sadie blinked, then nodded. She looked miserable. "I shouldnae hae gone in, but ye had told me to fetch 'im. I didnae expect to see what I saw."

"Both times you opened his door, I suppose," Liza couldn't help but remark.

Sadie was silent, and Liza stared into the cheerful flames. She considered this development. If Aaron and Daphne had indeed been having an affair, that gave Matthew a strong motivation for murder. She thought about Rabbie's aggressive words—the reference to the shackles Matthew had attached to his niece. If Rabbie had also discovered the affair, was it possible he might have killed Aaron to keep Daphne safe? Perhaps Rabbie's own secrets would have been at risk. But did Rabbie Rose have the capacity for murder?

Liza turned back to Sadie who was slumped forward, her head in her hands. "You said you opened the door this morning because you thought you heard someone crying?"

Sadie nodded. She looked as if she might burst into tears herself.

Liza spotted a decorative box of tissues on the sideboard and fetched it for Sadie.

Sadie took one of the soft tissues and used it to dab at her nose before she spoke. "At first, I thought it was the same...*sounds* I'd heard last night." Her face flushed. "But when I listened more closely, I could tell it was cryin'. Wailin' even, but soft."

"The door was locked?"

Sadie nodded. "I had tae use my house key."

"But when you entered, it was only Aaron you found? His body?"

"Aye, ma'am. There wasn't anyone else in that room."

"What is it that you think you heard?" Liza asked. Then quickly added, "Besides Lady Catherine. Because something tells me Lady Catherine wouldn't mourn for

Aaron Scott."

"I don't know, Ms. Ramsay. But now I'm wonderin' about Ms. St. James."

"What do you mean?"

"Well, if she was in love with Mr. Scott, and now he's dead…might she end up dead too? It's like Romeo and Juliet."

Liza knew that intimacy did not always equate to love.

Sadie though, seemed like a romantic. And her embarrassment in discussing intimate matters didn't necessarily mean that the girl wasn't experienced herself. Perhaps in the small village where she'd grown up, matters of the flesh were not routinely talk about. Particularly not with the person who provided you with a paycheck.

There wasn't much more to say on the topic. She considered giving Sadie the afternoon off, then thought better of it. Maybe it was better for the young woman to have a task to keep her mind off mayhem and murder. "Would you mind making sure Mr. Rose gets a cup of tea, and then arranging for refreshments to be served in the drawing room before lunch?" Liza asked. "Get yourself some tea, too."

Sadie stood quickly, eager to be dismissed. "Aye, ma'am."

As the girl opened the door to walk into the hall-way, Liza said, "Sadie?"

The young woman turned back.

"Don't share any of the information we discussed with anyone in the house."

"I would never speak tae the guests on subjects such as this."

"Don't share it with anyone else in the house either," she said. "Not Mr. McClaren, Mr. Baxter, or Mr. Fraser."

Sadie's brows drew together.

"Sometimes the less people who know something the better. At least until we can talk to the police."

"The police, ma'am?"

Sadie was still under the impression that Aaron's murder had been a terrible accident, and that Daphne was lovesick and in mourning.

"As a precaution," Liza assured her.

"Should I be worried, ma'am?"

Liza did her best to give her a reassuring smile. "It's all going to be fine," she said.

Sadie nodded.

"But be sure to lock your door."

The girl stared at Liza for a second longer before leaving the room. Liza hoped she was right, and everything really was going to be fine.

She wasn't sure the Ramsay Castle could survive one more dead body. She wasn't sure *she* could either.

Chapter 14

The midday meal was a tray of assorted meats, cheeses, and bread laid out on the sideboard in the dining room, with a hearty chicken and leek stew on the side. None of the castle's current inhabitants opted to sit at the table or even in the adjacent drawing room. Instead, most of the guests took plates to their rooms. Not one of them wanted to be either in the castle or with each other.

The lone person Liza encountered in the dining room was Carolyn Turner, who glanced at Liza over her shoulder as she entered.

Ms. Turner set a fresh pot of tea on a side table and said quietly, "I'm concerned that the men haven't returned."

Liza gazed out the window at the barren white landscape. Even the trees looked like pale cloaked figures on the horizon—beautiful and eerie, icy and ominous. She was also concerned about Lachlan and Bruce, but she was not yet panicked. The hike into town through the wooded path would have taken some time for the two men to navigate. And by the time they'd found a friendly villager to allow use of a telephone, made contact with Detective Chief Inspector Dean, and then allowed time for Dean to secure transport to the castle before making their way through the impassable streets, many hours may have passed. No, Liza was not yet panicked, but she was becoming increasingly anxious.

And that anxiety manifested in a sharp question. "What do you propose we do?"

"There's nothing to do but to wait. The guests are restless, but a coup hasn't begun." Carolyn Turner looked at the empty doorway and wet her lips. "I'm most concerned about Mr. Bothas. He is a man used to being in total control."

"They all are," Liza said grimly. "That's what this meeting was all about—their need to exert control over each other." In any way possible, Liza thought, but didn't say it out loud.

"But that one..." Ms. Turner tapped a finger against her chin. "...Petrus. I've met plenty of men like him before. He is a wild card."

Liza doubted Ms. Turner had met anyone exactly like Petrus. She changed the subject. "How is Daphne?" she asked instead.

"She'll live," Ms. Turner said grimly then arched one of her fine, nestlike eyebrows. "I trust Sadie informed you of what she saw last night."

It wasn't exactly a question, but Liza nodded anyway. The two women exchanged a look. Liza imagined that Ms. Turner had similar thoughts to Liza's regarding motives for murder. More and more people just kept emerging as suspects.

Sergei Popova walked into the room, florid and perspiring. A thin layer of sweat beaded his upper lip, and he licked it off.

Liza's stomach turned, and she looked away from the man.

A casual observer may have assumed he was inebriated, but Liza had given up on guessing if that was the case. He seemed to always look the same—damp, boisterous, boastful, and unsteady on his feet.

He didn't bother with pleasantries. "This is all there is?" he demanded in his heavy accent, sweeping his meaty paw above the array of food.

"We didn't think it was necessary to prepare a full meal, but if you'd like a different dish, I can ask the kitchen to fix something," Ms. Turner said evenly and amenably, the picture of a dutiful server.

"Bah," he said, and grumbled under his breath, as he took a plate and piled it high with rare roast beef, smoked turkey, and Havarti cheese.

He swayed. Liza thought he looked a bit more flushed and damp than usual. His breathing was heavy and audible.

"Are you feeling all right, Mr. Popova?" she asked.

He did not answer her question. "Is there something besides tea to drink?" He spat the word 'tea' as if it were the foulest of expletives.

"I can brew you some coffee," Ms. Turner said.

"Or perhaps you'd like some water," Liza suggested. Beneath Sergei's florid complexion, she saw a pallor she didn't like. She didn't wait for his response, but poured him a glass of iced water from a metal pitcher on the sideboard and thrust it in his direction.

To her mild surprise he didn't argue. He took the glass and swallowed the liquid without comment. She refilled the drinking glass for him.

"It might be wise to take a break from the whisky," she said.

He grunted in response, looked around the empty room, and walked out with his plate, most likely back to his bedroom and his Scotch or vodka. Liza didn't want to know how he'd been passing the hours.

"This is a disaster," Liza muttered.

"Well, it's certainly not your fault." Ms. Turner's voice was high and crisp. It did not make Liza feel comforted.

Liza frowned at the food in front of her. She should eat something, but she had no appetite and knew her stomach wouldn't completely settle until Lachlan returned.

"I'm going to check on Shaun," she said, fixing the footman a sandwich and a mug of the strong black tea.

Ms. Turner nodded. "We should also keep a closer

eye on Sergei. We don't need another medical emergency on our hands."

Liza bit her lip. She said nothing else before she left the room and climbed the stairs to the third floor.

The piercing notes of a saxophone shrieked into the stairwell, startling Liza and causing hot tea to slosh over her hand. The volume increased as she alighted the steps on the third floor. The noise was coming from the lounge. As she edged closer, the shrieking instrument shifted to a quick staccato, and the saxophone was joined by a thrashing, jazzy piano and the rhythmic beat of the double bass.

She frowned as she approached Shaun who was sitting on the floor in front of Aaron Scott's room, the back of his head resting against the door. The young man's eyes were closed, but his foot tapped the air in front of him in time with the discordant music.

God, Liza hated jazz.

As if Shaun sensed her coming, he opened his eyes, then eyed the plate of food gratefully. "For me, ma'am?" he asked.

She nodded and handed him the plate. She set the mug of tea on the floor beside him. "Would you like a chair?"

"Nah." He bit into the sandwich and chewed for a moment. Then he said around the partially masticated mouthful, "Sadie offered me a chair, too."

Liza hitched her chin toward the lounge. "What's

going on in there?"

"Mr. Carter, ma'am. No' much to listen to, but it's better than silence, I suppose."

Liza didn't know about that.

"Everything all right here?" she asked, pointing toward Aaron's door. She hated to think about the body on the other side.

"Aside from that arsehole Sergei who keeps summonin' me for random requests, it's been pretty quiet." He took another bite of his sandwich.

"What does he want?" Liza asked.

Shaun took a drink of tea. "The usual—more vodka, more whisky, refresh his fire, run his bath. Mostly, I think he's just lookin' for someone to brag to about his money and his women, to tell ye the truth."

"Did he return to his room?"

Shaun shrugged. "Haven't seen 'im for a while."

"Has anyone else been around?"

"Mr. Bothas left a bit ago, then came back again. Ki might be in there with him." Shaun's gaze slid away from hers, and he made a face as if he knew for a fact that Ki was in Petrus's room.

Liza expected she knew exactly how Shaun knew of Ki's presence. As thick as these old walls happened to be, sounds carried.

"I'm going to have a quick word with Mr. Carter," she said and nodded his head toward Shaun's plate. "I'll return for that."

"That's not necessary, ma'am. Sadie's been checkin' on me regular." His voice had softened, and Liza blinked. Another romance, she thought glumly. There was entirely too much romantic tension in the castle.

"I'll be back for the plate," she said more firmly than she intended. Shaun looked at her for a second and then nodded. "Of course, Ms. Ramsay."

Liza knew her own face was drawn. Her hair was no longer sleek and stylish. Instead, it looked tousled, brittle, and full of static from the dry air.

She couldn't say she much cared. Still, she smoothed her long black top over her slim jeans that seemed to have loosened around her hips before walking into the assault of jazz permeating the lounge.

Matthew sat on a sofa upholstered in a soft green fabric. A small tumbler of whisky rested loosely between his fingers as he stared into the distance. He didn't immediately acknowledge Liza in the doorway.

In the corner, an old gramophone scratched over the grooves of a vinyl record. The jazz wasn't modern; it had a distinctly 60s or 70s feel with its discordant horns, halting, jarring rhythm, and dissonant harmonies. The record must have belonged to Callum.

She placed a hand to her clavicle, and the slight movement seemed to alert Matthew to her presence, and he glanced at her and sat up straighter.

"Mind if I turn that down?" she asked over the music, already moving toward the record player. She twisted the knob, but didn't completely cut off the sound, even though she wanted to.

The sleeve of the album cover sat on a table next to the player. A clean-cut young man with short coiffed hair posed with a saxophone. The white letters on a red background read 'Tubby Hayes Quintet'.

"The silence was killing me," Matthew said, then seemed to realize the implication of his words. "You know what I mean."

"Have you eaten, Mr. Carter?"

"Not much of an appetite." He held up his glass. "At least not for food." Then he sighed. "Not for this, either." He sat the glass on the small side table next to him. "I just want to get out of here," he said. "No offense."

"None taken. Have you checked on your wife?" she asked.

Matthew's face turned hard and grim. "Why should I? Uncle Rabbie is with her."

Liza didn't know if Matthew had any idea his wife had taken an overdose of sleeping pills. She was sure it wasn't her place to inform him. "Well, you may want to check on her, all the same."

He inhaled then exhaled all the air from his lungs before he spoke again. "I had my people do a background check on you, Liza, before we came here. I know you know what it's like to be in a relationship that appears to have run its course."

Liza kept her expression neutral. "If a relationship has run its course, there are ways to set each other free."

"But that's just it. I don't want to be free of her. I love her so fucking much." This, Liza realized, was a rare show of vulnerability from the man. All at once, his normally level voice was filled with such emotion, Liza thought it might spill over into tears. He swallowed. "I keep hoping she'll come to her senses. I can make her happy if she'll just let me."

Moved in spite of herself, Liza sat down on the edge of a chaise lounge.

Matthew's large square head was turned away from her, and she stared at his black hair.

"Does she know how you feel?"

Matthew shrugged.

This man was old enough to be Daphne's father. And though he was handsome in a rugged and moody way, like a boxer or a warrior, she didn't know if a young woman like Daphne was ready to settle for a man as intense and possessive as Matthew was. Which may have been why she'd been having an affair with the married Aaron Scott—as an act of rebellion that could not tether her as her marriage to Matthew had.

Then again, what the hell did Liza know? She didn't know these people and didn't understand their lifestyles. Her sage and naïve advice had no place in their world.

She continued staring at this rich man-child in front of her—at his brooding expression and self-pitying misery. Her sympathy was quickly tilting into disgust. How dare he act the victim? This man, with his billions, preying on a sheltered girl like Daphne St. James, for her youth, her looks, and her family.

Liza knew she shouldn't poke this particular bear, but she couldn't help herself.

"I'm sure Daphne is just upset about Aaron's death."

She said it in an innocent enough voice, but the man's expression darkened immediately. He glowered in her direction. Then he growled, "What's that supposed to mean?"

Liza tried to match her expression to her innocent voice. "She seems to have a sensitive nature, and a death in the house—even if accidental—is likely upsetting to her. She's not much more than a child, after all."

He ignored the comment about his wife's age. "What do you mean, 'if accidental'?"

"Well, we can't know what happened for sure."

"That idiot killed himself engaged in some stupid sex game. That's what we know for sure." He emphasized the last two words.

Liza wondered if Matthew suspected his wife may have been a part of those games, and if he might have staged Aaron's death in a way to not only embarrass the man but to send a message to Daphne. She shivered. With the way he was glaring at her now, she didn't doubt he was capable of violence.

There was something menacing about Matthew Carter. The dark, square shape of his head and body. The deep-set, brooding eyes. The quiet aggression bubbling just beneath the surface.

There was also something possessive about his relationship with his wife. Despite his tearful claims of love, Liza's observation was that he treated Daphne more like an accessory. Or his property. Did he abuse her? Maybe not physically. But Liza had no doubt the young woman felt imprisoned by the union.

The conversation with this man felt surreal, especially given the environment—the music, the fire, the warmth. Liza felt as if she were in a cocoon.

"What if it wasn't an accident though? What if someone actually killed him?"

"You can't be serious."

She lifted a shoulder. "It wouldn't be the first murder in this house."

"And who do you think would have wanted him dead?" His voice held a note of humor or incredulity, as if he couldn't believe what he was hearing.

Liza didn't look at him. "You, for starters," she said softly.

She could feel his gaze burning into the side of her face.

The notes of the tenor saxophone on the phonograph danced in harmony and then clashed with the staccato notes of the piano. It was a rambling, tumbling duet, and Liza had no idea where the resolution would come.

"You're suggesting I killed Aaron Scott?"

Liza didn't respond. She let the notes wheel and whirl in her head. There was something compelling about the music's journey, but her brain struggled to keep up with the composition.

"Why on earth would you think I'd want Aaron dead?"

"Because your wife was sleeping with him, and I think you wanted it to stop. Not because you loved her. Because you wanted to show her what you were capable of."

Chapter 15

Matthew laughed. He laughed long and loud, nearly doubling over, drowning out the sound of the jazz. When he finally stopped laughing, he wiped away nonexistent tears of mirth. "You actually think I'd kill someone for sleeping with my wife?"

"You were just now nearly weeping because you said she wanted to leave you."

The laughter subsided, and the hardness returned. "It's true that I want Daphne to love me as much as I love her. The only reason she's still with me is because she can go out and do as she pleases. So can I." He shrugged. "I'm afraid your theory is ridiculous, Ms. Ramsay."

"Aaron Scott, the man with whom your wife was having an affair, is dead."

"You have no proof she was having an affair with him."

"Oh, but I do."

His eyes turned nearly black, and for just a second, Liza thought he might lunge at her. But as quickly as the cloud flickered over his features, the look of hostility passed.

Matthew shrugged. "If Aaron was indeed murdered, he certainly wasn't murdered by me. I wouldn't risk my life and my career over that good-for-nothing, arrogant dud of a human."

"Even when your wife was sleeping with him, and everyone knew it?"

He scowled. "*Especially* if she were sleeping with him."

"What if she was in love with him?"

Some of Matthew's bravado faltered. "So what if she was?" His voice was only slightly strained.

"That doesn't bother you? A beautiful, bright young thing like Daphne, intimate with a man like Aaron? He was richer than you, wasn't he? Had more respect? More power?"

Matthew chuckled, and this time, it seemed genuine. He took a long swallow of his spirits. "I'm not sure what you're hoping to accomplish by goading me, Ms. Ramsay. Even if Daphne were in love with him—and she most certainly was not—I would not have murdered anyone." Liza thought she caught the slightest emphasis on the word 'I'. "And, just for kicks, suppose I had wanted the man dead? I certainly wouldn't have done it in the sick way he was found."

They sat in silence. The notes of the saxophone squealed then faded. No one moved or spoke. The needle of the record skipped on the last song before the arm of the gramophone lifted and moved itself back to its starting position.

The silence was disquieting.

Matthew drained his glass and stood up. "You'll have to excuse me, Liza. You've reminded me that I need to check on my wife."

Liza nearly said something about his wife's condition—the pills, the convulsion, the vomit—but she sat quietly until Matthew had left the room. Then she stood and walked to the gramophone, slipped the slim black disc back into its case, and switched off the machine.

She walked from the room. Shaun Fraser was in the same position, head against the door that separated him from the dead man's body. God, she hoped Lachlan would return soon.

If she hadn't been panicked before, the edges of alarm had now begun to lick at her back.

She descended the staircase, intent on finding Ms. Turner, but when she reached the first floor, heading for the kitchen, instead she found Petrus dressed in the outfit in which he'd arrived. He was pulling on a pair of thick black boots over black jeans. His knit cap was pulled down over his ears; he didn't hear her coming.

"What are you doing?" she asked, approaching from behind him as he bent over.

He startled, then straightened, frowning. "You shouldn't sneak up on people like that."

"You can't go out wearing that."

"You don't like it?" His tone was teasing, and he held out his arms and looked down at his own body, pretending to critically assess his outfit.

It was Liza's turn to frown. "There are several feet of snow out there. You'll freeze to death."

He shrugged. "I came in wearing this exact outfit."

"It had just begun to snow when you arrived, and you were half frozen."

"I only need to get halfway down the drive before the men see me." He dismissed her, his flirtation gone. He intended to do what he wanted, regardless of her desires.

As he laced up his boots, Ki appeared at the top of the staircase, looking down at the two of them.

"Where is Lachlan, Liza?" she asked. Her bright accent sounded out of place and eerie as it echoed off the high ceiling of the grand hallway.

"Yes," Petrus said, looking up at her. "Where *is* Lachlan?"

Liza faltered. Ki's voice again filled the space. "You said he was fixing things in the chapel, but he isn't there. And he hasn't been there. I've been checking."

"Why is it you're checking in on my fiancé?"

"Because we'd like to know where he went," Petrus responded for his girlfriend.

Again, Liza wished she'd taken time to master the art of deception. Or at least tell a decent fib.

"If you must know," she said with a dramatic sigh, "he's still sleeping. He was exhausted from last night and wasn't feeling well. Since we're all confined together, he decided not to expose everyone to illness, should his condition be contagious." Even to her own ears, the excuse sounded too elaborate. Too contrived, too affected.

Petrus and Ki exchanged a glance.

"I don't think that's true, Liza," Petrus said. "I think he's left the castle. I think, based on your misguided notion that Aaron was murdered, that Lachlan has gone to attempt to summon the police. And that, my beautiful friend, was a bold move—sending someone you allegedly love out in this weather. I just have to make it down the drive. How far does your boyfriend have to hike?"

Liza narrowed her eyes. "So what if he's gone to get help? It's still not clear to me why you're so eager to cover up Aaron's death. That is not the action of an innocent man, in my opinion."

"Lucky for me, your opinion doesn't count." He finished tying his boots and stood.

Desperation rose in her throat. "We need a doctor, too. Daphne isn't well."

Petrus looked skeptical. "Like Lachlan isn't well?"

"Daphne is in her room," Ki said.

"Are you aware that Daphne took pills?"

Both Ki and Petrus looked at her blankly.

"I think she tried to kill herself."

"And did she?" Petrus said.

"Did she *what*?"

"Kill herself."

Liza stared at him. "Well…no. But she needs medical attention."

He sighed. "My men can take care of it."

Liza didn't ask how. She didn't want to know.

He went to the door, but before he could open it, the sound of a loud, deep engine reached them from just outside the walls.

Liza's heart leapt into her throat. Either the police had finally come to help, or Petrus's men had decided to make their way up the drive unbidden. Petrus's face creased with displeasure, and Ki uttered a soft, "No."

The door opened. Lachlan stood on the other side. Liza felt tears of relief and utter exhaustion well up in her eyes. She wanted to fold herself into his arms and press her face into his stiff black coat that looked as if it smelled of woodsmoke and snow.

But she didn't. She couldn't. There were other priorities right now. And before she could throw herself into his arms, she needed to ask him about Ki. She needed to be sure nothing had happened between them.

Bruce Baxter's surly voice cut through the silence. "It's pure baltic out there," he exclaimed. "Didnae know if we'd see ye all again."

"Thank *god* you made it back," Petrus said.

Liza noticed two things—the way Ki was staring at Lachlan, and the way that, just maybe, he was looking back at her.

Then she saw the looming figure behind the men. It was Detective Inspector Alex Lawson.

Liza looked behind him, expecting to see Detective Chief Inspector Dean.

DI Lawson saw the direction of Liza's gaze. "DCI Dean has her hands full at the station," he said. "The weather brings out the worst in people."

Liza could relate to that. She nodded, attempting to hide her disappointment. She didn't have anything against Lawson. But the last time she'd encountered him had been during that nasty business with Callum, Charlie Campbell, and Brodie Graham. She'd found Lawson silent, brooding, and less than impressive. In fact, in the few minutes since he'd entered the house, he'd already spoken more than she remembered during the entire prior investigation.

At least Ms. Turner was here, she thought ruefully, as she silently condemned Marion Dean for abandoning her.

Ki had sidled too close to Lachlan, and Liza went to him, gently pulling him off to the side, away from the nubile body of Petrus's girlfriend.

Lachlan continued to peel off his layers of outerwear, ignoring or unaware of Liza's agitation.

"Are you okay?" she asked, as Bruce Baxter shouted to no one in particular, "N'er seen it that bad. No' in my sixty years."

Lachlan gave her a small smile that made her heart twist in her chest. "I'm fine. I could use a break from Bruce," he said. "And I could use a hot meal and a strong drink."

Petrus pushed past Bruce to stand in front of Lawson. "Where are my men?" he demanded.

"Yer men are right where we left them. I haven't decided yet if I'll have them arrested when backup arrives."

Petrus laughed, but it was a mean and brittle sound. "On what grounds?" he asked. Then added, "I'd like to see you try."

Lawson ignored the implied threat. "For interferin' with an investigation." Lawson peeled off his own coat and gloves. He stood face to face with Petrus. The detective was just as burly, just as tall, just as confident. Neither of them seemed to be the least bit intimidated by the other.

"Investigation of what?"

"The death of..." The detective hesitated before Lachlan supplied, "...Aaron Scott."

Petrus threw up his hands. "You people and your damned conspiracy theories. There's nothing to investigate. The man hung himself. Autoerotic asphyxiation. An accident."

"Neither of those things seems accidental to me," Lawson responded.

Ki had retreated from Lachlan, but she hung back. Liza thought she looked just a bit worried.

"I'm goin' tae get somethin' hot in me," Bruce said.

"I'll join ye," Lachlan added. But before he went, he said to Liza, "Everything else okay here?"

She shook her head, but she didn't want to discuss the day's events with this cast of characters around them. And she certainly couldn't leave Lawson alone with Petrus.

Lachlan gave her a grim look. "We'll need to talk soon," he said, then turned and walked away.

Liza's anxiety tingled. What was that supposed to mean? She wished more than anything the two of them were alone in this castle, and they could just shut themselves away in their cozy room.

Ki watched Bruce and Lachlan go, but she stayed by Petrus's side, biting her lip.

The detective turned to Liza. "Can ye take me to the body, ma'am?"

Liza nodded and started walking toward the staircase, aware that both Petrus and Ki were also following.

"I thought you'd have an investigative team with you," she said to Lawson. And Dean. They could all use Dean's no-nonsense, calm demeanor right about now. She'd know how to handle a houseful of billionaires.

Lawson lumbered behind her on the stairs. His breathing was heavy, but not because he was out of shape. It was simply because he was such a big man.

"Wish it were possible," he said. "I had to use one of the M-RAVs to make it through the snow. The others will have to follow once the roads are cleared. We've got all officers on public safety duty right now. Cars stuck on the motorways—three deaths from carbon monoxide poisoning, from what it seems."

Liza glanced back at him, wondering if he were indicating that the death of a billionaire, and perhaps a suicide, at that, was not worth the time of the other officers. On the other hand, this particular death had the potential to attract a lot of attention. Perhaps Dean had sent Lawson alone to avoid unnecessary eyes and wagging tongues. She hoped that was the case and that there was some strategy behind their decision.

They emerged on the third-floor landing, and nearly ran headlong into Sadie, who startled, sloshing tea from a cup in her hand. "Pardon me, ma'am," she said. She glanced up at Lawson, looming tall over her in his authoritative police uniform. She shrank back.

"Sadie, Mr. McClaren and Mr. Baxter are back," Liza said, attempting to redirect the girl. "Would you mind making sure they get a hot meal and a good stiff drink? They're in the kitchen now."

Sadie nodded and hurried past.

"And can you send up Ms. Turner?" Liza asked

after her.

The girl mumbled a clipped, "Yes, ma'am," and Petrus said, "Why on earth are you sending for the help?"

She didn't bother to answer.

"Did you tell my men what was going on?" Petrus's question was aimed at Lawson.

"Don't know what's goin' on myself yet," Lawson said evenly.

"But surely they asked what you were doing here?"

Lawson seemed to consider the question. "I don't think they did, after all. Tried to prevent me from drivin' through. I told them I'd shoot first, and if they shot back, they'd likely all rot in prison. We might have abolished the death penalty in Scotland, but the citizens don't look kindly on a bunch of Americans killin' their public servants. After that, we didn't get far in discussin' the purpose of my visit."

Petrus opened his mouth as if to argue, then thought better of it. He looked incredibly perturbed that his men had lost their argument against this big, thick-looking police officer.

"Besides, wouldn't make a very flatterin' story for ye, Mr. Bothas, would it now?"

"Petrus," Ki said, her small hands on her boyfriend's large arm.

Petrus shrugged her off, and they all continued down the empty hallway. Shaun was no longer in his position. Liza frowned and stopped outside Aaron's unguarded door. When she tried the door, she found it locked, at least, but she didn't have her master keys.

A second later, Shaun came hurrying from the servants' staircase near the opposite end of the passageway.

"I'm sorry, Ms. Ramsay," he said, out of breath. "Mr. Carter had me take his luggage up to Ms. St. James's room."

"Why?"

"He said he's stayin' with her for the rest of their time in the castle."

Liza sighed. She was quite certain Matthew was the last person Daphne wanted in her room.

"Is he with her now?"

"Aye."

"Where's Mr. Rose?"

Before Shaun could answer, Liza spotted Rabbie walking toward the group, a worried look on his face.

Rabbie glanced at Lawson. "I hope tae god he's here to sort out this mess so we can all get out of this godforsaken ruin and go home." He remembered himself. "No offense, Ms. Ramsay, but my niece's life may depend on it."

"What's that?" Lawson asked.

Liza turned to Shaun first. "Mr. Fraser, please open Mr. Scott's room." She looked at Lawson. "One issue at a time, detective." Finally, she turned to Petrus and Ki.

"I will accompany the detective alone." Shaun opened the door, and before the others could protest, Liza silently steeled herself and marched inside. After Lawson walked in behind her, she shut the door firmly in the faces of her guests.

She let out a breath.

"Where's the body?"

Liza whirled around. "It's right—" Her words were abruptly swallowed by the still, empty air of the room. The bed, where the body had lain, was unoccupied, the blanket smooth and undisturbed.

Liza stared at it, blinking. For a split second, she wondered if she were in the right room.

Her heart pounded in her ears. She moved toward the closet where the body had been found and flung open the doors. The space was empty except for Aaron Scott's luggage, two sweaters, and a pair of pressed trousers neatly folded over a hanger. A small suitcase had been rolled against the wall. Gone also was the belt that had been around Aaron's neck.

Liza reeled around wildly. She rushed into the washroom. Empty. She moved to the other side of the bed and knelt on the floor, looking beneath the furniture.

There was no body in the room.

Lawson watched her. "Are you sure we're in the right room?" He rubbed his chin with his massive hand, looking at her like she was insane. Or stupid.

Despite wondering the same thing herself only seconds earlier, Liza snapped, "Of course this is the right room. And the body was right here." She gestured toward the bed. "We all saw it."

Lawson frowned. "I thought the guy hung himself in the closet."

"He did."

"Then how did the body get on the bed?"

Liza jerked her hand toward the door. "They moved it."

"Who?"

"Them," she said to Lawson. "The rest of them."

Lawson finally took a small notepad and pen from the front pocket of his shirt. He scribbled something on the page.

Liza pulled open the door to find Petrus, Ki, and Rabbie still standing outside. Was it her imagination, or was there a smug look of satisfaction on Petrus's face?

She turned her attention first to Rabbie, the one of the trio she trusted most. "He's gone," she said.

Rabbie frowned. "Who?"

"Aaron."

"What do ye mean, lass?" he asked, pushing past her into the room.

The old man looked around, just as stunned as Liza.

"Well then," Petrus said from the doorway. "Nothing to see here after all."

Liza glared at Petrus. "What did you do with him?"

"What on earth are you talking about, Ms. Ramsay? This door was locked—you tried it yourself. And I certainly don't have a key."

She pushed past him. "Where is Shaun?" She was talking mostly to herself.

Lawson poked around the room skeptically, shifting items with the tip of his pen and scribbling meaningless notes. Without a body, what use was an investigation?

Shaun appeared from the staircase again, and Liza grasped his arm. "Who went into that room?" Her voice was loud, verging on hysterical.

Shaun looked alarmed. "What do ye mean?" He disentangled himself from her grasp. "I was outside the whole time."

"No, you weren't," Liza said. "You weren't here when we arrived. And you were the one who lit the fires this morning and tended to Sergei throughout the day. You left this post on multiple occasions."

"Not long enough fer anyone tae smuggle a body out without me or anyone else as a witness. Besides, the door was locked the whole time."

Liza whirled around, feeling unsteady on her feet.

Where was Aaron Scott?

She was about to ask the question aloud when a long and somewhat inhuman groan wailed through the passageway. The sound was followed by a loud, heavy thud that seemed to shake the walls of the castle.

The group stared at each other.

There was a light scraping, followed by another moan, quieter this time. Weak and tragic. It came from across the hallway. Sergei's room.

Lawson led the way, pushing the door open with authority. Liza was behind him, struggling to look past his large frame. When she did, she nearly crumbled.

Sergei lay on the floor, his head broken open, blood painting red the white hearth of the fireplace. The man's sightless, glazed eyes stared back at her. That lifeless gaze was the last thing she saw before blackness encroached and she dissolved toward the floor; before the strong arms of Petrus Bothas caught her before she hit the ground.

Chapter 16

The blackness had enveloped Liza for less than a second, and she quickly scrambled out of the billionaire's grasp. He let her go. Still, she shivered.

All of the people in the room had turned away from the badly injured Sergei Popova and were instead bending toward her.

"We have to get him help," she said, forgetting Petrus and squinting at the man on the floor. She took a few deep breaths and placed her hands against her temples.

The group turned their attention back to Sergei.

Lawson's face was grim. "Seems to me that one's beyond help." Still, he went to Sergei, and peered into the man's horrible, glazed eyes. Then Lawson put two fingers against Sergei's neck, straddling the pool of blood that extended from the hearth onto the ancient hardwood of the floor, making a permanent stain.

Lawson's frown deepened, and he shook his head. "How much had he to drink?"

Shaun spoke up. "Dinnae ken if he ever stopped drinkin', tae tell the truth."

"Probably should have been cut off." Lawson cast an accusing eye toward Liza.

Liza opened her mouth to dispute the comment, but it was Petrus who interjected. "Ms. Ramsay isn't his babysitter, Officer. Besides, I don't know that I've ever seen Sergei sober. The man was a highly functional alcoholic. It didn't affect his professional life one bit."

Lawson rose and looked at Petrus. "It's 'Detective Inspector'," he said, a note of indignation coloring his words. "What exactly was his profession?"

"Sergei?" Petrus gave a little laugh. "He was an oligarch."

"But what does that *mean*?"

"You don't know what 'oligarch' means?"

"Of course I know the meaning of the word itself," Lawson said. But his voice was defensive, and Liza doubted he actually did know the definition. "In terms of how this man made his money, what does it mean?" Lawson demanded. His round face had reddened, and he was looking at Petrus with an expression of blatant animosity.

Petrus ignored the hostility and shrugged. "I'm afraid I'm not the most qualified person to answer that question. Sergei had a lot of contacts, but even more political power."

"And ye didn't take advantage of that political power?"

Petrus snorted. "I didn't need his contacts or his

influence. I have my own. If you want to talk to someone who knew Sergei's business—or rather who was profiting from Sergei's connections—you need to talk to Matthew Carter."

A startled exclamation from the door made everyone turn.

Anne Kane's elegant hand was at her throat. "Oh my," she said, her eyes wide. "Yet another body."

Lawson must have decided that there were quite enough spectators. "Okay, people," he said. "Let's all take a pause and meet in the first-floor drawing room. I need to alert my team that we have one confirmed death in addition to the other reported death." He herded them out of the room using his big frame. Then he turned to Liza. "Can we lock the door before this body disappears, too?"

Anne whirled around. "What does that mean?"

"Aaron's body is gone," Ki supplied helpfully.

"Gone where?"

Ki's eyes were wide. "Nobody knows."

Someone knew, Liza thought.

"Well, it can't have gotten up and walked off itself. We all saw Aaron in that dreadful position."

"I don't want any speculation," Lawson said, watching as Shaun locked the door with his substantial set of keys. Then Lawson pulled out his mobile phone. "I'd like to talk to everyone in the drawing room at half past the hour." He looked at Liza. "Is there a private place I can make this call?"

She nodded, still feeling a bit unsteady. She pointed Lawson to the lounge where she'd sat with Matthew what felt like hours ago. "I'll round everyone up," she said.

"Perhaps ye can get someone else to do that, Liza." His deep brogue was filled with concern, and Liza looked up at him.

"When's the last time you ate anything?"

She thought of the meager meal she'd had earlier. She didn't answer his question.

"Get some food in ye. We'll get this all sorted out." He gave her a meaningful look. "Ye need to take care of yerself."

Sorted out, she thought to herself. As if two bodies—one of which had disappeared into thin air—was a minor inconvenience or misunderstanding.

As Liza ascended the stairs, she wasn't so sure they'd get it sorted out. Where on earth could Aaron's body have gone? Had Petrus managed to give his men access to the castle without anyone knowing? It wouldn't have been impossible, but it would have been difficult without witnesses. And even if he *had* managed it, why then had he been preparing to go out in the snow to summon his team? Could that have been an attempt to draw attention away from himself?

But Petrus did not seem like the type of person to go to great lengths to fool anyone. He didn't seem to care that much what anyone thought of him. Besides, he'd been extremely open about his desire to take care of the circumstances of the death himself. Why then would he have bothered keeping it a secret after the deed had been done?

Her thoughts turned to Sergei splayed unceremoniously on the ancient hearth. His death appeared to have been a tragic accident. The man was unhealthy and overweight. Not to mention permanently inebriated. He could have easily stumbled due to the drink, hit his head on the stone mantel or hearth, and died due to his own foolish gluttony.

Alternatively, he could have had a heart attack or a stroke. She thought of his gray complexion when he'd collected his food from the dining room earlier. He'd appeared unhealthy in a way that had nothing to do with his alcohol consumption.

But there was something else niggling at the back of her mind. Something she couldn't quite place her finger on that was bothering her about Sergei's death. It tickled the edge of her thoughts, but each time she seemed to approach the memory, it danced away from her so that it slipped from her recall.

As she walked down the hallway toward Daphne's room, she saw Rabbie at the door. He spotted her at nearly the same time.

"Ah, my dear," he said. "I was just coming up tae collect Daphne and see if she's feelin' well enough tae join us in the drawing room."

"Is Matthew in there with her?"

Rabbie frowned and nodded once. "Unfortunately."

While she certainly didn't think Daphne had anything to do with Sergei's death—nor Aaron's, for that matter—she didn't like the idea of the woman being left alone in the room, unaccompanied and unprotected.

Rabbie rapped sharply on the door with one knuckle and without waiting for a response pushed his way inside. Liza followed close behind.

Before Matthew spotted Liza, he shouted at Rabbie, "I thought I told you to leave. I'm quite capable of taking care of my wife." He was sitting in an armchair near the window, and had risen half from his seat. When he saw Liza, he straightened. "Ah, Ms. Ramsay too." His voice was lowered, but his eyes were thunderous.

Liza ignored him and looked to the bed where Daphne lay. Her eyes were open, expression despondent. "How are you feeling?" she said to the young woman.

Daphne made a movement that might have been a shrug under the sheet. She didn't speak.

"Everyone needs to come to the drawing room," Rabbie announced. "Daphne can stay here and rest."

"Actually, I'd like Daphne to come too," Liza said.

"Neither of us are going anywhere." Matthew gestured toward his wife. "Just look at her. She's in no position to be moved. This wretched place has destroyed her."

Liza winced, but managed to suppress her stronger reaction to the insult. "Be that as it may, Mr. Carter, Detective Inspector Lawson has requested the presence of all the guests, including your wife, in the drawing room."

"The police?" Matthew exclaimed. "Surely this isn't about that business with Aaron? I know you have your conspiracy theory, Ms. Ramsay, but as I told you earlier, the man was an idiot, and his actions were his own."

Daphne made a soft keening sound that her husband pretended not to notice.

Rabbie approached Liza and said softly, out of Matthew's earshot, "Perhaps it wouldn't hurt for Daphne to stay here."

"And who'll stay with her?" she asked the old man.

He gave a brief nod of acknowledgment when he understood her meaning.

Matthew sliced the air in front of him with his hand. "I will not be questioned about the death of that good-for-nothing socialist who wanted to mechanize the world at the expense of the human race. He caused me nothing but problems when he was alive, and he continues to complicate my life in death."

Liza wondered if the problems Aaron had caused Matthew extended beyond the affair with his wife. But she didn't ask. "It's not a request, Mr. Carter."

"And what are you going to do about it, Ms. Ramsay? Have me arrested for tending to my wife? Tell this detective he can come up here if he wants to question me about Aaron Scott." He sat back down and picked up a book from the side table. His nostrils flared.

Daphne had begun weeping softly.

Liza hadn't wanted to let Matthew know Sergei was dead. Not yet. But she supposed he'd find out soon enough. If he didn't already know. "This isn't just about Aaron," she said. "There's also the matter of Sergei Popova."

Matthew glanced up from the book. "What matter with Sergei?" he demanded.

"The matter of his death."

He stared at Liza, open-mouthed. After a moment, he sputtered, "What on earth are you talking about?"

Was it Liza's imagination or did his shock seem just a bit contrived—a bit dramatic?

Rabbie offered, "His body was just found in his room. Looks like he fell and hit his head on the stone of the hearth."

The color drained from Matthew's face. "That…That just can't be. I saw him not half an hour ago. He was fine."

"He's not fine now, Mr. Carter."

"I don't believe it." The man's mouth had shifted from slack disbelief to hard defiance.

"No one's forcin' you to believe it," Rabbie said. "But it's true. Saw it with my own eyes."

Matthew looked from Rabbie to Liza. "You're serious," he said. "Sergei Popova is dead?"

Liza nodded once.

Matthew rubbed a hand over his mouth. "Who knows about this?"

"Petrus, Ki, Rabbie, and I were in the room with Detective Lawson."

"Anne came in too," Rabbie added.

"Petrus…" Matthew said, his words trailing off. He stood. "I have to get out of here." He began moving toward the door. "I have to make calls. I need my phone…"

Liza blocked the doorway. "You can't leave."

"You don't understand." The man looked desperate. "This is urgent, Ms. Ramsay."

His wild look caused Liza to say gently, "I know it's urgent. The police are taking it seriously. Let's all go down to the drawing room, and you can tell Detective Lawson what you know." She had no doubt the man knew *something*.

"This goes far beyond an investigation by a small-town cop."

Liza had no idea to what Matthew was referring, but his words reminded her of something Carolyn

Turner had said earlier. She'd indicated she'd been put in place after being tasked with gathering knowledge related to another issue. Could Sergei Popova be that issue?

Liza couldn't reveal Ms. Turner's true purpose in the castle, but she said instead, "Detective Lawson will be calling in reinforcements. It's a place to start anyway."

Matthew didn't appear to be listening. He'd begun to pace the room, and the lifelike eyes embedded within the portrait of Lady Catherine Ramsay followed him as he moved.

Liza said quietly to Rabbie, "We can't leave her in this room alone. She's too vulnerable, and there have been too many accidents. Besides, I don't trust her husband."

"Nor do I," said Rabbie. He went to his niece. "Daphne, do you think you can come to the drawing room for a bit?"

The young woman gave a small shake of her head.

"It'll be safer for you there," said Rabbie.

Liza saw Daphne's eyes flit to Matthew.

"A police officer is now in the house," Liza whispered.

The woman's eyes traveled from Rabbie to Liza and back again. After a minute, she placed her smooth hand into Rabbie's gnarled one and managed to sit up and slide her legs over the side of the bed.

His attention caught by the movement, Matthew rushed over. "She's not going anywhere."

"She's coming with us," said Liza. "Strange things are happening in this castle, and Daphne will not be the next victim of wrongdoing."

Matthew wet his lips, considering. "Do you truly believe there is a murderer among us?"

He hadn't believed that Aaron may have been the victim of foul play. The man was acting much differently now that Sergei was also dead. Liza had no idea what to make of his change in attitude, but she would take advantage of it. "I don't know, Mr. Carter. But I certainly don't want to test out the possibility with Daphne's life."

His eyes shifted from side to side. "No," he finally said, some resignation in his voice, along with a touch of paranoia. "No, we do not."

Daphne was standing now, unstable and supported by her uncle. She recoiled faintly when Matthew grasped her upper arm, but she allowed his touch. He guided her away from Rabbie.

As he led his wife slowly to the hallway, Rabbie hung back with Liza.

"Do you think he could be a murderer?" Liza asked.

"I wouldn't hae put it past him tae kill Aaron, especially if Daphne had been havin' an affair with the man. But there's no way he had anything to do with Sergei's death."

"Why's that?" Liza asked.

"Because Matthew and Sergei were in business together."

"Plenty of business deals go wrong."

Rabbie hesitated, weighing his words. Finally, he said, "I don't know much, Ms. Ramsay, but I do know that this deal involves two very powerful governments, some defense contracts and weapons deals, and some very dangerous men. Without Sergei, Matthew is in a precarious position."

Liza stared at the old man who was looking off into the distance.

"If someone wanted Sergei dead, it wasn't Matthew. But, suspectin' what I do, there's a good chance Matthew Carter might be next."

Chapter 17

They all watched each other, suspicion on their faces. Petrus was sprawled on a rather worn loveseat that had been a gift from Oliver Cromwell. Ki perched on the narrow wooden armrest, though she was so slight, Liza didn't worry much about any damage.

Anne Kane's arms were clasped behind her back, the elegant fingers of one hand wrapped around the opposite slender wrist. She was staring wistfully out the window as if she were imagining herself out there—anywhere but within the high walls of the Ramsay Castle.

Daphne had reclined on a more modern and functional sofa, and Matthew sat near her bent knees, the short fingers of his hand absentmindedly caressing her leg.

Bruce and Lachlan were helping Sadie carry a trolley piled with plates of sliced chicken, baked potatoes, and Cullen Skink into the drawing room. They set the plates, along with pitchers of water and soda, on a table. Rabbie was the only one who helped himself to a plate of sustenance, preparing a small plate for Daphne as well.

Liza knew she should also consume something, but even though her mind was telling her to eat, her body was still reacting to the sight of both Aaron Scott and Sergei Popova. And those thoughts led her to remember the bodies of Brodie Graham and Callum Ramsay. Four bodies at the castle in the space of less than a year. Not to mention poor Charlie Campbell who had died in the creek not a mile away. To speak nothing of her own brush with death deep beneath the castle floors.

She was the proprietor of a house of horrors and haunts.

Lachlan came to stand near her. "Ye need to eat, Liza," he said, echoing the earlier words of the detective inspector.

"I feel so responsible. I should have been more mindful of Sergei's drinking."

"Ye couldnae have known the fool would drink himself tae death."

"You don't understand," she whispered, her voice intense. "This is *my* castle now. It bears my name. And I'm the one who made the decision that these people should come here." She didn't bother to mention that the alcohol had been provided by her. By *them*.

Lachlan didn't respond. His arms dangled at his sides and a muscle ticked in his jaw.

"How are you feeling?" she asked, changing the

subject. "Have you recovered from your sojourn?"

"The food still needs servin'. I guess it disnae matter much that I'm tired, Liza."

She was the reason Lachlan had been out in the cold for as long as he had. She opened her mouth to say as much, but from the doorway, Carolyn Turner said, "Ms. Ramsay, a word please?"

Liza looked up at Lachlan and saw the rippling of a barely concealed anger. "Come with me," she said.

The corner of his mouth lifted, but the smile didn't reach his eyes. "Nah, I'm not the Ramsay laird o' this castle," he said.

"What does that mean?"

"Ye ken what it means, Liza. Ye're the one who belongs with these people, not me. Ye're the one who owns this place, who makes the decisions."

She opened her mouth and shut it again, bewildered. This had something to do with Ki. She knew it. "I thought we were a team."

He shook his head. "If we were a team, ye wouldn't be playin' alone. Since this gatherin' started, I've been helpin' tae set up fer the show, trudgin' out in the cold, carryin' in the food and drink. I'm part of the house crew," he said. "Maybe it's where I belong, and that's okay. But if it's true, I probably don't belong in yer bed."

Liza was flabbergasted. She tried to think what she could have done to bring this on. It was true Lachlan had been doing a lot of the drudge work required during this disaster of a weekend. But it wasn't as if she was having a picnic. She'd been dealing with all of these horrible personalities, these bodies, these deaths.

They'd been playing separate parts, but deep down, she'd thought they were in this macabre production together. Even with the complication of Ki's presence.

"That's not fair," she whispered, and opened her mouth to continue.

"Ms. Ramsay," Ms. Turner said again from the doorway. "We need to speak with you, please."

"Ye'd better go," Lachlan said. "Ye're needed to help with the investigation. I'll just be at the back o' the room, makin' sure the food doesn't get cold."

He turned away from her. A wave of anger rose up along with a wash of color into her cheeks. She wanted to stay and fight it out, but that was impossible with everything else going on.

She took a shaky breath and turned. As she did, her eyes met the intense gaze of Petrus Bothas. He couldn't have heard the exchange she'd had with Lachlan, but he could well have observed the tension between them.

As Liza approached the door, Ki rose, slow and leonine, from her perch on Cromwell's loveseat. Liza didn't turn around, but she knew that Ki was going to Lachlan. Why wouldn't Petrus stop her?

Perhaps the more important question was, why wouldn't Lachlan?

Frazzled, sad, and angry, Liza approached Ms. Turner with a deep frown. If the other woman noticed, she didn't let on. They walked across the hallway to the conference room tucked away at the front of the castle. It was the same room in which Detective Chief Inspector Dean had questioned her about Lachlan and the possibility he'd murdered both Charlie Campbell and Brodie Graham.

This time, it was Detective Inspector Lawson who motioned her to have a seat.

"I've had a chance to speak with Dean," he said when Liza was seated. Ms. Turner sat to her left. "She filled me in on Ms. Turner and her true purpose here."

Liza waited for him to continue. He glanced down at a yellow legal pad filled with scrawled notes.

Finally, Liza asked, "Will she be here soon?"

"Dean?" Lawson shook his head. "She and the forensics team won't make it until tomorrow."

"Tomorrow!" Liza exclaimed. "But we have two bodies in the house."

"One that we're sure about."

Liza looked at Ms. Turner. "You saw Aaron's body."

She nodded grimly.

"Shouldn't we at least search for him?" She stared at Lawson. "We need a whole team here. Aaron Scott was a well-known man. You can't get anyone here faster?"

"The temperatures have dropped, and the roads are still impassable. It's gettin' late, and much of the town is without power. Those who still need savin' take precedence over the already dead. And Aaron Scott's body isn't goin' anywhere if it's still in the castle. We'll get a team out here tomorrow. The city is workin' on clearin' the roads."

"*You* managed to get here," she said to Lawson.

"I did," he agreed. "And I'm not goin' anywhere. I'll make sure nothin' else happens until the rest of the force arrives."

Liza considered Petrus's men at the end of the driveway. Perhaps the man had been right; his team may well have been more competent than these locals. As much as she respected DCI Dean, she was shocked and angry that the woman had left them in this vulnerable position.

"Perhaps Mr. Bothas's team can be of assistance." She started out of her seat. "They can at least offer some assistance with the search—"

Ms. Turner held up a hand. "That's not an option, Liza."

"Why not?" she demanded. The two women stared at each other before Lawson and Ms. Turner exchanged a look. Neither of them spoke.

A realization occurred to Liza. "Is Petrus the person you were assigned to observe?" she asked quietly.

Ms. Turner didn't answer directly. "It would seem

that Petrus has major conflicts with each of the guests in this castle. His feud with Aaron Scott was certainly the most prominent conflict, but Sergei invested heavily in one of Mr. Bothas's rival space companies and then poached three of Petrus's top engineers. Similar to what Aaron Scott had done with Ajna. Petrus was livid, and it set back his development work at Kephalē." She paused for effect. "I should add that Matthew Carter was a silent partner in and supporter of Sergei's investment."

Liza remembered Matthew's fear when he found out Sergei was dead. "And you think Petrus killed both Aaron and Sergei?"

"We can't prove anything of course," Ms. Turner said. "Not without more investigation. But that might explain why Aaron's body disappeared and Sergei's death looked like an accident."

"If we bring in the force now," Lawson said, "We won't be able to prove anythin', and if someone *did* kill those men, they'll likely get away with it."

"So you're hoping he kills again?"

"I'm hopin' he shows his hand."

Liza couldn't think of a better way to show his hand than to try to harm another of his rivals. "You said he was feuding with Aaron, Sergei, and Matthew. What about the other guests?"

"Rabbie likes to pretend that he's innocent," Ms. Turner said, "But he helped Hugh St. James, Daphne's father, short stock a number of Petrus's public ventures. Petrus has taken personal offense."

"What about Anne?"

"Early in his career, Petrus asked Anne's father for funding and help for his first startup. Anne's father turned him away."

"Anne's father is dead," Liza said.

Ms. Turner nodded. "He is. But Petrus was dating Anne at the time. In fact, Petrus had hoped to marry her. When Asher Kane rejected Petrus's request for money, he essentially closed the door on any relationship between Petrus and his daughter. Anne didn't fight for the relationship. Petrus's ego has never recovered from that slight."

"You think he'd kill Anne because of it?"

"I didn't say that," Ms. Turner said. "I'm not certain that he's killed anyone, in fact."

"He's the one with the strongest motive," Lawson added.

Liza shook her head. "What about Matthew? Aaron was having an affair with his wife, for god's sake."

"Did he have motive to kill Mr. Popova?" Lawson asked.

Rabbie told her that Sergei and Matthew had been business partners. Wasn't it possible the relationship had soured? She remembered Sergei's comment earlier, something to the effect that Matthew had gone back on a promise or an agreement. And Matthew's paranoid reaction to Sergei's death was over-the-top enough to have been an act.

"The point is," Ms. Turner said, "we just don't know what has happened."

"If anything," Lawson interjected.

Ms. Turner nodded. "And if we get more police here, we may never know."

"So you're purposely keeping them away." Liza shook her head slowly.

"Everythin' I said earlier is true," Lawson protested. "The roads *are* nearly impassable, and there are other emergencies out there."

But Liza knew he was making excuses. "So why are you telling me this?"

Another glance was exchanged between Ms. Turner and Lawson.

Ms. Turner spoke first. "Petrus seems quite taken with you."

Heat flushed into Liza's cheeks. She honestly couldn't tell how Petrus felt about her. Nor could she tell how she felt about him. And it didn't matter. She was in love with Lachlan, and she hated that he was angry with her. The last thing she wanted to do was explore any confusing feelings she might have about another man. "I don't see what that would have to do with anything," Liza said, her voice tight.

"We wouldn't be askin' ye to do anythin' uncomfortable," Lawson said.

"What on earth are you talking about?"

Ms. Turner spoke next. "He might open up to you, Liza."

She looked from Ms. Turner to the detective. "You're asking me to cheat on my fiancé? After all we've been through together?"

"No, of course that's not what we're suggesting," Ms. Turner said. She looked at Liza levelly. "In my line of work, there have been times that I've had to put aside personal convictions for the good of the job. Especially when I was young and attractive...there were times I was able to use those qualities to my advantage in order to gain the trust of a target."

"I'm not in your line of work." But Liza knew that she had considered this very game earlier in the day. She had thought she might be able to use Petrus's attraction to her to get information.

"No, you're not. But this is your home, Liza. And two people have died here so far. Do you really want this to be known as the place where people perish without explanation?"

"We're just asking that you try to gain Petrus's trust. Talk to him. Try to get any information from him that might indicate what could have happened."

"And what if nothing has happened? What if he's innocent of these suspected crimes?" Liza asked.

Lawson shrugged. "Then no harm has been done. Ye've lent a friendly ear."

"What am I supposed to tell Lachlan?" she asked.

"I think Lachlan may be a bit distracted himself."

Liza's head swiveled to Carolyn Turner. She didn't need to ask for her meaning. She knew exactly what the woman was referring to.

After her initial burst of anger had subsided, she felt incredibly sad. Were Lachlan's feelings for Ki the reason he'd picked a fight with her? Had he been attempting to assuage his own guilt by transferring his shame to her? She wasn't sure. And the fact that she wasn't sure made her sadder still.

She also didn't trust her own motivations when she exhaled and looked from Lawson to Ms. Turner.

"Okay," she said with a note of resignation. "Tell me what you want me to do."

Chapter 18

Liza led the way back to the drawing room, the detective and Ms. Turner right behind her. To her surprise, the guests had obeyed orders and stayed in the room. Most of them seemed to have eaten.

She noted Lachlan sitting on the sofa, Ki close, whispering to him in earnest. They were almost, but not quite, touching. Liza felt a deep spreading pain within her chest. She wished she could demand that each and every one of them leave her home this instant so that she and Lachlan could work this out. Whatever *this* was. She had no idea how they'd gotten here.

She did know that Ki was energetic, eccentric, uninhibited—all qualities Liza did not possess. At least not to the degree of the spritely woman who had no issues roaming around with no clothes on.

But she couldn't think about any of this right now. There were two dead men in the castle, one of whom was currently missing.

God, she hated these people.

Detective Inspector Lawson held up his hands. His deep voice boomed. "Listen up…"

Liza turned away from him to prepare a plate of the now tepid food. She forced herself to take a few bites.

"I know ye all have questions and would like to go home," Lawson said. "We're goin' to get ye all out of here as soon as possible."

"Thank *god*," Anne Kane exclaimed.

"My wife needs medical attention," Matthew said, speaking over Anne.

Lawson nodded. "Aye, if ye can just wait one more day."

"She's taken pills, detective. I don't know if we have one more day."

Liza exchanged a glance with Ms. Turner. She would never forgive herself if anything happened to Daphne. Daphne was a sweet girl who'd been born, raised, and married into a tangle of money, power, and ego. From the outside, she might have appeared to have it all, but Liza didn't wish her life on anyone.

"Help is on the way. I promise," Lawson said.

Petrus stood, his hands shoved into the pockets of his black jeans. Even slouched forward as he was, he seemed imposing. More so than Lawson with his round face and soft middle. "And do you believe that foul play has occurred, detective?" Petrus asked.

"I wouldn't be able to answer that, Mr. Bothas. I'm not an expert in forensics, and we seem to only have one body to examine."

"What do you think happened to the other body?"

Detective Lawson looked intently at him. "You tell *me* what ye think happened to it."

"I'm sure I don't know."

The two men stared at each other for a long and tense moment.

"Are we suspects in these deaths?" Rabbie asked.

Lawson broke his gaze first. "As I said—I don't know that any crime has been committed."

Anne Kane's lips twisted up. "You didn't answer the question, detective."

"As far as I'm concerned, we can't have suspects without proof of a crime."

"A rather weak response," Petrus said.

"How do we know we're safe?" Matthew asked. "I'm worried for my wife."

Liza studied him out of the corner of her eye. Again, she wondered if his concern was all an act. Or if perhaps it was himself he was worried for.

"I'll be stayin' here tonight," Lawson said.

"I'm sure we'll all sleep better for it," Petrus quipped.

"Well, despite the death, I'm going to try to make the most of it," said Anne. "Perhaps I'll do some more exploring of this beautiful place."

Liza shot the other woman a grateful look. She knew it shouldn't matter, but hearing her beautiful home called 'evil', 'godforsaken', 'dreadful', and 'wretched' had started to affect her. Even if these guests never again mentioned their experience at the Ramsay Castle, Liza knew there would be knowing glances and whispered offenses that would prevent anyone of their ilk from returning. While Liza wasn't necessarily displeased with that, she still worried about their future plans. Perhaps a business letting out the castle for special occasions wasn't in the cards after all.

But in the end, she thought, looking at Lachlan whose head was bent close to Ki, this castle may be all she had left.

To think, just two days earlier, her biggest concern was whether or not the chapel would be ready in time for her wedding. Now, she wasn't sure there would even be a wedding.

Lachlan met Liza's eye, then looked away quickly.

Carolyn Turner was flitting around the space, picking up discarded dishes and carrying them to the dumbwaiter on the other side of the dining room. Not one person in the space noticed her watching them closely.

Liza finished the unappetizing food on her plate and drank a large tumbler of water. She felt bone-tired and wanted nothing more than to get some sleep.

"Ms. Ramsay," Lawson said, approaching her. "Can I borrow yer footman—Shaun, I think it is—to search the rooms?"

"All resources are at your disposal," she said, waving her hand toward the door. Shaun had not joined them in the drawing room, and Liza assumed he'd transferred his position to outside Sergei's door. Perhaps she shouldn't assume anything. She had lost control of the situation.

"Don't forget what we discussed," the detective said, before leveling a meaningful glance in Petrus's direction.

Liza hadn't forgotten anything, but she wanted to talk to Lachlan first.

After the detective had left the room in search of Shaun, Liza approached the sofa where Ki and Lachlan were seated. She ignored the woman as best she could. "Can we talk?" she asked her fiancé softly.

Ki stared up at Liza with her big eyes, but Lachlan kept his gaze averted. "I dinnae have much tae say tae ye right now, Liza."

"It's important." She stood her ground; she wasn't going anywhere.

Nor, it seemed, was Ki, who made no move to give them privacy.

Lachlan finally exhaled and stood.

Liza breathed a bit easier as they moved to the doorway at the back of the room. Once alone, she gave him an abbreviated and lightly modified account of the conversation she'd had with the detective, careful not to reveal any information that might compromise an investigation or cast suspicion on any one person. She wasn't concerned with Lachlan having information, but it pained her to admit she was a little worried what he might inadvertently reveal to Ki, who had become a confidant.

She ended her retelling with, "And so the detective would like to see what I might be able to learn from Petrus."

"Learn from Petrus," Lachlan repeated slowly.

Liza gave a short nod, noting his dark tone. Her hackles were immediately up.

"And I suppose ye were just fine with this plan."

"I understand why they're asking me to do it." Her voice was tight, defensive.

"Do ye now?"

She stared at her fiancé.

"I suppose ye've noticed the way he looks at ye. The way he finds a reason to touch ye."

She shot back, "The way you do with Ki?"

Lachlan gave a bark of laughter, but he didn't argue with her. Instead, he said, "I knew it might come tae this—this rift between us. I just didn't want tae see it this quickly. Ye have the opportunity tae be with a billionaire. I'll never be much more than the groundskeeper here. I'm happy with who I am, but I can't compete with the allure of Petrus Bothas."

"I'm not asking you to compete with him," she said.

"Then what is it ye're asking me tae do? Stand back while ye pretend tae seduce him? Or will it be fer real,

Liza?"

"Of course it's not real. And it's not…seduction."

"Just a bit of flirtin' then. Harmless, right?"

"It's just talking. Same as you're doing with Petrus's girlfriend."

"Ki has been kind tae me. She's seen the dynamic between us, and she recognized it. She's been nice enough to offer me a friendly ear."

Liza shook her head. "If you have a problem with our relationship, you should be talking to me, not another woman."

"And when would I do that, Liza? When ye're busy running around trying to be a hero? When ye're asking me to risk my own life for the good of this castle? I've known this place much longer than ye have, and I love it, too. But I'd give it all up fer ye. I don't think ye can say the same. Ye've bought into the status of land and money." He turned his back on her, but not before saying, "Do what ye want with Petrus. But yer actions have consequences. Remember that."

She didn't yell after him. She just watched his broad, retreating back.

When she walked back into the room, Ki was still seated on the sofa, and Petrus stood by the buffet, eating Cranachan from an etched whisky glass.

She picked up a glass of the oat, berry, and cream dessert, along with a spoon, even though she had zero appetite.

Petrus eyed her, and she clinked the spoon clumsily against the side of the glass. "Liza," he said, drawing out the sound of the 'a' at the end of her name. "How are you holding up?" His tone wasn't so much concerned as almost…amused.

Liza looked up at him. Though his expression was unreadable, his dark eyes were sharp and observant. She detected no misplaced humor. Perhaps she'd been imagining things.

"I'm tired," she found herself admitting.

"I imagine you are. It's hard to believe so much has happened in just a day."

Liza glanced out the window. In the winter evening, the sun had sunk long ago, and the sky was an inky black. While the castle to her had become a refuge, tonight she felt uneasy and isolated. Lawson's presence in the building did nothing to assuage her fears. Or her loneliness.

"I'm surprised your men haven't ventured up here," Liza mused. "Especially with the arrival of Lawson."

"I've given them strict instructions not to approach unless they're summoned."

"You were ready to summon them earlier."

"I was."

"Why not now?" Liza took a small bite of her Cranachan.

"Now that the police are here, what would be the

point?"

Liza thought about that. What had been the point *before*? she wondered. To smuggle the body out? That's what he'd wanted to do. And now, the body had mysteriously disappeared.

"They could offer some additional protection, I suppose." She glanced over at Matthew, who was frowning deeply and staring off into the distance beside an expressionless Daphne. "There are people in the house who are afraid. Aren't you?"

Petrus looked back at her, studying her face so intensely and openly that she had to look away. Then he offered a half a smile. "Why would I be afraid, Liza?"

She didn't respond.

"Are *you* afraid?"

Liza shook her head. No, she was not afraid. If the deaths were a result of homicide, she did not think she was a target. What had anyone to gain from her demise?

Petrus, on the other hand, was a more likely focus for a killer. She imagined everyone in this house had a reason for wanting Petrus dead. Including Lachlan, she realized.

The fact that he wasn't afraid, even without his security team, was telling. She glanced at Matthew, who had shifted his attention to Petrus and was watching him surreptitiously.

"Our significant others seem to have found a spark in one another," Petrus said, pulling Liza out of her thoughts. She placed her half-eaten dessert on the table. "I'm sure you've noticed."

Though she remembered her mission, she couldn't bring herself to trifle with this man. He was too dangerous, and she didn't trust him. Or herself, she realized.

Instead, she glared at him. "What is your point, Mr. Bothas?"

"No point, Liza. Just an observation."

She turned to walk away, and then turned back around. "Doesn't it bother you?"

He finished scraping the rest of the cream out of his glass. "Doesn't what bother me?"

"That she cheats on you?"

Petrus slowly put the glass next to Liza's. "What does that word mean exactly—*cheat*?"

"That she is unfaithful to you."

"You think it's unfaithful to give your body to another person?" With the tip of his tongue, he licked a spot of cream from his upper lip.

Liza watched this and then looked away. "That is generally considered the definition of cheating."

"Then I think the definition needs to be changed. Ki's body is not mine to own, and it's hers to give as freely as she would like."

Liza again didn't respond, and he came to stand

close to her. She could feel the heat of his body—the energy—pulsing between them.

"I don't control Ki's body any more than she controls mine. And to think I could tell her what to do with something she was born with…" His words trailed off, and his breath warmed Liza's ear. "That would be just archaic to me. Monstrous."

Liza felt too paralyzed to move.

"Do you think you own Lachlan's body, Liza?"

She gave a small shake of her head.

"Do you think he owns *yours*?"

"I think I owe him an explanation about what I choose to do with my body."

"Why is that?"

Liza had no good answer for this. "He's my fiancé," she said quietly. "Soon, we will be married."

"Would it make you love him any less if he chose to share his body with another? Even if his heart was yours?"

This time, she looked directly at Petrus. "Yes, I think it would. If he chose to join intimately with another, then yes. How can he love me the way he says he does?"

Petrus looked back at her for a long moment. His gaze was slow, smoldering. Liza shivered.

"I think you've got it backward, Liza."

She waited.

"It's not whether Lachlan promises his body to you

in the good times that matters. It's whether he'll stay with you in the difficult times. Will he stand by your side when everything is falling apart? Will you do the same for him? That's what makes a lasting love."

Petrus was so close to her that Liza swore she could feel the steady pulsing of his heart. She swallowed, but she couldn't bring herself to look at him again. "Will Ki do that for you?" she asked, her voice breathless.

He chuckled. "Ki will do anything for me," he said.

This made her look up. He brought his face close to hers, and she thought he might kiss her. She did not turn away.

"Anything," he repeated.

Then he brushed his lips softly against hers. It was just a touch more than it was a kiss.

At Liza's widened eyes and catch in her breath, he smiled. "Go get some sleep, Liza. You aren't cut out for this game."

Chapter 19

"**M**s. Ramsay!"

The voice of Rabbie Rose caused Liza to jump back, away from Petrus, who seemed amused by her reaction.

"Yes, Mr. Rose?"

"We need tae take Daphne back tae her room. Just lettin' ye know."

Liza nodded, glad for the excuse to walk away from the man who so unsettled her. "Has she eaten anything?"

"We got a bit of food in her, but she still needs tae see a doctor."

Liza looked at the forlorn figure of Daphne, so diminished compared to the vibrant young lady who had reminisced about the castle the day before. "Will you keep an eye on her?" she asked Rabbie.

"Aye, I'll do my best. But Matthew seems intent on stayin' by her side."

Liza thought of Petrus's words. *Will he stand by your side when everything is falling apart?* Would Matthew do that for Daphne?

To Rabbie, she nodded, then said quietly, "Do what you can. Hopefully, tonight will be uneventful."

Rabbie gave her arm a squeeze. "Watch yerself, my dear."

It was a gentle warning, but it felt ominous…foretelling. Liza tried to smile. She was letting the situation get to her. She needed to stay calm. Lawson was here; she was safe.

She watched Rabbie follow Matthew and Daphne out of the room. Ms. Turner and Bruce were gone to tend to the kitchen staff and the house. Sadie hadn't made an appearance after dinner had been served, and Ki had also disappeared without a word. Where was Lachlan?

The only ones left in the drawing room with Liza were Anne, who was sipping a martini, and Petrus, who appeared to be waiting out Anne. Was he waiting for Liza? A small thrill ran through her. She wasn't proud of it. She didn't want to explore it.

Will he stand by your side when everything is falling apart?

Suddenly it was all too much: the deaths, the heartbreak, the exhaustion, the isolation. She needed to get out of this room. Without saying another word, she hurried into the passage and down the hall to her apartment. Unlocking the door with shaking fingers, Liza hoped beyond hope to find Lachlan inside.

The room was empty.

She bolted the door behind her and switched on the lights. If nothing else, this space was familiar. Liza made her way to the washroom, where she shed her clothes and stood under the spray of the shower until her skin was raw.

Despite the circumstances, she knew that tomorrow would bring resolution. Tomorrow, the police would be here in force. Tomorrow, Detective Chief Inspector Marion Dean would arrive with her team of investigators and forensics experts. Tomorrow, these people would be gone. Tomorrow, she and Lachlan could get back to normal.

She just needed to get through one more night.

She exited the shower, dried herself, and dressed in her comfortable silk loungewear that felt like liquid on her clean skin. She let her auburn hair dry naturally into its soft waves. Gone was the sleek hairstyle and careful makeup. Instead, she became herself again, fresh-faced and with full hair grazing her neck. Instead of the polished and posh castle owner, she was the rustic girl from across the pond. She was innocent and naïve and uncomplicated. She liked this person. She had missed this person. Maybe Lachlan had been right. She'd been trying to be someone else.

Her body clean and her mind more relaxed than it had been all day, for the second night in a row, she climbed into an empty bed. She wished Lachlan were beside her, the reassuring rhythm of his breathing giving calm to her soul.

Where was he?

Could he have been in a bedroom on the second floor?

Despite her exhaustion, sleep would not come. Each time she began to drift away, images floated, ghostlike, into her field of vision: The bloated figure of Sergei Popova. The distorted face of Aaron Scott. The supple, naked body of Ki, whose real name was Stephanie. The slow smile of Petrus as he leaned ever closer…

Liza finally drifted into a fitful slumber, but at some point during the night, she was pulled her from her sleep by a loud, grating noise that stole into her consciousness.

Her eyes snapped open and she listened to the silence. Perhaps she had dreamed the sound.

After a moment, she inched her hand carefully over the empty mattress beside her. She stared up at the ornate ceiling of the laird's apartment. *Lady's apartment,* she corrected herself silently. She was the lady of this castle.

The small clock next to the bed read 2:00 a.m., and Liza turned away and curled into herself, willing sleep to overtake her once more. Then she just barely heard the sound—was it what had woken her?—the faint sounds of music vibrating through the still night air.

She listened closer, and thought she detected the tune of 'The Parting Glass', a traditional Scottish folk song. Was it Lady Catherine, reminding them of her presence? Was it Callum?

A whisper of a breeze against her skin; a soft rustle next to the bed.

Liza stared around her in the dark as the music played on.

And gently rise and softly call...

She couldn't tell if the lyrics were in her head. She rose, plucking her long silk robe from the end of the bed and wrapping it around her shoulders as she shivered. She shoved her feet into her soft slippers, and padded to the doorway to her apartment. The music increased in volume.

She was most definitely not imagining the song. Carefully, she pushed open the door, stared down the empty hallway at the shadowy doorways and alcoves. Her eyes often played tricks on her and showed movement that may or may not have been her imagination. Tonight was no different. The ghostly shadows danced in front of her as if she were watching a scene from centuries ago. The spirits were unaware of her presence.

Liza wished the shadows peace and followed the sound of the notes to the small sitting room just in front of the library. A phonograph was playing, this one smaller and quieter than the machine played earlier by Matthew Carter. A figure was sitting in a chair, its back to Liza. A steady stream of smoke rose above the head of silver-blonde hair.

Anne Kane.

Liza didn't think she'd spoken the woman's name aloud, but Anne twisted around in her chair, the scented cigarette held gracefully between two long fingers.

"Liza," she said, a distracted smile on her face. "I hope the music didn't disturb you."

"No," Liza said. "Something woke me, but it wasn't the music. How long have you been here?" She moved around the chair and sat on a red velveteen loveseat across from Anne. Anne offered Liza another of her flavored cigarettes. Liza accepted.

"I'm not sure," Anne said. "A while."

Liza noticed the woman was still wearing the same outfit from earlier in the day. She took a long drag of the fragrant warm smoke. It filled her lungs and her head, making her feel pleasantly dizzy.

"Is anyone else awake?" Liza asked.

"The detective and your man had been searching rooms, but that seems ages ago."

Liza didn't know if Anne meant her footman Shaun or Lachlan.

"They're having an affair, aren't they?" Anne asked.

Liza looked at Anne. Her stomach dropped. Who?" she asked cautiously.

"The boy and the girl. Shaun and Sadie."

Relief coursed through Liza. She waited as her heartbeat returned to normal.

Anne stared at the smoldering tip of her cigarette as if recalling a long-ago memory. "Young love. To have that again, eh?"

"Lachlan and I are in love," she murmured. It wasn't an old love, but it was a connection that had felt as old as time and inevitable. How had they lost that so quickly? If their connection was that tenuous, had it been meant to last at all?

Anne arched an eyebrow. "What about Petrus?"

In the soft lamplight, Liza stared at the swirling gray smoke of the cigarette. 'The Parting Glass' had finished its turn on the vinyl record and gave way to 'The Trees They Grow So High'.

"What about him?" Liza asked.

Anne studied her. "I never thought Ki was good enough for him. He has a tendency to date these insubstantial girls who fancy themselves artists. Or whatever." She waved her cigarette around her head. "But Petrus needs a woman who knows when to challenge him."

"Like you?" Liza hazarded.

Anne's rich, full laugh filled the room. "Ah, that ship sailed long ago." Despite the laughter, the words had a note of sentimentality to them. A tinge of yearning.

The two of them had embarked on a voyage, Liza thought. At least the start of one. Liza folded her legs beneath her on the sofa. "What happened?"

Anne stubbed her cigarette out in the same stemmed glass from which she'd been drinking earlier. "We were young," she said. "Petrus was ambitious, but not yet successful. A mutual friend had introduced us, and there was an attraction. Not long after we began dating, I suggested he ask my father for a loan to get his first tech startup off the ground. My father wasn't as taken with him as I was."

"So the relationship ended?"

She lifted a shoulder. "I knew Petrus would be successful, but back then…When Asher Kane said no, it meant no for everyone." She exhaled. "It was for the best. It wouldn't have worked out."

"Why not?"

"Petrus and I have different ways of looking at the world."

"Because of his perspective on artificial intelligence?"

The smile faded from Anne's face. "Excuse me?"

"Because AI could one day destroy the concept of art and the need for artists. Did you say that yesterday? I'm sure someone said that."

There was a long silence. "No, Ms. Ramsay. That

has nothing to do with it. Or anything, for that matter. Despite whatever computer programs these fools create, art will survive."

The music of 'The False Bride' began to play on the phonograph. She wondered if Anne still loved Petrus, despite everything else. She thought of a young and elegant Anne Kane who would have been a perfect match for a tall, handsome Petrus Bothas. What a force they could have been.

"Was it religion then?" she asked, emboldened by the image of them together, the late hour, and the quiet intimacy of the library.

"Religion?"

"Samuel Cohen?" Liza asked. She remembered the odd way Anne had reacted when Liza had first mentioned the subject. She hadn't understood then, and she didn't understand now. Surely a simple internet search would reveal the truth of Anne's lineage. And for all her talk of history and heritage, the woman certainly seemed loathe to talk about her own.

"I suppose your art professor told you that, too?"

"As a matter of fact, he did," Liza said. "We studied the influence your family has had on the art world. At Harvard," she added with emphasis, before Anne could again question the legitimacy of her education. "Dr. Rosovsky dedicated an entire lecture to the Cohen collection that had been lost during the Great War."

"Dr. Rosovsky," Anne said quietly and reverently.

"Did you know him?"

Anne didn't answer, and instead asked a question of her own. "And what did he say had happened to this collection?"

"That it had been stolen by…" Liza's words trailed off. Anne was staring at her intently.

"By whom?" Anne prompted.

Liza shook her head. The skin on the back of her neck prickled. "It doesn't matter." She stubbed out her flavored cigarette in Anne's glass on the table between them and pulled the silk robe tighter over her chest.

"I'd like to know, Ms. Ramsay, what you've learned of my family. What you've learned of me."

Liza swallowed. "It was a long time ago."

"The past is always closer than it appears, and you seem to remember well what you've learned."

Liza thought of Sergei, his body decomposing directly above them as they spoke. She thought of the blood drying on the hearth and hardwood floor. Of his limbs stiffening with rigor mortis. The sweet smell of decaying flesh. Her stomach roiled from both the image, the cigarette, the lack of sleep.

"Tell me," Anne said.

Liza eyed the doorway. Anne was on the edge of her seat as if poised to pounce.

Liza made a decision, and began to speak. "It was suggested that many pieces of Jewish art were eradicated, but that countless more collections were stolen by the Russians and are currently held in St. Petersburg," Liza said, her voice barely a whisper. "Dr. Rosovsky believed this is what drove you to become a collector."

"And what do you think of that, Ms. Ramsay?"

"I—I hadn't thought anything of it, really. Other than you had chosen a noble cause."

The record ended and the needle scratched against the grooves before the arm retracted and replaced itself. The silence was deafening.

Liza thought of Aaron Scott, and his allegiance to creating an advanced intelligence. It was why Petrus had called this meeting in the first place. It was also why Anne had decided to join the conversation, despite having no formal business interest in the topic. There may have been no reason she was there from a retail perspective. But there was certainly a reason she may have joined from an *art* perspective.

Anne was watching her closely. Could she see all the pieces click in Liza's head?

"I need to get to bed," Liza said, and as she stood up, so did Anne Kane.

"Oh, but our conversation was just getting interesting," Anne said. She took a step toward Liza.

A movement from the door caught Liza's eye. It was Petrus. He glanced from Anne to Liza.

Liza moved quickly past Anne and stood close to Petrus, who raised an eyebrow. Liza looked up at him, relief seeping through her limbs. Only once had she been as happy to see someone as she was to see Petrus. And that was when she'd been rescued from the dungeon of her own castle as the place was about to burn down around her.

Chapter 20

Petrus seemed happy to place an arm around Liza's shoulders as she huddled against him. "To what do I owe this surprise?" he asked as Anne frowned at the two of them.

"We were just having a conversation," said Anne.

"It's over now," Liza offered, trying to herd Petrus from the room. She wanted as far away from Anne as possible. The woman was as beautiful and sophisticated as she was cold and calculating. Liza should have seen it before. "Would you mind walking me down to the kitchen to get some tea?" she asked.

With another curious look back at Anne, Petrus followed Liza from the room. "What was that all about?" he asked quietly as they walked down the dimly lit corridor. Though most of the lights had been extinguished, the glow from the moonlight reflecting off the snow shone an eerie radiance into the high windows and lighted the shadowed hallways.

They walked down the grand staircase and into the kitchen, where at this hour, the room was abandoned. "Did the staff trek back to the cottage?" she asked.

Petrus nodded. "Bruce, Lachlan, and Ki helped them down."

"And they're not back yet?" she asked, referring to the two Scots and Petrus's girlfriend.

He shrugged. "Not that I'm aware of."

Liza set about brewing two mugs of Scottish Blend. She wished Lachlan was back, but she was more upset about the encounter with Anne than the idea of Lachlan spending time with Ki. She only had so much energy to expend at the moment, and all of her resources were currently consumed by self-preservation.

After a moment, Petrus said, "Look, it's none of my business, but what on earth did I walk into up there?"

Liza poured boiling water into a mug and then dunked the teabags into the hot liquid. Simply the routine of brewing the cup had begun to calm her nerves.

"How well do you know Anne now?"

"I've known her for years."

"And you dated her."

Petrus stared at Liza. "Decades ago. Why?"

"She's still in love with you."

Petrus barked out a laugh. "That's preposterous. Anne and I have both had many, many relationships between us over the years. We've stayed friendly, but never once has either of us attempted to rekindle our romance."

"Did you ever ask yourself why?"

Petrus paused, and Liza poured cream into her tea. She took a sip of the scalding liquid.

"I don't think it matters," Petrus finally said.

"She had motive to kill both Aaron and Sergei."

Petrus's expression shifted from puzzlement to surprise. "Anne?"

Liza nodded and repeated the conversation she'd had with Anne in the library. The woman's deep distrust of artificial intelligence and its effect on the art world. Her belief that Sergei may have had knowledge, and even possession, of her family's art collection.

Petrus listened to all of this quietly as Liza's words flowed from her lips.

"And if she believes that Matthew may have something to do with the deteriorating geopolitical situation, who's to say he won't be next?" Liza asked. She shivered.

"That all seems a little...far-fetched," Petrus finally said. "Anne is a smart woman. Too smart to kill a bunch of people who are trapped under one roof."

"So what do you think happened?"

Petrus shoved his hands into his pockets and leaned against the large center island. He looked off into the distance. "I always think that the simplest explanation is the most likely explanation."

"And what is that?"

"What I've believed from the beginning. That Aaron accidentally killed himself and Sergei fell and died in a drunken stupor. Not everything is a crime."

"Then where is Aaron's body? Why would someone go to the trouble to hide it?"

"We've been through this. To save his family the embarrassment. To let the man go with some dignity."

Liza shook her head. None of this made any sense, and speculation was useless.

She had to admit that she didn't really know who else had a strong motive to kill both men. Anne for sure had motive. But so did Matthew. And Sergei had mentioned a possible betrayal by Matthew. Perhaps Matthew killed Sergei before Sergei could kill *him*. Perhaps the murder of Aaron Scott had been a crime of opportunity.

Even Rabbie could have had motive to kill Aaron, if he'd thought Daphne might be putting his own wealth at risk through her affair with the man. They all knew Petrus had motive to kill Aaron, and according to Carolyn Turner and Detective Inspector Lawson, Petrus was the most likely suspect.

Liza glanced up and found Petrus watching her closely. A wave of unease coursed through her body. She'd been so eager to escape Anne that it had escaped her reasoning; she was now alone with the prime suspect. He smiled at her—a slow, feral smile. It might have been an attempt at seduction, but in the dim light of the kitchen, his grin seemed sardonic and evil.

Liza put the cup down slowly, pondering her escape.

A loud bang near the entrance of the kitchen startled her, causing the china to clatter against the saucer and liquid to slosh over the edge.

Petrus straightened and looked to the door from where the noise had just come. He frowned and started to walk toward the exit.

Liza saw her chance and took it. "I'll check it out," she said, hurrying in front of him. But when she got to the doorway, there was no one in the passage. The front door remained resolutely closed, and she detected no movement. No presence.

Another loud thump, this time from the kitchen, made her whirl back around. Petrus was no longer standing where she'd left him, and she found herself completely alone.

"Petrus?" Her voice was tentative. Was he hiding from her? Trying to scare her?

Trying to *kill* her?

Perhaps Anne Kane had come to find them. Perhaps Petrus and Anne were working together.

She was about to step out of the room to try to get back to her apartment as quickly as possible, when another movement caught her eye. A shadowy figure toward the darkened back of the kitchen. Liza froze, her heart in her throat. The figure moved like a woman, quick and feline, but when Liza saw the face, she relaxed.

"Ms. Turner, thank god," she said. She put her hand to her chest and breathed. "I'm so happy to see you."

"What on earth are you still doing awake?" Ms. Turner asked in her Queen's English.

"Anne Kane," Liza began. "I think she may be the killer. She had motive and opportunity. I know you believe it's Petrus. But I don't know that he would risk it."

"You've gotten a little crush on him, have you?"

"No, of course not."

"None of them are good people, Liza. If you only knew the pain they'd inflicted on each other. On the world. Every last one of them." Ms. Turner shook her head as if she were deeply disappointed.

"Did Lawson find Aaron's body?"

"No. He and Shaun will resume searching at first light."

"And Dean will be here. I need to talk to Dean," Liza said. "I need to hash this all through with her. She'll listen to reason and take a closer look at Anne. She'll find the truth."

Liza was starting to feel better. Maybe this would work out after all. Then they could get everyone out of here and she and Lachlan could go back to planning their wedding. One thing was for certain—they would host no other guests before their union took place.

Carolyn Turner was watching her. Liza shrugged. "Sorry, I'm just looking forward to everything going back to normal."

Ms. Turner nodded but offered no other response.

"Have you seen Lachlan?" Liza asked.

"No, I haven't."

Liza hesitated, frowning. Her unease returned. "What are *you* still doing awake, Ms. Turner?"

"Someone has to make sure that everything is going according to plan."

"According to plan?"

"Yes, Liza. There's always a plan. Especially when a group of people such as this is involved."

At first, Liza thought Ms. Turner was talking about logistical planning—food, arrangements, entertainment. But those plans had been abandoned long ago. Now they were only focused on maintaining order. Weren't they?

"What plan?" she asked slowly.

"Oh, Liza. You're far too naïve to understand, aren't you?" The older woman made a *tsking* sound with her tongue. "It's a shame it must come to this."

Before Liza could ask another question, Ms. Turner raised two arms over her head. Liza had just a split second to notice the object in her hands. It was a heavy cast iron skillet. She didn't have time to react; Ms. Turner brought the weapon down hard on Liza's head. She fell to the floor, and before she lost consciousness, she saw the inert form of Petrus Bothas lying face up and unmoving beside her.

Chapter 21

Liza opened one eye, then the other. Her brain pulsed against the confines of her skull as she found herself staring into inky blackness.

She was back in the dungeon.

She reached out. Her fingertips brushed gritty sandstone on both sides. The walls were close, and this space was too warm for the winter months. This wasn't the dungeon.

She tried to sit up and her body was wracked with a wave of nausea. She breathed in and out slowly, willing it to pass. When her stomach settled, she touched her hairline. A huge goose egg had formed on her head. It took her a minute to remember. Then the scene came rushing back.

Carolyn Turner. Ms. Turner had done this to her.

Liza remembered the woman's distorted face as she'd brought the heavy skillet down on Liza's head. She thought she remembered crying out.

Had she cried out? Had any of that even happened? Was it possible she was imagining all of it? She tried to recall the details, but her mind was foggy and her memories blurred at the edges. The darkness was not helping. And the pounding in her head kept causing the waves of nausea to roll through her.

She blinked and looked around, searching for even a sliver of light. Where was she? She could hear muffled movements, thought she could hear voices.

She called out, "Hello?" The vibration of her voice made her head pulse more intensely. Wherever the voices were coming from, Liza didn't think they were close.

Despite the pain in her head, she tried to stand. When she got to her feet, she hit the top of her head on stone. Crying out, she stumbled backward, coming down hard on her backside and tailbone.

Stunned by the second blow to her head, Liza sat still for a moment and attempted to puzzle out her situation. But in the utter blackness, she began to feel as if the walls were closing in around her. She yelled, "Help! Help me!" She yelled over and over again, despite the pain in her head. She yelled until her throat was raw.

Then she stopped. Listened. There was no response, no reaction. She may as well have been screaming into the abyss.

She swallowed hard, another wave of nausea overtaking her. It wasn't just the blow to the head, she realized. She hadn't eaten enough. She was dehydrated. She felt weak and dizzy, and the air was thick.

She blinked hard, trying to detect even a small amount of ambient light, but the dark surrounding her now was as black as the dungeon.

Liza lifted her head and ran her fingers over the stone in the space around her. It was tight and cramped. It seemed as if she were somehow tucked away inside the castle walls.

A thought came to her. Something Daphne had said about exploring secret places when she'd visited the Ramsay estate as a young girl. Were there secret passageways Liza didn't know about? If there were, surely Lachlan would know about them and would think to look for her.

Liza had no idea if Lachlan was even interested in trying to find her. But she knew she couldn't just sit here and wait to be found.

She rose to her feet, struck her head again, then crouched forward. With her hands in front of her body, she hunkered onward slowly, touching the walls. Moving in the darkness was disconcerting; Liza anticipated slamming into a dead end at any moment.

The air was dank and dark. And while it wasn't freezing, a damp chill cooled her skin. She imagined this is what it must have felt like all those centuries ago to walk through the furthest reaches of the castle where heat from the large fireplaces did not reach.

Even then, there would have been light—torches affixed to the walls to guide the way.

Liza felt as though she were trapped in another time, so close to her modern-day counterparts, and yet a world away—years away. *Lady Catherine*, she whispered in the darkness. In her ghostly world, did her ancestor feel a part of the same black haze that Liza did right now?

She fought to stay focused on the world of the living. She needed to keep her wits about her.

This was not some ghostly realm. This was real life. Evil in the flesh and blood. Carolyn Turner had done this to her.

Ms. Turner was someone she'd trusted, someone Marion Dean had recommended to keep them all safe. To protect them. Just what were Ms. Turner's intentions?

Liza tried to concentrate as she slowly, deliberately, moved through the narrow passageway.

Ms. Turner had worked for the late Queen and had extensive dealings with the Royal Family. She'd described herself as an observer, a listener. She'd said she had no authority to act.

Liza hadn't thought to ask on whose behalf Ms. Turner had been listening. Not that the woman would have told her anyway. Was it the Royal Family or was it the government? And if so, which government?

Still, the answers to those questions would not explain why anyone would have wanted Liza dead. Even if Ms. Turner had been working for some person or entity who had ordered the murders of Aaron Scott and Sergei Popova—or if Ms. Turner herself for some reason wanted those men dead—Liza could think of no good reason Ms. Turner would have wanted Liza dead as well.

Liza stopped moving. Unless…Unless Liza, in her conversations with Anne and Petrus, had started to get too close to some kind of truth. Was it possible Anne Kane was tangled up in Ms. Turner's plans to kill these men?

Liza needed to get to Dean. Even though Dean was the one who'd installed Carolyn Turner in the castle in the first place, Liza refused to believe Dean was part of a larger scheme. Dean was too transparent and straightforward for that type of subterfuge.

Detective Chief Inspector Dean had to be her savior, and Liza felt a weak emergence of energy thinking about the woman. Chief Inspector Dean had become her north star.

She moved steadily forward, feeling as if she were on a gradual upward plane. As if the floor of the passageway was slightly inclined. Liza imagined that these hidden corridors may have been built as a refuge, for passing through the castle in times of siege. Women and children would have needed a safe place to hide. What better place than tucked away within the thick walls?

Given the estate's importance as a stronghold and

gateway to the rest of the Scottish country, someone in the Ramsay lineage—perhaps the founder of Clan Ramsay, Simundus de Ramesia himself—had ordered the construction of secret rooms and passageways within the walls.

Liza found it hard to believe that neither Callum nor Lachlan would have thought to mention this surprising feature at some point during their early conversations. She could only hope the thought occurred to Lachlan that his fiancé might be trapped.

Her heart fell at that realization. Even if he had been looking for her, why would he ever think to look for her *here*?

But she had to press on. She continued her slow climb. After a time, she dropped to her knees and began to crawl. Her head throbbed mercilessly. Periodically, she called out, but no response answered her cries.

She heard intermittent scrabbling around her—above her, below her. She imagined rats, hungry for abandoned flesh. She imagined ghouls, taking up residence from where they could easily observe their living counterparts.

Liza shivered, and stopped to rest and consider her progress. Simply moving forward was not going to help, she realized. She needed to find an escape. Someone had placed her in here. If there was a way in, there must be a way out.

She tried to imagine Ms. Turner dragging her unconscious body into the passageway. It wasn't impossible, Liza supposed. But she couldn't help but wonder if the woman had been working with someone else. Could it have been Detective Inspector Lawson? It quite literally could have been anyone. Anyone but Aaron Scott or Sergei Popova.

Liza yelled out in frustration.

A flash of a memory: Petrus's lifeless body lying on the floor of the kitchen next to where Liza herself had fallen. Was Petrus dead too? She felt a sorrow deep within her that nearly squeezed the breath from her chest.

Was she going to be next?

No. There was no way she would allow herself to perish in these walls like a rodent. All the anger she'd felt last summer, when Margaret Boyle, Kenneth Morrison, and Robert Douglas had thrown her into the dungeon like some kind of discarded object, surged through her. To them, she'd been nothing more than a nuisance to be thrown away and then burned.

Liza would not allow that to happen again.

Those three people were still in prison. Whoever had done this to her, and whoever those people may have been working for, would meet the same fate.

Oh, how she wished Lachlan were here. What story had Ms. Turner told to him and the others?

Liza again began to crawl along the passage. She

ran her hands over the walls until her fingertips were raw and oozing, looking for some sort of snag in the stone, a latch that may have led to an escape.

If Liza had been the designer of the castle centuries ago, where would she have put an entrance to a secret passage? She was no architect, and she wished she'd paid more attention to the building's construction than she had to the paintings and antiques within.

She thought of Lady Catherine's chambers, where Daphne had been housed. Where Liza had slept last year during her first visit to the Ramsay estate. There was a fireplace at the front of the room with two ornamental inserts next to the hearth. It was certainly possible those inserts could have been small doorways.

She continued the tedious search, ignoring the pain in her fingers. She felt nothing against the smooth walls and fought the desperate hopelessness of her task in the pitch dark.

She began to weep softly with the knowledge that she was becoming weaker and weaker.

After what could have been minutes or hours, she crawled into an object; an obstacle. A heap in the passageway.

Her fingers reached forward and touched cloth, then the rubbery texture of skin.

Liza's nose begin to twitch as the faint sweet odor of decay wafted into her nostrils.

She had found Aaron Scott.

Liza jumped back, scrabbling away from the stiff limbs of the missing man.

Her body crawled with revulsion, and she wretched into the disconcerting dark space.

She sucked in deep breaths of the damp air, but the smell of this rotting body fed her continued nausea.

Pull yourself together, Liza, she ordered to herself, and managed to calm her racing mind enough to attempt to think.

She imagined she was somewhere close to Aaron Scott's bedroom and tried to orient herself to the layout of the castle. That meant she was now on the third floor, between rooms with likely few inhabitants.

She had to assume hours had passed since she'd spoken with Petrus in the kitchen. Since Carolyn Turner had hit her with an iron skillet. Which meant it may be well into the next morning. At this point, no one would be searching for Aaron's body in Aaron's room.

If her speculation was correct—and she had no idea if it was—any remaining guests and residents would now be on the second floor, perhaps in the drawing room or the dining room below. But for all she knew, they could have all been gone.

In the blackness, Liza still had no sense of direction or perception. In fact, she had no idea from which direction she'd just come. She decided to just press forward, dead body be damned.

Liza steeled herself and climbed over the corpse. She could tell that the limbs were stiff, and the skin had become waxy. She also knew that even in this isolated location, insects and parasites would have already begun to eat away at the flesh and internal organs. Bile rose in Liza's throat, but she didn't stop moving. She said a silent prayer for this man who she'd known for only a short time, but who seemed like a decent person.

Once she'd overcome the obstacle, she moved slowly, in case she encountered any other dead bodies or ancient bones in the passageway. She wanted to believe that the hidden maze had been cleared at some point, but at least two people had become trapped in the walls in the last two days. There could have been many, many more throughout the years.

The thought of decaying corpses with their unseeing eyes and tangled manes of hair made Liza loathe to continue her quest for freedom.

But she kept going, feeling her way forward, even though she suspected that eventually the passageway would end, and she wouldn't be any better off than she was right now. She tried hard to retain hope, though it was nearly impossible, given the hopeless set of circumstances in which she currently found herself.

At some point, a sound met her ears. It was faint, but it was something other than the silence of darkness. It was a soft muttering. Perhaps weeping.

Liza listened closely, cautioning herself against

becoming too optimistic. She could be hallucinating. Or the ghosts of the Ramsay Castle could be playing tricks on her again.

After a moment, the sound stopped. Liza touched the walls with her raw fingertips. She could not feel any difference in the stone. There were no secret latches, no hidden fasteners by which to shift the walls.

Breaking through the silence, the sound came again. Liza took her chance. She began to yell and scream.

"Hello! Help! Help me!" Over and over again.

Even though her throat felt as if it was on fire, she shrieked and shouted until she had no voice left.

She stopped. The sound she'd heard had also stopped. Silence and darkness.

Her heart sank and pitched her into a deep despair. This time, she would die in the recesses of her home. This time, her ghostly Ramsay ancestors would claim her as their own.

She surrendered to the darkness.

Then she heard another sound; a deep sliding and scraping noise very close to where she'd crumpled on the passageway floor. Light flooded the space, blinding her with its brilliance. Liza started to weep.

A call. "Hullo? Is someone there?" It was a British voice; Liza's blood ran cold. She stayed silent.

"Hiya? Am I hearing things then?"

The voice was soft and the accent was distinct, but

it was not the Queen's English. This was a voice Liza knew.

Liza managed to drag herself forward. She crawled toward the light, through a small doorway, and finally into the room that had belonged to Lady Catherine. And she collapsed on the floor in front of the fireplace in front of a pale and shocked Daphne St. James.

Chapter 22

Liza hadn't realized just how weak she was. Perhaps it was the relief, but in the brilliant daylight streaming through the windows, Liza could barely lift her head.

Daphne held Liza's face between her hands. "How did you get in there?" the younger woman asked. Without waiting for an answer, she said, "My god, what's happened to your head?"

Liza couldn't make the words come, and she certainly couldn't stand. She needed water, and she managed to communicate that request to Daphne, who hurried to the washroom and brought her a tumbler of tepid liquid.

Liza gulped it down. Then shock set in, and she began to shake all over. Her teeth chattered violently.

Daphne said, "Let me call for Ms. Turner. She's been looking everywhere for you. Everyone has been searching."

Liza reached forward, smearing her bloody and worn fingertips red against Daphne's pale wrist. "Please, no," she whispered. "Don't let them know I'm here."

Daphne stared at Liza with gaunt, haunted eyes. It occurred to Liza that the woman in front of her was no longer a beautiful model and influencer. This woman was as worn, as exhausted, as defeated, as Liza was. The past two days had changed them all.

Daphne appeared to recognize that, too. She nodded in response to Liza's plea.

Liza wrapped her arms around herself to try to quell the shaking. When her body started to settle, and she trusted her speech again, she said to Daphne in a weak voice, "How did you know about the secret passageway?"

Daphne wet her lips and looked toward the opening in the wall. "It was a long time ago. When I was here before."

"The boy that you explored with…" Liza said.

After a pause, Daphne nodded.

"Was he a member of the Royal Family?"

She hesitated. "Yes."

Liza continued to shiver, and Daphne pulled a quilt from the foot of the bed. She wrapped it around Liza's shoulders then brought Liza another tumbler of water.

Liza drank it down, then asked, "Was it the boy who told you about the secret passageway?"

"I…I think so. He'd heard it from someone in the Royal Household. Perhaps a confidant of his grandmother or something. I'm not sure."

Someone like Carolyn Turner, who had been installed in Her Majesty's Household for decades.

"But you remembered the passageway, didn't you? You remembered being inside the walls all those years ago. It was the reason you wanted this room—the one directly above Aaron's room."

Daphne's pale face regained a bit of color. "I don't get the chance to be with him often. It was an opportunity for us to be together." Daphne's eyes reflected her deep sorrow.

"You loved him," Liza said.

"I loved him," Daphne repeated softly.

She'd loved him enough to try to end her existence without him, Liza thought.

"What about Matthew?" she asked.

A bitter little laugh tore through Daphne's suffering. "Matthew could care less what I do. Matthew cares only about Matthew."

But Liza remembered the man's angst yesterday in the sitting room. She didn't think that was true at all. She thought perhaps Matthew loved Daphne as much as Daphne had loved Aaron.

"Daphne, did Matthew kill Aaron?"

Daphne's lips twisted. She gave a small shake of her head. "He wouldn't put himself at risk like that. It's not his style."

"Do you know who killed him?"

She hesitated. Then she nodded.

"How?"

"I was…in the passageway when it happened. I'd been with him when we heard someone at the door. I'd only just time to hide myself."

"Was it Anne Kane?"

A crease formed between Daphne's delicate eyebrows. "Why would Anne want Aaron dead?"

"Because he was trying to advance artificial intelligence."

Daphne lifted a shoulder and gave a dismissive flip of her wrist. "Everyone wanted Aaron dead for that." Then she said, "But Anne didn't kill Aaron." There was a long pause, then the young woman said in a small, wistful voice, "It was my uncle Rabbie."

Liza gaped at Daphne. Of all of the people in the house Daphne could have mentioned, this name shocked Liza the most.

"But…why?"

"He's broke. He and Spirits Rose are completely bankrupt. My father has bailed him out a million times over." She gave a shaky sigh. "It was my father who arranged my marriage with Matthew, and my family won't let that connection end. I'm sure Rabbie saw this as an opportunity to eliminate Matthew's competition or do a favor for my father." Tears welled in Daphne's eyes. "He would have done it as repayment if my father requested it."

"That's it?" Liza asked, then she realized how insensitive those words sounded. She spoke quickly to cover her dismissiveness. "Aaron was involved in some serious and suspect technologies. You admitted it yourself—a lot of people would have liked to have seen his demise. Like Petrus Bothas," Liza added.

Daphne dashed the tears away with the back of her hand. "More people want Petrus dead than they do Aaron. And what better way to set up Petrus than to blame him for Aaron's murder? That's what they're doing, you know. Blaming Petrus for everything. No one knows what I've seen."

And no one knew what Liza knew either, she thought to herself.

"What about Sergei?" Liza asked. "Did Rabbie kill him, too?"

"I don't know, and I don't care. Sergei was a pig. He and Matthew are involved in some crooked weapons deals with government leaders. They think I don't listen. They think I don't know." A look of intense revulsion spread across Daphne's pretty features making her look severe and mean. "I hate them both, and I'm glad Sergei is dead. I just wish someone had killed Matthew too."

Liza leaned forward. "You can't tell anyone any of this, Daphne. Do you understand?"

Daphne set her jaw. "I am done taking orders. I want to tell the world about how awful all these people are. I want to tell the world what they did to Aaron."

"If you tell anyone, they will kill you. You are not safe."

"Rabbie would never hurt me."

"Maybe not. But there are others who will."

Seconds later, Rabbie Rose entered the room. "I've brought ye some tea—"

His words abruptly halted when he spotted Liza sitting on the floor, blanket wrapped around her shoulders. She was still wearing the silk pajamas and robe she'd been wearing the night before.

In that split second, his face was a mask of shock and horror. And in that instant, Liza knew that even if he'd had nothing to do with her attack, there was a good chance he'd known about it. Exactly what was this man's connection to Carolyn Turner?

The old man recovered quickly. "Liza, my dear. We've all been worried sick about ye. Where have ye been?"

Liza put on her own best bit of acting. "I...I don't remember much. I was in the kitchen with Petrus, and then there was blackness."

Liza saw Daphne start to speak. She gave an almost imperceptible shake of her head, and to her relief, Daphne kept her mouth shut.

Rabbie didn't appear to notice Daphne's reaction, but he *did* seem relieved at Liza's words.

"The basturt," he spat. "The police think he's the one who killed Aaron, ye know. And likely Sergei, too.

He's denyin' the whole thing, of course. But DCI Dean has just placed him under arrest. He's been taken away, along with all of his crooked men."

Liza tried to cover her dismay. "Dean took him to prison?"

"One of the men took him, but she put him in the cuffs. We're all so lucky to have Ms. Turner here. With any luck at all, Petrus will rot away in jail."

"Why would Petrus want to kill Sergei?"

"Accordin' tae Ms. Turner, Sergei was actively workin' against Petrus with both the Russian and the United States governments. Petrus's ego couldn't take it. He saw an opportunity to get rid of an obstacle and make Sergei's death look like an accident."

"Ms. Turner told you this."

It was more of a statement than a question, but Rabbie nodded. "She's been watchin' Petrus for quite a while. It was only a matter of time before he slipped up and hubris got the better of him."

A thought occurred to Liza. "Have you found Aaron's body?"

The pleased look faded from Rabbie's face, replaced with one of concern. "We think Petrus's men must have somehow gained access to the castle and taken him away. If that's the case, the police will find him soon enough." He didn't look convinced.

She realized no one knew where Aaron's body had gone. But Liza knew exactly where it was.

She glanced at Daphne who had averted her eyes. Liza realized Daphne knew too.

Liza turned back to the old man. "Is Dean here now? I think I should speak with her about what Petrus tried to do to me."

Rabbie nodded. "Aye, the other detective just left with Petrus, thank the lord. Let me summon Dean and Ms. Turner fer ye." He peered at the nasty gash on her head. "It looks as though you could use a doctor. Just like our Daphne. Ye might be concussed."

Liza didn't respond to his false show of concern. And she didn't tell Rabbie she did not want to talk to Ms. Turner. In fact, she *did* want to see her, if only to witness the look on Ms. Turner's face when she saw Liza, very much alive and well.

When Rabbie left the room, Daphne said, "I have no reason to defend Petrus Bothas, but I don't think he had anything to do with any of it."

"He didn't. They're setting him up."

"Why would they do that? Why wouldn't they just kill him too?"

"Petrus's investments, his companies, his interests, his wealth—they threaten all the people in this castle right now. His *friends*. But he's a prominent name, if elusive, figure. Much more well-known than Aaron Scott and Sergei Popova. If they kill him, they make him a martyr. By changing the narrative and throwing him in jail, they can paint him as the most hated man in the world." It was pure speculation on Liza's part, but it made sense.

Daphne didn't react, and Liza knew this might be too much for her to process. She couldn't see far beyond Aaron and her own motivations and love for the man. Liza shifted the direction of the conversation. "Why did you hide his body?" she asked softly.

Tears sprang into Daphne's eyes anew, and she took a moment to compose herself. "I couldn't stand what they were saying about him. I couldn't stand to know that the world might view him poorly and whisper behind his back. He was a good, loving, decent man. He had a family. He had children."

Liza was touched by her sincerity, and it made her think of Lachlan, whom she loved just as deeply as Daphne loved Aaron. She had been so wrapped up in her own plans lately, in the castle and the chapel, that she'd forgotten to tend to the devotion between them.

"Liza, what happened?" Detective Chief Inspector Marion Dean exclaimed, rushing into the room. Carolyn Turner followed closely behind.

Dean knelt down next to her. "Where've you been?" Her eagle eye spotted the gap in the stone next to the fireplace, but she offered no comment.

Liza, though, had shifted her gaze to Ms. Turner. The woman was doing her best to appear concerned, but Liza detected the fury beneath. She held herself very tall and straight, and Liza had no doubt if Ms.

Turner could get her alone, she'd finish the job she started.

Still, she managed to put on an award-winning act. "Liza, dear, are you all right? It looks like you took a nasty blow to the head."

Liza stared at the woman. They engaged in a visual showdown.

Liza suspected Ms. Turner knew what she was thinking, just as Liza knew what Ms. Turner was thinking. But Liza could give as good as she got. "I…I think so," she said, her ruined fingers gingerly touching the gash on her head. "Rabbie filled me on what has happened." She paused and pulled the blanket tighter around her shoulders. "I wish I could remember more. One minute I was with Petrus in the kitchen, and the next thing I knew, I woke up in darkness."

"What were you doing with Petrus?" Dean asked.

"I'd shared my suspicions about Anne Kane—that she might have killed both Aaron and Sergei."

"Anne Kane?" Dean exclaimed. "Why on earth would you think that?"

"I thought her revulsion of artificial intelligence may have caused her to kill Aaron Scott. In addition to that, Sergei may be in possession of the stolen Cohen art collection from World War II."

"Cohen?" Dean asked.

"The given name of Samuel Kane, Anne's grandfather."

Dean looked at Ms. Turner. "Ye didn't mention this piece of information. It may be something we need to explore," the chief inspector said to the other woman.

"No," Ms. Turner said quickly. "Anne has absolutely nothing to do with any of this. It was Petrus from the beginning. He's done his best to install all the friends who may have motive in the house so that he has plausible deniability. We know he's not a twit. I'm telling you, Marion. We've got this one right. Now we just need the people in charge to take care of this in the best way possible."

Dean looked skeptical, but she didn't say anything.

Ms. Turner turned back to Liza. "My dear, I think you may be concussed, with all this nonsense." She used the same phraseology Rabbie had just used.

Then she leaned toward Liza; Liza backed away. Ms. Turner saw it and pursed her lips.

"I understand. You haven't had much sleep over the past few days, and you have that nasty bump. It's a good thing you're a hardy girl." She peered at Liza's head. "A blow like that could have killed you."

"I believe that may have been the intent," Liza muttered.

"Come now. I'll take you to your room." Her fingers closed around the flesh of Liza's arm.

It was Dean who interrupted. "That's quite all right,

Ms. Turner. I'll accompany Ms. Ramsay. Liza, if you're up for it, we have some things to discuss about the implications for the castle."

Liza did not feel up to it, but she wanted to tell Dean what she knew as quickly as possible. She nodded.

Ms. Turner looked as if she might argue, then said, "I will join you. Since I've been here from the beginning. I can fill in any details that Liza might recall incorrectly, due to her injury."

Dean exchanged a glance with Liza.

There were still details that didn't make sense to Liza. If Rabbie Rose had killed Aaron, then how and why was Ms. Turner involved? And if Aaron's murder was a crime of passion or revenge, how had a plan to frame Petrus been hatched? And by whom? Liza didn't have answers to these questions, and neither would Dean.

Liza got to her feet. Her legs felt like jelly. It was partially the time she'd spent cramped inside the passageway, but it was also the blow to her head, dehydration, lack of proper sustenance and rest. It was Dean who steadied Liza. She turned to Ms. Turner. "Do ye think ye can get her some food and water?"

Color rose high on Carolyn Turner's cheeks. "I'm not the help."

So, the charade was over for Ms. Turner. She was no longer playing a part. Rather, she wasn't playing *that* part—the part of servant.

"I didn't say that ye were the help." Dean's voice was patient. "But I did ask if ye could help."

Ms. Turner hesitated. Finally, with a huff, she stalked away toward the front stairs. At the same time, Lachlan came barreling toward them from the opposite direction.

"Liza!" Ignoring Dean's presence, he swept her into his arms. "I've been looking all over fer ye."

Lachlan's hands and face were cold. His thick clothing felt damp.

"Were you outside?" Liza asked at the same time that Lachlan said, "What happened to yer head?"

Dean stepped in. "Let's go down to the room we've set up to get this sorted." Then she deferred to the way Lachlan was looking at Liza. "I'll go check on that food for ye first," she said and walked away.

Lachlan held Liza close. She pressed her face into his shoulder and began to cry, partly from exhaustion. But the larger part of her wept with relief.

She finally had her Lachlan back again. And she didn't want to ever let him go.

His embrace was tight, and he made soothing sounds as they moved down the stairs and across the corridor. The guests who were left—Rabbie, Anne, and Matthew—gaped at them from the drawing room. Shaun and Sadie looked on, unsure, yet hopeful.

In the conference room where Lachlan finally set

her down in a seat at the long polished table, she scrubbed her face with her hands and took a shaky breath. He sat close to her, holding her hand.

"Where's Ki?" she asked, and while she hadn't meant it to come out in an accusatory way, she feared her insecurities betrayed her.

"DI Lawson allowed her to ride with Bothas to the station. She's upset and worried, but she needs tae leave that monster. No amount of money or notoriety is worth what he's puttin' her through."

"Petrus didn't do this."

A look of stark rage spread across Lachlan's face. "Ye can't be serious, Liza. He didn't do that tae yer head?" He didn't wait for an answer. "And where hae ye been? Petrus kept sayin' he didn't know, but Ms. Turner and Lawson ken he was lyin'."

"He wasn't lying, Lachlan. He didn't do anything they're accusing him of. Someone put me in the castle's hidden passageway, but it wasn't Petrus."

A deep frown creased Lachlan's forehead. "Hidden passageway?"

"Why didn't you tell me about them? Are there more?"

He looked mystified. "I have no idea. How did ye get out?"

"Daphne let me out."

Before Lachlan could ask more questions, Carolyn Turner walked into the room with a tray of tea and sandwiches. She was followed closely by Detective Chief Inspector Dean.

Ms. Turner set the tray down roughly, and tea sloshed out of the small serving vessel while the dainty china cups rattled on their saucers. Liza reached forward to pour herself a cup—she was parched and starving. Then a memory rose from the depths of her mind, and she stopped.

"I'd like to have a word with DCI Dean alone," she said.

Ms. Turner balked at that. "Ms. Ramsay, I needn't remind you that I am here at the behest of His Majesty's Government. Crimes have been committed upon this soil, and I am responsible for reporting them to the best of my ability."

Liza looked at Dean for help.

"Carolyn," Dean said evenly, "Liza and I have a history. It might make sense for her to talk to me first."

"I'm afraid that I must insist I be here." She scraped a chair back from the table and installed herself in the seat, glowering at Liza. Lachlan was looking at her curiously, and he reached forward to pour a cup of the tea.

"Don't," Liza warned.

"Don't what?" he asked, the peat-colored black tea flowing from the spout.

"Don't drink that," she said, ready to knock it from his hands.

"What are ye talking about?" he asked, but he set the small pot and cup back on the tray.

"Are you implying that I've put something in your tea, Liza?" Ms. Turner said. Her tone was amused, but her face was clouded with anger. She gave a laugh that sounded like the breaking of glass. "Do you think I would be so reckless?"

Even Dean now looked alarmed. "I think we need to start at the beginning."

"I've told you all you need to know." Ms. Turner took the cup of tea Lachlan had just poured and sipped it, a superior look on her face.

Dean watched her, frowning, then turned to Liza. She opened her mouth and shut it again. "Okay, then. Let's start at the end. Who did that to yer head, Liza?"

Liza hadn't wanted to lay her cards on the table this way, but now she had no other choice. She cleared her throat. "The representative of His Majesty's Government, Carolyn Turner did, detective."

Chapter 23

"**Y**ou must be mad," Ms. Turner said, laughing.

Lachlan's expression ran through a gamut of emotions. "Liza, are ye sure what ye're sayin'?"

"I'm quite sure."

Dean sighed. "I really think I should talk with Liza alone."

Ms. Turner shook her head. "Oh, it's no trouble to me, Marion. I'd like to hear this tale that Ms. Ramsay has woven around these events. She seemed quite taken with Mr. Bothas, by the way. As her significant other has been with Mr. Bothas's consort. So, yes…I'm very interested in this story."

Liza's cheeks colored at the implication, but she knew Ms. Turner was trying to twist the narrative and goad her down a path that ultimately led nowhere.

Lachlan started to interject, but Liza held up a hand. "I do have a story to tell, actually."

And Liza told it, from start to finish. She told Dean of Sadie discovering Aaron's body, of the movement of the body and its subsequent disappearance. She told Dean that most of the guests had thought Aaron's death a tragic accident, but that Ms. Turner had been the first to insist foul play was involved. She told Dean of her conversations with Petrus and with Matthew. Of finding Sergei's body, and the reactions of the guests. She told Dean about her conversation with Anne and encounter with Petrus.

Finally, she told Dean about her last memory in the kitchen—Ms. Turner's face warped with rage as she slammed the heavy object into Liza's head before she'd awoken alone in the dark passageway.

Dean was momentarily speechless. She looked at Ms. Turner. "Do ye have anything to say?"

The woman's face was serene. "Most of what Ms. Ramsay has said is pure speculation. As for her claim that I hit her—well, that's just not true at all. As I've told you, Marion, I'd heard a noise in the kitchen and found Petrus staggering around, saying that someone had struck *him* in the head. Perhaps he placed her in the passageway and injured his own head in hiding her body."

"Why would I be defending him if he's the one who hit me?" cried Liza.

Lachlan ran a shaky hand through his hair. "Ma heid's mince. Pure chaos, all o' it."

Only Dean was quiet. Finally, she said, "How did you know about the hidden passageway, Carolyn?"

Ms. Turner opened her mouth to say something, then shut it again.

Liza smiled. The woman had tripped up. "I never said in front of you that I'd been left in the passageway, Ms. Turner. Only the person who put me there would know that."

Ms. Turner swallowed then sat up straighter. She took a sip of her tea. "Your claims mean nothing, Ms. Ramsay."

Dean placed her hands flat on the table's surface. She sighed. "Let's, just for a minute, go back to yer claims of Petrus's involvement in the other two deaths, Ms. Turner. Ye have no proof, and Liza has brought forth at least one other theory that perhaps Anne Kane needs to be considered."

"Preposterous. You can talk to Rabbie Rose about that."

"I understand you haven't yet located Aaron's body, is that right?"

"Aye," Dean said on an exhale. "We think maybe Petrus's men have him."

Liza hesitated. Then she wet her lips. "They don't have him."

Ms. Turner let out another snort of derisive laughter. "And how would *you* know?"

"Because I know where he is."

All eyes were on her.

"The passageway," Lachlan said.

Liza nodded. "I climbed over his body."

Ms. Turner looked shocked, and for the first time,

she seemed nervous. "Well, *I* certainly didn't put him in there."

"You're not the only one who knew about the hidden passages. Apparently, you were here over a decade ago with Her late Majesty, and you shared your knowledge with her grandson, who shared *his* knowledge and a few stolen kisses with one of the young guests who was here that night. That guest was Daphne St. James."

Ms. Turner blanched, and Dean said, "Are you saying it was Daphne who put Aaron's body in the passageway?"

Liza gave a small nod.

"Why would she have done that?"

She leveled a glance at Dean. "Did Ms. Turner tell you how we found his body—its position? It was an obscene and embarrassing way to die. And Daphne loved him. She didn't want the world to remember him that way. In fact, neither did Petrus, who moved the body to the bed himself. It's why he wanted his men to deal with the situation. He was trying to be *kind*."

"Tampering with the scene of a crime is a crime in itself," said Ms. Turner.

"So is murder," Lachlan exclaimed.

Ms. Turner held her hands in front of her chest as if she were physically pushing away his words. "I didn't murder anyone."

"You certainly tried," said Lachlan.

Dean stood up. "Enough," she said, her voice betraying the frustration. "I've had enough of the finger-pointing. I need to know who killed Aaron Scott."

Ms. Turner raised her eyebrows but kept her mouth clamped tightly shut.

Lachlan looked mystified.

Liza let out a deep sigh. It pained her to have to be the one to make this announcement because she genuinely liked the man, and wanted to believe he'd done this deed because he felt he had no choice. "Rabbie Rose killed Mr. Scott."

"Rabbie?" Lachlan barked. "But that's impossible."

"That's a serious accusation, Liza," Dean said. She lowered herself into her seat and leaned back, frowning deeply. "Are ye sure?"

"There's a witness," she said quietly. They all knew it could be only one person, but Liza spoke the name aloud anyway. "Daphne was in the secret passageway and watched the entire act."

After a shocked silence, Ms. Turner spoke. "Do you actually believe that the girl will testify against her own uncle?" The pitch of her voice was raised.

Liza lifted a shoulder. "She admitted it to me. I don't see why she'd have any trouble testifying. She loved Aaron that much."

"Love," Carolyn Turner scoffed. "What a useless sentiment."

"Let's pretend for a minute it's true," Dean broke

in. "If Rabbie really did kill Aaron, how does the plot to frame Petrus fit in?"

It was a question Liza had asked herself. And she had a theory. She asked Dean a question in return. "Who put you in touch with Ms. Turner for this assignment?"

"Marion and I have known each other for years," Ms. Turner said.

But Liza hadn't been talking to Carolyn Turner. She kept her eyes trained on Dean, who said quietly, "Rabbie Rose."

"I think the killing was a favor to Hugh St. James, Daphne's father. But I think Ms. Turner knew about it all along and planned to frame Petrus, who made it all too easy."

"Absurd," Ms. Turner said.

"And Sergei Popova?"

Liza thought about the motives of everyone in the castle for wanting Sergei dead. Each of them had their reasons—some more than others. But she also remembered Sergei's gray pallor and unhealthy perspiration, combined with the drink. "I think Sergei's death was a happy accident for Ms. Turner and another opportunity to blame Petrus. An autopsy will probably reveal as much."

Dean looked at Ms. Turner who had become smugly silent. "Do ye have anything to say for yerself?" the detective asked.

"Marion, you're an outstanding detective, and you deserve more than a position in a bit of a hole in the middle of nowhere. I can make that happen for you," Ms. Turner said. "But I can't do it with these ridiculous accusations, none of which can be proven. Without the testimony of Daphne St. James, you've got absolutely nothing."

Both Liza and Lachlan looked at Marion Dean. She was a good and decent woman, but an offer of a promotion from Scotland Yard might be more than she could resist. Besides, Ms. Turner was right—all they had was speculation. Petrus could go on trial, and a jury of his peers would find him innocent or guilty. But Ms. Turner, her superiors, and their counterparts across the globe, likely had the power to influence the decision. And there wouldn't be anything any of them could do about it.

Liza's heart sank as the silence grew longer. She knew Lachlan wanted to say something, but she silently willed him to remain quiet. This wasn't their decision to make.

Finally, Dean said, "You may be right, Carolyn. I've got nothing on the murder or accessory charges without Daphne St. James. But what I *do* have is a charge of attempted murder on Elizabeth Ramsay."

Liza glanced up sharply. A smile spread across Lachlan's face. "Fek aye, ye do," he nearly yelled.

"Are ye willing to testify against Carolyn Turner?"

Dean asked Liza.

Liza gave a resounding, "Fek aye," in return.

Dean nodded once, rose from her chair, and guided Carolyn Turner to her feet.

"Ye do not have to say anything. But it may harm your defense if ye do not mention when questioned something which you later rely on in court. Anything you do say may be given in evidence."

Carolyn Turner sputtered, but didn't fight as Dean reached into her back pocket and pulled out a slim plastic zip-tie, securing the woman's wrists.

"You know this won't hold up, Marion," Ms. Turner said. "Your career in law enforcement will be over. You've messed with the wrong people."

"Aye, maybe I have." Dean began to walk Ms. Turner from the room. "But I know in my heart I've made the right decision, and sometimes that's all ye can do." She looked back and winked at Liza and Lachlan. "I'll have Dr. Patel come up and take a look at yer head. As soon as the forensics team finish up with Sergei and take possession of the body of Aaron Scott, we'll be out of yer hair. For now."

"For now," Liza said with a small smile.

"Ye certainly know how to get yerself in trouble."

Liza shut her eyes. "I have a feeling this trouble may follow us for quite some time."

"I wouldn't be so sure about that," Dean said. "People of this caliber have a tendency to take care of their own problems quietly."

But Liza didn't see how they could sweep murder under the rug forever.

When Dean and Ms. Turner had left, Liza turned to Lachlan. They stared at each other for a long moment.

Then he rose and folded her into his arms. All she wanted to do was sink into him and stay there forever. But she pulled away and looked up into his green eyes.

"Are we good?"

"Aye, we're good," he said and buried his face into her tangled auburn tresses, careful to avoid the large knot on her head. "I have an idea—let's pretend the last few days never happened. It was all a strange, wild dream."

Liza lifted her head so that he could kiss her. "Deal," she said. "But I feel like this nightmare may not be completely over yet."

"Ye're probably right. But a nightmare with ye is better than the sweetest dream alone."

Liza smiled, and he smiled back, his eyes crinkling at the corners. "Do we need to talk about the wedding?" she asked quietly.

He nodded once. "We probably do." His voice was soft.

Her heart sank. But she understood.

"When Bruce got his phone back, he had a voicemail sayin' the stained-glass order was bein' rushed, and it would be done in plenty of time fer the ceremony. So ye can go ahead and send out the save-the-date cards, or whatever they are, this week."

A surge of relief gushed through her, making her dizzy and giddy and embarrassingly emotional all at once. "Oh, Lachlan," she said. "Are you sure you still want to marry me?"

"I've never wanted anything more in my life."

Chapter 24

Two weeks later the snow had melted, the runoff flowing into the Creagan River below the castle. The river rushed so high and loud that Liza was sure she could hear the whoosh of it inside the thick walls of the fortress.

She was sitting in the empty drawing room, scrolling through the news on her laptop, when two different articles caught her attention.

The first was breaking news out of Silicon Valley in the United States. Entrepreneur philanthropist Aaron Elliott Scott had died in a freak scuba diving incident while vacationing with close friends in Indonesia. There was no word yet on cause of death, but the outlets were being told that his death was accidental, and thoughts and prayers were with his wife Marissa and two young children.

The second piece of breaking news was that British-American influencer and heiress Daphne St. James and her husband Matthew Carter, businessman and founder of the cloud application and infrastructure system, Sibyl, were expecting their first child together.

Daphne was doing well but would be out of the spotlight for a period while she dealt with some pregnancy-related health issues. Despite those minor complications, both mom-to-be and baby were expected to be fine. The couple were said to be over the moon with happiness.

Liza let out a snort of disbelief. Was Daphne actually pregnant or was the pregnancy an excuse to address her depression over the loss of Aaron Scott? Liza supposed she'd find out nine months from now. If there *was* a baby, Liza took small comfort in the thought that perhaps the father might be Aaron Scott. A secret incarnation of the man who had left them much too soon at the hand of Daphne's uncle.

Liza searched the headlines, but there was no mention of an arrest of Rabbie Rose. From what she could tell, he was safely back in the Highlands, overseeing his bankrupt business.

While Liza was glad the Ramsay Castle had escaped unscathed from what could have been an absolute disaster, she was appalled that the deaths which had occurred had been so casually dismissed and no one held responsible.

On a whim, she typed in the name 'Sergei Popova'. A Wikipedia page on the man popped up. It gave scant information about his family and his connection to the Russian government, but there was no mention of his death. Liza suspected that one day the page would disappear, just like Sergei had.

The deep chime of the doorbell signaled a visitor, and Liza sat up straighter. She hadn't been expecting anyone at the main entrance, and she wondered if one of the workers from Fleming Stained Glass had become confused looking for the chapel, where full construction had resumed. She heard Sadie's voice, but she couldn't make out what the young woman was saying.

A minute later, Sadie's footfalls sounded on the staircase before she entered the drawing room.

"Are ye agreeable to welcoming a visitor, Ms. Ramsay?"

"Who is it?"

"It's Mr. Bothas, ma'am."

Liza's heartbeat quickened. The last time she'd seen Petrus, he'd been lying on the floor of the kitchen, knocked out cold by Carolyn Turner. She knew he'd been released from police custody, but she never expected to hear from him again. She certainly didn't expect to come face to face with him.

"I...I suppose you can send him up."

Liza wasn't dressed for meeting guests. In fact, she hadn't even bothered to shower that morning and was wearing jeans and a vintage David Bowie T-shirt with 'Hunky Dory' printed in gold letters above a photograph of the late entertainer's face.

But she stood and tried to look calm and confident, as Sadie showed Petrus into the room then discreetly disappeared.

Petrus smiled warmly when he saw her, and the first thing he said was, "Cool album."

It took Liza a moment to realize he was referring to her shirt. She glanced down and then smiled back. "Yes, it is." Then she said, "What are you doing here?" at the same time as Petrus said, "I just came to say—"

They both stopped and laughed awkwardly. But something about the misstep had broken the ice, and Liza felt more relaxed.

"Would you like to sit? I can have Sadie bring us some tea. Or coffee," she added, remembering his preference.

He shook his head. "I can't stay." He remained standing and shoved his hands in his pockets and hunched forward, minimizing his height. He looked around the room. "It really is a beautiful place," he said. "I wish I'd been able to enjoy it properly."

"I'm sorry—" Liza started to say, but he shook his head.

"I'm not here for an apology."

"They nearly locked you away for good."

"They certainly tried, didn't they? It won't be the last time. I threaten them. My voice threatens them. The truth threatens them."

"What is the truth?"

He seemed to consider that. "It's anything that goes against the narrative, I guess. But what do I know? I'm just a nerd who likes to tinker with software, robots, and rockets. I've got no authority."

They both knew that wasn't true.

"What I really came to say was, thank you."

Liza ran her palms down the sides of her jeans and let out a laugh. "Thank you for nearly getting you killed and arrested? You're quite welcome." She gave a little bow.

"I know it was you who went to bat for me with Detective Dean. You really pissed off Scotland Yard. And a whole bunch of other people you don't even know about. You didn't have to do that."

"Of course I did. You hadn't done what they were accusing you of."

"No, but a lot of people would have just stayed out of it."

"Carolyn Turner tried to kill me for messing up the narrative."

"I told you—they like their narratives."

Liza nodded. "Well, you're welcome. It was the very least I could do."

The same uneasy energy crackled between them. Liza thought it might have been the isolation in the castle during the snowstorm, the underlying macabre nature of the deaths, and the suspicions. But they were no longer trapped, snowed in, or under attack. Still the energy pulsed.

She cleared her throat. "Is Ki with you?"

"Stephanie has gone back to New Zealand for a while. We're taking a break."

Liza noted the use of the girl's given name, and wondered if their 'break' had anything to do with events at the castle. Or with Lachlan. But Petrus's next words surprised her.

"Anne and I have decided to give it another go after all these years."

"Oh, wow," she exclaimed. "Good for you. For both of you." Liza meant that, too. Truly.

"She sends her regards, and her thanks."

"I nearly accused her of two murders she didn't commit. I'm not sure why she would be thanking me either."

"Because if she'd had the moxie, she'd loved to have killed both Aaron and Sergei. She's glad they're both dead. And she's flattered you thought she'd have the nerve to do it herself."

It was an odd thing to take as a compliment, but Liza understood it. Kind of.

"Surely you didn't fly all the way over here just to thank me," Liza said.

"I'm actually here for Detective Dean."

This was another point of guilt for Liza. After Dean had arrested Carolyn Turner, the woman had been freed and absolved of all charges by her superiors. She'd then made good on her threat to destroy Dean's career, and Dean had been summarily dismissed from her duties, replaced by Alex Lawson.

Dean had not blamed Liza for her fate, however, and seemed to have taken the entire ordeal in stride.

"What do you need Dean for?" Liza asked.

"After you brought up the lost Cohen art collection, Anne realized it was time to track it all down. She needs a partner to do that—a detective—and we happen to know Dean has just become available. So she'll be working for us." Petrus leaned forward conspiratorially. "And I hear the pay's a lot better than Police Scotland."

Liza's laughter rang out, and she was still laughing when Lachlan walked into the room with a scowl on his face. "Mr. Bothas," he said. Liza could tell that Lachlan was doing his best to keep his voice light and friendly, but her fiancé was not happy to see the billionaire.

Petrus bent forward at the waist and nodded. "Mr. McClaren," he said. "I'd just come to thank you and your fiancé for your hospitality."

Lachlan nodded but didn't respond further, and Petrus said, "Well, I'd better be going. I have businesses to run and contracts to sign."

Liza said goodbye, and Petrus showed himself out. When the door had shut and the castle was quiet again, Lachlan looked at Liza. "I'm not goin' tae lose ye to a billionaire, am I?"

Liza smiled. "To quote Robert Burns: 'Though

fickle fortune has deceived me, She promis'd fair and perform'd but ill'."

"What's Rabbie Burns got tae do with anythin'?"

"I was blinded for a minute by money, power, and fame, and I was trying to be something I'm not and impress people who didn't matter. I got singed for it, but the worst punishment of all would have been to lose you. So no, you're not going to lose me to a billionaire. In fact, I'm pretty sure you're stuck with me."

"I'll take it, Mrs. Elizabeth Ramsay-McClaren."

"Very, very soon," said Liza. "But let's hope there are no more deaths or murders at the Ramsay Castle before the wedding."

"Ach, don't dare say it, *mo luaidh*. The spirits must be on our side now since we've given them our own fair share of souls."

Liza was skeptical. Something told her though the spirits of the Ramsay Castle enjoyed their bit of mischief, they welcomed the new souls into their realm. She just hoped that Aaron Scott and Sergei Popova would be friendly entities as they settled into their new life with the otherworldly Ramsay Clan.

A cool sigh brushed the back of Liza's neck, and she swore she heard a woman's laughter.

THE END

Acknowledgments

I hope you enjoyed reading "Of Mistress, Friends, and Wealth" as much as I enjoyed writing it. While "Perils Past" focused on the budding romance between Liza and Lachlan in the midst of a murderous rampage, its sequel is meant to explore the challenges that arise in a new relationship, especially when the temptation of lust, power, and money are introduced. Along with more murder, of course.

You may think you recognize some of the personalities on which Petrus, Aaron, Rabbie, Matthew, Sergei, Anne, Ki, Carolyn Turner, Sadie, Shaun, and Daphne were based. Maybe you do and maybe you don't. I will say that each one of the fictional characters morphed and changed throughout the writing of this book, and every persona is a complete figment of my imagination, though inspiration certainly existed throughout.

As always, I'd like to thank my family for their endless support for this hobby of mine. Jim might call it an obsession, but it's a healthy obsession. I think. But all my love for putting up with it.

Thank you to Rachel, Noah, and Adam. Thank you to Mom, Sue, Nate; Sydney, Dave, and Mary. And for Lydia and Gracie—my heart.

To the staff of the Dalhousie Castle on which the

Ramsay Castle was based. Thank you for your encouragement and willingness to feature an unknown independent author who once spent a night in your beautiful hotel and was inspired to tell a story. I hope that the spirits of the Ramsay Clan that drift through your passageways are pleased with their portrayal.

Continued sincere appreciation to my dedicated friends and readers who read and review every new book and story. I can't list you all, but you know who you are. And you are the best.

I am grateful to my editor Paul Carson at Seminal Edits. The care and humor with which you edit my wacky stories is so appreciated. (And if you're in the market for an editor, give him a shout.)

And for my BFF Robert who responded to a random LinkedIn message from me two years ago, and since then has truly changed the course of my life. Thank you.

There are so many others to thank—friends, supporters, readers. Love to you all.

Stay tuned for Book Three in the Ramsay Castle Mystery series, tentatively titled "From Thee, A Light Emerges." A special thanks to Bernt André Nergård for the inspiration. I hope the finished product does justice to your vision.

I love hearing from new readers. You can reach me at sarah@sjcunningham.net or visit my website at www.sjcunningham.net. Until next time!